Lars Holger Holm

Come Snow

A Psychic Thriller

Leo Publishing
Heleneborgsgatan 44
117 32 Stockholm
Sweden
Telephone: +46 86 69 46 16
www.leo.infosite.tc

ISBN 91-974968-1-2

© Lars Holger Holm, 2006
Cover and graphic design: John Eyre
www.johneyre.com

Printed by Standartu Spaustuve Ltd., Vilnius 2006
All rights reserved

"Only a monster can permit itself the luxury of seeing things as they really are."

          E. M. CIORAN

To the unborn soldier

Sankt-Anna Klinik, Schwarzwald, September 7, 1939.

From a distance, the clinic seemed a tranquil haven for tormented souls. Spacious lawns, overshadowed by trees, meandered towards a lake accommodating rowing boats and black swans. From the roadside, an iron gate crowned by the imperial eagle led to a drive-way flanked by two one-storeyed annexes housing gardeners and chauffeurs. Beyond these quarters, a canopy of linden trees created the illusive impression that the main building was little more than a spacious villa in the midst of opulent greenery. From all other directions the Black Forest descended a halo of thorny pines to girdle its ridges; beyond these, the sky presented its forever shifting scenery.

On this day of late summer, the sky was the same shade of greyish-blue as the pair of inscrutable eyes that stared into it from a window on the top floor of the main building. Chief psychiatrist Hans Schröder stood in his office, facing the open window through which the distant pines spread their resinous fragrance. Resisting this subtle call, he picked up the telephone and asked the nurse to find him assistant chief psychiatrist Claus Uhland. While Schröder prepared his arguments, a messenger was sent off. Soon Schröder was overcome by the disturbing sensation that what he was about to experience had in fact already happened to him – not only once, but innumerable times before. He was merely the impersonator of a long-completed, presently irrelevant monodrama. Only in his memory did it live on, over and over again, like a maniacal obsession, a feverish dream, a compulsory psychosis. As if waking up to the crack of a whip, he heard his colleague open the door. In the moments before his first words were actually pronounced, Schröder mouthed them to himself as he threw a last glance at the immutable, only all-too-familiar, pine forest. "Now," he thought, "it begins all over again. The same senseless repetition; the same interminable labyrinth, the same, the same, the same …" He then turned round to hear the words he already knew. Instantly, his sense of déjà-vu disappeared. He no longer remembered his life.

*

– Dr. Schröder, how can I be of service?
 – Have you seen this?
Schröder pushed the order across the table. Uhland picked it up, read it through and looked at his superior.
 – You realise what it means?
Uhland nodded.
 – I have heard of this. The decision is general and concerns all German physicians, but in particular those within our jurisdiction, if I may so express myself.
 – That was very poignant.

– It was not my intention to sound witty.

– No, but you hit the nail on the head. We are being ordered to act as a court martial in matters of health and disease. What do you think about that?

– In view of the present war situation, there is, as far as I can see, no room for negotiation.

– So you recommend that we start implementing it?

– I don't recommend anything, I follow orders.

– So you are first and foremost a soldier, not a physician?

– With all due respect, Doktor, I should prefer it if you continued to regard me as a helper of human beings, but I must draw your attention to the fact that failure to execute orders issued in the name of the Führer will be regarded as treason.

– You can always submit your resignation.

– And what would I live on then? My good conscience? Excuse me, Doktor Schröder, but I'm thinking of you. I obey, and at this clinic, you are in charge.

– You will consequently abide by my decision?

– Of course.

– Because you know that you will not have to take responsibility for it?

– No, because I was brought up to respect and obey my superiors. Tell me, where would Germany be today if loyalty to the Fatherland hadn't helped us overcome egotism time and time again?

Schröder, realising that he would soon find himself deadlocked, decided to approach the issue from a different angle.

– And what do you believe personally, your professional code of honour set aside, to be the right thing to do?

– Between the two of us, I don't know. On the one hand I have often wondered if what we are trying to do here is in reality nothing but a hopeless struggle against natural selection. Only in our time has it occurred to anyone to confer an abstract value on mentally defective members of our race; only in our time has it become acceptable that these individuals, at great economic sacrifice, are kept in institutions such as our own Sankt-Anna Klinik. Previously, they were perhaps accepted out in the countryside as village idiots that were somehow part of the whole, and as such tolerated. But that was all there was to it, and the majority of such severely handicapped or retarded children were as infants abandoned in the woods, and thus returned to mother nature. This practice was perhaps deplorable, but one has to admit that it spared families and small communities the trouble of finding some suitable occupation for their cretins. On the other hand, I find it in some ways quite understandable that nature, in her great abundance, produces both the genius, who stands above average man, and the idiot, who stands below him. We can't do much about that. But we can – and this is the revolutionary idea of the new German society – we can, just as we do in matters of agriculture and animal breeding, help to further the emergence of individuals capable of survival even in harsh circumstances. In this way, and in the long run, we facilitate human development toward a more highly evolved race.

– But wouldn't it then be enough to prevent our mentally ill and retarded from procreating?

– Of course. That's what I think as well, but how should that goal be achieved? Only a few of our criminals are incarcerated. Most mentally deranged people remain in our cities and mix with racial elements, the offspring of whom are not less but more prone to inherited weakness and handicaps. In our consulting rooms we see every day how children, once singled out to die by nature herself, are being saved for life by improved medical techniques. But what kind of life? Survival per se is no value criterion, there must also be a quality of survival, in other words, there must be standards determining to what level of physical or spiritual degradation life-sustaining measures should be extended. There has to be a limit here. During the last decades, especially the years following the Great War, when so many fertile men in their prime died, we have witnessed a steady increase of deficiency ailments previously unknown to science. Deficient genetic characteristics are not only inherited, but aggravated. New allergies are created, immunity, even against previously harmless diseases, is weakened. If this is the situation today, where are we going to be in a hundred years from now if we allow this development to run its natural course? We doctors will be forced to care for people who are born and die sick. How on earth shall we be able to care for people who completely lack the prerequisites for even leading a life? No, I can't see why doctors should acquiesce in trying to cure diseases, the evil root of which cannot be eradicated because they have their origin in the genetic material itself. To treat symptoms in order to create the illusion of a healthy population is an act of deliberate regression to darkness and ignorance, and this at a time when we physicians have the unique responsibility, and therefore obligation, to actually create health. This is, between you and me, my opinion.

– With all respect for your lucid vision of the future of medicine, Schröder interjected energetically, – Even I can agree that we have to start thinking about how to pave the way for future man. But this, unfortunately, is not the issue at stake. The question is, shall I today authorise and supervise measures aiming at the actual death of our patients, and at the same time pretend that I haven't murdered them, simply because I have in my hand a piece of paper that states that I have the right to kill them? I do see the grand ambition in the interest of the future of the human race. I simply ask myself how we can be so sure that today we know the genetic combinations which will eventually create and foster perfectly sound individuals? Wouldn't it be best to let nature take her course here too?

– And accept that thieves, rapists, murderers, homosexuals, Jews and niggers take over the country?

– And just what is it in the ordinary German that gives you such hope for the future?

– To a certain extent, his willingness to work, his sense of honour. But above all, his readiness to sacrifice himself for something higher, for the benefit and future of his country. In short, his idealism.

– Thank you Uhland, Schröder said, and stretched out his hand to receive the paper containing Hitler's order from his colleague. Dr. Uhland was on his way out when Schröder addressed him once again.

– And what would you really do if you were in my shoes? he asked, slowly putting the paper on the desk.
Uhland gave his superior a searching look. In a different, almost resigned tone of voice, he answered.

– God knows.

– And if I seek to be relieved of my present duties, then you will perhaps be the one having to …
– I can't imagine that you would make such a hasty and dangerous decision, Uhland replied, not allowing Schröder to finish, or perhaps saving him from that unpleasantness.
– One does not ask to be dismissed from a war, Doktor. Good day.

Once Uhland had left, Schröder went to the big mirror which he used in the examination of patients, and looked at his own reflection.

"Yes", he said, as if talking to someone hidden behind the cold glass, "I am now forty years old. I didn't exactly choose to become head of this clinic. I accepted it because it seemed to provide me with an opportunity to investigate what science calls the paranormal. As you know, I prefer to call it the fourth dimension, and its existence is no more strange than the fact that subliminal perception, the divination of the future and the correlation between simultaneous psychic and physical events also exist. That, and not ambition, or need for recognition, or greed, prompted me to accept this position. In no way did I foresee that the objectives and priorities of my research were going to be dictated by the state, and not just any state, but one which has sanctified its racial bias and vulgar Darwinism to the point of demanding that every single citizen oblige its dilettantish furore, or be accused of treason. Surely, there is a grain of truth in what they say. The real danger lies not in the ideas as such, but rather in the extremist and fanatical ways in which they are promulgated and carried out. If I begin here and now to give the most hopeless cases injections to facilitate their transition from this world to the next

– where, one would hope, they will lead a better life than the one they enjoyed here – I launch myself and my staff on a course of action which will lead in the end to there being no means of distinguishing between a death intended to end an individual's meaningless suffering and society an equally meaningless burden – and arbitrary genocide. Look at the order. Its only categorisation of victims is as 'very sick patients', but this obviously does not only, or perhaps not at all, apply to those suffering the terminal stages of physical disease. Its objective is to pave the way for the elimination of the unwanted in general, and it wants to make us physicians collectively responsible for its implementation. Our justification is to be that the nation is at war, and that we have to follow orders ... Yes, I am forty years old and I am afraid, just like all the others. Afraid, in particular, of what will happen to my family and myself if I don't obey."

He stared into the mirror, wishing that he himself had had the power to remain as unflinching as his own reflection, not betraying itself even in the blink of an eye. He went to the desk, opened the top drawer, placed the order inside, locked the drawer, put the key in his pocket and left the room.

Schröder began his routine daily rounds. When he arrived at the wards, the noise, even for a mental asylum, was unusually loud. One patient, as if he were a battering ram, kept running his head against a wall. Another sat in a chair pretending to read the newspaper, but what he was really doing – in fact the only thing he had been doing for the past twelve years – was turning the newspaper round and round in circles. A nurse came running and announced, out of breath, that Schneider had had another anxiety attack, and as a consequence had tried to hang himself with his own bed-linen.

– Give him a sedative, Schröder calmly responded, still wondering to himself if it wouldn't have been best for everyone if Schneider's attempt had actually met with success this time. Farther down the ward two male assistants threw themselves on a patient who had tried to rip the clothes off a manic-depressive girl. He was soon pacified and removed, strapped into a straitjacket.

For a moment Schröder remained immobilised, rendered mute by the enormity of the suffering around him. He felt like a commander encircled by the remnants of his wounded troops on the battlefield. Even though the sight as such represented nothing new, alien or shocking for him, on this day he had some difficulty in shaking off the feeling that he was staring straight into hell. Here, he too had been condemned to live out his life as an administrator, entrusted with the task of remaining at his post until every handicapped, invalid, retarded, backward, incapacitated, yes, every single damned unaccountable soul, had been flushed down the sewers to subterranean vaults, where their bodies were to be mummified, their skulls measured, their ribcages placed one on top of another like so many baskets, their teeth stripped of gold and their flesh burned.

Schröder asked Uhland to take over the rounds and descended the main staircase where the smell of wax polish blended with that of disinfectant. He emerged into the courtyard in front of the main hospital building, from which the canopy of linden trees stretched into the distance, like a corridor, an aisle, a visibly endless tunnel.

*

Beatrice had been working in the garden all day, and entered the house carrying with her the scent of moist earth and fresh flowers. She had Mathilde sorting and arranging the flowers on the kitchen table, while she washed and began to think about what to wear for the evening. For her husband this was to be an important gathering, though initially it had just been the result of a coincidence. The snowball had been set in motion one afternoon when Schröder, by chance as it were, ran into county minister Wolfmaul, and was invited to drink a cup of mocha with him. Soon they found themselves discussing important issues, such as the possibility of Dr. Schröder's moving on from his position as head of Sankt-Anna Klinik to that of director of an independent institute for research into occult phenomena. The creation of such an institute, perhaps somewhat surprisingly, turned out to be an important item on the Führer's agenda. So far there had been no more than loose speculation as to who the future head of the institute might be, but Schröder's name had been mentioned more than once, and Wolfmaul himself, who had been something of a godfather to Schröder since his arrival in town, thought the brilliant young psychiatrist an ideal candidate. Toward the end of their conversation, Schröder was even discreetly encouraged by Wolfmaul to invite him to his house. He was quick to seize the opportunity. An evening the following week was agreed upon.

The day before Wolfmaul was to visit the Schröder family, he telephoned regretting that he had been forced to accept another invitation, an urgent official meeting with Dr. Siegfried Rheinau at the Universitätsklinik. Schröder was of course willing to postpone their evening together, but then Wolfmaul himself came up with the idea of bringing Rheinau along to Schröder's house, in this way letting one meeting merge with the other.

– You see, Wolfmaul had added in a confidential tone, – If you obtain the favourable opinion of this man, it might just be your ticket to success. Only remember, he's a fanatic. Do I need to say more? Well, he's also a bachelor with a pronounced predilection for, you know, young actresses and so on. So, if by any chance you know some charming young lady, a friend of your wife's, perhaps, who could be invited as well, then I am quite positive that I could talk him into rounding off the meeting at your house instead of at the Ratskeller.

Although unwilling to let probable members of the Nazi party into his house, Schröder realised that Wolfmaul had just made him an offer he neither could nor should refuse. If he played his cards wisely now, he might soon be delivered from his dilemma at the clinic, since whoever was chosen to head paranormal research experiments would hardly be the same kind of physician as the one qualified to administer the euthanasia programme. At the same time, Beatrice must be kept unaware of the gravity of the situation. Her unknowing neutrality was at present the best weapon to counter any difficulty, the only problem being how to convince her of the necessity of inviting young, intelligent and attractive Laura Emming to dinner with two senior representatives of the state. Hans Schröder solved this problem by adding another couple to the invitation list, in this manner giving both his wife and the prospective guests the impression that their gathering was no more than a purely social occurrence. Of course, he couldn't know to what extent Wolfmaul would be obliged to reveal the real aim of the manoeuvre to Rheinau. Neither was it quite clear what Wolfmaul himself expected in return for his paternal recommendation.

Consequently, the person figuring in Schröder's mind was another contradiction in terms, namely a timid corporate lawyer, who a couple of years ago had helped Beatrice and he to acquire the patrician villa at 18 Fürstenbergstraße, their present address in the town of Freiburg im Breisgau. The man had ever since remained a legal consultant to the family, and he was an ideal decoy, insofar as Laura Emming, with her passionate and obtrusive interest in the law, would almost certainly, and much to the lawyer's embarrassment, force him to engage in a discussion on judicial matters. Blücher's simple-minded wife would help to confer upon the soiree an indispensable air of banality – Schröder had high hopes in this regard. Both Wolfmaul and Rheinau had no doubt been informed of the Führer's latest whim, and neither would compromise himself by bringing state secrets up for discussion at a dinner table at which ladies were present. However, a gentlemen's rendez-vous in the study was a more or less preordained matter. There the question could indeed be brought up, that is to say, he could mention it. It might even be expected of him that he make his personal standpoint on this question clear to Rheinau, so that he in turn, and without further hesitation, could recommend Schröder for the new appointment. But this piece of theatre also entailed some considerable risk in the event of Rheinau's deciding not to go along with Wolfmaul. Suppose, for instance, that Rheinau was only interested in hearing him express his commitment to the new programme, to make sure he was kept at his present job. That was a distinct possibility, since from what Schröder had heard about Rheinau, his loyalty was to principles, never to human beings, except, of course, to the Führer himself. In the name of secrecy he could perhaps simply remain silent and wait for someone else either to bring the issue into the open, or to gloss over it. The order had certainly been made known to all physicians in executive positions, and it was perhaps applicable to all branches of medicine. However, he could hardly be mistaken in assuming that it entailed a downright imperative to mental asylums and other institutions for the spiritually debilitated. In moments of weakness, Schröder had toyed with the idea of going 'insane' himself. But then it struck him, what an irony of fate it would be if he were then imprisoned in his own hospital and 'mercifully killed'. He finally concluded that he must boldly advance to face danger. It had become too late to turn back. The enemy was already at the gate.

*

Beatrice was somewhat at a loss; she couldn't quite make head and tail of the assorted company expected at the evening's buffet. "Since the guests will probably arrive at different times of the evening, cold cuts will suffice", Hans had said. "After all, we must show some solidarity with soldiers going to the front, and not flaunt the blessings of domestic life," he had added with a smile which made Beatrice laugh. She posed in front of the mirror as she remembered his words, confident in her choice of dress, an elegant greyish-blue flannel creation crowned by a bow. But then the mere thought of Laura Emming – who for some reason knew that a bachelor doctor had been specially invited – made her change her mind and settle on something less conservative. For some years hers and Laura's friendship had been close, but of late Laura had begun to behave capriciously, sometimes even insinuating an intimacy with her husband that Beatrice found oddly out of place – especially in view of the unlimited hospitality she had always enjoyed as a guest in their home. Deciding to straighten her out, if necessary, Beatrice nonchalantly threw a colourful shawl over her bare shoulders, assuring herself that a princess, no matter how charming, was not to be favourably compared to the queen.

She heard Hans at the front door. He entered the house, and she went downstairs to greet him. He heard her coming too and tried to control himself so that she wouldn't notice how excited and nervous he was.

– How has your day been, dear? she asked casually, giving him a kiss and putting his hat away.

– Oh, another day at the mill. A few attempted suicides, inedible food, paperwork from the Medical Board ... They want to cut down on our staff. Sankt-Anna is too expensive.

– Sounds like another of those days, then.

– Hmmm, absolutely. Even the weekly threat of closing down the hospital has become routine ... But you look lovely, let me see ... That's beautiful.

– You haven't forgotten that we have guests tonight, have you?

– Oh, no, of course not. I just need to finish this letter to the board about the transfer of two patients to another clinic, that's all. I'll soon be done.

Schröder went into his study, but instead of sitting at his desk, he began walking aimlessly to and fro across the room. Dissatisfied with his vagaries, he opened a small cabinet, took out a bottle of brandy and poured himself a generous measure. Just as he finished his drink, the bell sounded. Mathilde announced that a guest had arrived. Schröder hurried to make himself presentable. When he entered the salon he saw that it was Dr. Rheinau, and he alone, who had arrived. His surprise was instantaneous – where on earth was Wolfmaul?

– Professor Rheinau, I presume. I am Dr. Schröder. It is a great joy and honour for me to receive you as a guest.

– The honour and pleasure is all mine, Doktor Rheinau responded.

– Can I offer you something to drink, a schnapps, perhaps, or a whisky?

– I would prefer mineral water, if that is possible.

– But of course. Mathilde, would you be so kind as to make sure that the professor has some mineral water? Turning to his guest again, he continued, – Do please make yourself comfortable. I'm sorry, but I shall have to leave you alone for just a moment. There is one little thing I have to take care of.

– No need for excuses, Doktor. After all, I am a little early. It's not really my fault, though. County Minister Wolfmaul asked me to join him here, at this hour, but he also said he might be a few minutes late. We met at the Universitätsklinik earlier this afternoon, you see.

– I quite understand ... I'll be with you in no time at all ...

On the way to his study, Schröder met his wife in the doorway.

– Beatrice, dear. Let me introduce you to Professor Siegfried Rheinau, the world-renowned thorax specialist. We are indeed fortunate to have such great men here in Freiburg. Professor Rheinau, may I introduce Beatrice, my wife. Now, please excuse me for a moment.

Rheinau moved forward respectfully and feigned a kiss on her hand.

– So you are the famous Frau Schröder of whom we have all heard so much. I would never have imagined that marriage could make a woman so beautiful.

– Then you should have seen me before I got married!

– I don't even dare to think about it!

– You really know how to flatter a woman, Professor. May I ask, are you married yourself?

– No, I still belong to the incorrigible and inglorious assembly of bachelors, and I shall, alas, probably remain a desert island on an old and forgotten map.

– Oh, that would be entirely up to you to decide. I can't imagine ... women must be running after you ... a handsome Professor of medicine ... world-famous, too ... you are teasing me!

Professor Rheinau smiled, quite satisfied with his own coquetry. It was true that he didn't look a villain. And as far as marriage was concerned, possibilities had not been lacking. But Rheinau was a man of lofty principles. His lifestyle was simple, and he was in his own mind totally dedicated to the progress of science. Not only did he expect from a woman obedience and loyalty, but also that she understand the importance of subordinating herself to a higher cause. He had found most women too superficial and frivolous to accept the commitment required in the service of something beyond family and social position. So he had remained unmarried. Of all the women he had met, however, none had made a greater impression on him than Frau Schröder. He could see now why she was so admired all over Freiburg. Her physical constitution showed nothing of the sturdiness characteristic of so many of the women of the region, even the most beautiful. She was tall and slim, yet at the same time voluptuous, and her features combined in a seductive manner Nordic and Oriental traits; heavy eyelids contrasted with blond hair and delicate eyebrows, olive-tinged skin with full red lips and a slightly aquiline nose. There was in her countenance an enigmatic blend of cool northern aristocracy and the passionate temperament of the Mediterranean. Rheinau experienced something of a wild, burning sensation that was in violent opposition to his controlled and mannerly bearing. It struck him that there might be reason to envy Dr. Schröder in one respect at least – it even occurred to him to regret that she was already married. But then his self-discipline came to his rescue and he suppressed his feelings.

Arriving guests, Wolfmaul among them, now began to crowd the hallway. Schröder had felt much relieved on seeing the minister enter the walkway, his cane swinging. Counsellor Blücher and his wife arrived at the same time, and as Schröder stepped into the salon to resume his conversation with Rheinau (who again had difficulty taking his eyes off Beatrice) he received a long dark glance from Laura Emming, herself newly arrived.

Glasses of Sekt were served – even Rheinau accepted

one and Schröder was only too keen to interpret this as a good omen. The county minister, who felt he had to make his jovial presence felt, returned Schröder's salutation and welcome with an energetic and altogether sincere,

– A toast to the Führer, the Fatherland and their future victories!

Schröder knew Wolfmaul to be a liberal of the old school, that is to say, someone who still in this fateful year of 1939 regretted the fall of the Weimar Republic and sincerely wished for its resurrection, or at least for some sort of functioning democratic as well as capitalistic system. But he was also a sworn anti-Bolshevik, and it was quite possible that, confronted by two evils, he would prefer what was apparently the lesser. His patriotic exclamation, on the other hand, had nothing to do with this, but served the purpose of convincing Rheinau that in this house he was among reliable, thoroughly dedicated people. "Whatever you do," Schröder thought, as he saw Beatrice instinctively playing out her role of keeping Rheinau entertained and flattered, "Don't be deceived by his compliments, and, above all, don't tell him any more than he needs to hear."

The meal, frugal enough so as not to offend the sense of wartime decorum, was served in the adjoining room. Soon the conversation had exhausted the subject of wind and weather; even the compulsory eulogies of the German army had abated. It now took a decidedly provocative turn with Laura's passionate objection to something Counsellor Blücher had just said.

– Personally, I simply don't understand how anyone, even as a jurist, can allow himself to defend a cold-blooded murderer or rapist. How would you react, for instance, if you knew a man to be guilty – maybe he had confessed to you – of murdering children, and you were charged with the task of defending him in court?

– I have never accepted such a case, Blücher said, so much taken aback by the vehemence of Laura's words that he quite forgot to remind her that he was a corporate lawyer, and never had dealings with criminal cases.

– Would you be able to? Laura said, fastening her deep brown eyes upon him. – Suppose it was a really well paid assignment, or that the trial was a matter of national importance that could greatly enhance your reputation?

– As I said, I have never accepted such a case and I can only answer the question hypothetically. In principle, every human being, regardless of his crime, has the right to be assigned a public defender, and I think it would be wise to make a distinction between the lawyer in his capacity of civil servant and as a private citizen.

– So you mean that although you might find a crime abominable – you may even privately wish the defendant sentenced to death – you must at the same time do all in your power as an officer of the court to have the man acquitted. As a lawyer, in fact, you have a further duty to try to influence the legal proceedings so that any sentence handed down will be as lenient as possible, isn't that correct?

– Yes, that's correct.

– How on earth could you do that, if at the same time you are absolutely convinced of his guilt, and you despise, reject and loathe his deed?

– I would have to try.

– And what would you feel if you were to succeed in freeing a man who you knew to be a bestial child-killer? How could you live with yourself as a human being if you knew that, thanks to you, this man was free to roam the streets again, and that the next headline announcing the murder of yet another child is proof that the same killer has struck again? Would you then just continue to say your Lord's Prayer and wish for sweet dreams during the night, or what?

– What I said was simply hypothetical!

– Yes, I know, and I'm trying to understand that hypothesis, Laura countered.

She would doubtless have continued her attack had the general conversation not quietened for a moment and all attention centred upon Siegfried Rheinau, who now came to Blücher's rescue.

– Dear young lady, the duty and responsibility that the legal code lays upon a court official must necessarily overrule considerations of personal preference and taste. Of course, the lawyer is as convinced as the prosecutor that justice must be done. The task of the attorney is not to conceal the truth but to give the defendant a chance to defend or justify his actions, no matter how disgusting they may seem. No one in the court-room cares what the lawyer personally thinks or feels. Jurisdiction and the irreproachability of the court rest on the premise that all investigations are conducted in the hope of uncovering the truth of the matter, and, on the evidence presented, providing the basis for an appropriate sentence. However, to arrive at this final stage of the trial, it is absolutely indispensable that the words of the accused are heard by way of his counsel, and duly acknowledged.

– I understand that too! Laura impatiently exclaimed.

– But that's not what I'm talking about. I wanted to know if Counsellor Blücher could live comfortably with himself knowing that a child-murderer, partly thanks to him, had escaped the law.

– You don't seem to have a very high opinion of our legal system, Fräulein Emming. However, I must emphasise that your question is impossible to answer, and irrelevant too. If a person charged with the murder of children is declared free to go, it means that the court considers the evidence against the defendant to be insufficient for the pronunciation of 'guilty as charged' in compliance with the requirements of the law. Furthermore, it also means that such circumstantial evidence pertaining to the case as has been adduced has not been considered trustworthy enough to link the accused to the crime 'beyond all reasonable doubt'. When this happens, the court has no alternative but to set the defendant free, cleared of all charges brought against him. Now, if the court has decided that a person accused of murder is from the standpoint of the law innocent, then he is, or should be, innocent in the eyes of society. This holds true regardless of what you, Fräulein Emming, or anyone else, may choose to think about it. No court of justice can be ruled by assumptions. As in scientific matters, there has to be evidence, and for evidence to be introduced into court there must be facts. Without facts we are unable to determine the existence of practically anything, let alone to declare a man guilty of murder.

Professor Rheinau's words were not received with general approbation, but they were nonetheless sufficiently authoritative to put an end to the discussion. Although Laura would have gone on to question this ostensibly logical but absurdly idealised image of the legal system, she was in effect forestalled. Beatrice, in announcing that coffee, tea and cake were to be served in the next room, took the opportunity to bring the discussion to an end. Here the guests formed separate conversing groups, and the gentlemen, after a few minutes, withdrew to Schröder's study. Once the doors had closed behind the group of four, and Wolfmaul was comfortably seated, brandy and cigar at hand, Rheinau wasted no further time.

– The minister has had the kindness to inform me that your preferred subject of research is not so much part of traditional psychiatry as it is of, shall we say, the 'occult' sciences. Now, if this is the case, how would you best describe the nature of so-called paranormal studies?

– Well, first of all I think psychiatry, in itself a quite recent offshoot of the mighty tree of natural science, has always in some manner had dealings with what are sometimes referred to as paranormal phenomena. The French system of psychiatry, for instance, was based on results of experiments obtained from research into 'animal magnetism', that is hypnosis, and other mental states in which the patient finds himself in some kind of trance, for instance, a somnambulistic fugue or at least a considerably lowered awareness. The experiments conducted and the theories propounded by Charcot at La Salpêtrière were extremely influential, not only in France, but in Austria and Germany, too. Although unwilling to admit it, both Kraepelin and Bleuler were influenced by that charismatic French professor. Janet, Wundt and Freud are in direct succession to Charcot, and in the Zurich school the phenomena of psychophysical parallelism have become almost an obsession. Now, Jung and his colleagues might be accused of employing methods that are not entirely scientifically approved, and of relying more on speculation and the purely anecdotal evidence provided by folklore and literature. The fact remains, however, that scholars from all over Europe, yes, and from America too, are interested in this treatment of the subject. I mean, we have the scientific Journal of Parapsychology by the Rhines at Duke University ...

– I understand, Rheinau interrupted, but you see, it is exactly the international nature of these ventures which is seen as harmful and counter-productive to our own, national, branch of psychiatry. The Führer is above all interested in seeing the results of paranormal research put to use in the service of the Reich. Is there, for instance, a way in which intelligence operations could be enhanced by the aid of telekinesis?

– At present we don't know enough about telekinesis to determine whether it could be put to any kind of practical use. Besides, the study of the human psyche knows no borders. It is not merely international, it is supranational. It follows that scientific inquiry in this domain would benefit to a great degree from the free exchange of ideas and experimental results.

– That, I'm afraid, is out of the question at present, Dr. Schröder. Paranormal research has been classified, meaning that any results obtained within research centres designed to study such phenomena must be kept top secret, the province of the Ministry of Internal Affairs, which appoints local officials as well as heads of clinics. As our friend Wolfmaul has explained, there are plans to establish such a research centre here in Baden-Württemberg. The position as head of that clinic is still vacant, and my question to you – purely consultative and informal, of course – is: do you think it possible to create a national institution for paranormal research which would have as its prime objective the enhancement of the efficiency of our conventional methods of warfare and the provision of another valid resource in Germany's battle for peace, prosperity and victory?

Schröder looked at Wolfmaul, who, although he remained immobile in his chair, let the affirmative show in his eyes. Blücher, realising that he had involuntarily witnessed the discussion of state secrets and had therefore become implicated by association, didn't dare look anyone in the face. All too aware that the question was a trap and not to be taken at face value, Schröder forced himself to deliver the ludicrous answer, "Yes, I think so," in a tone of voice sufficiently composed to seem wholly sincere. But as soon as he had spoken, he knew that he had turned himself into a sitting target. The only thing Rheinau would have to do now in order to make a fool out of him, would be to ask the simple question: "How?"

There was no "how". Schröder knew it. He also knew that Rheinau knew it. But to his great surprise, the question was never posed. Instead Rheinau calmly continued,

– What exactly was it that prompted you, a clinical psychiatrist accustomed to the rigours of science, to become so fascinated by these apparently random and ephemeral phenomena?

– Actually, it happened as a consequence of personal experience. Ever since I was a child, I have had the feeling that I divide my existence between two worlds simultaneously, one material, the other of a more subtle composition.

I think of them as parallel, because in my experience, as in that of others whom I have interviewed on the subject, these worlds are closely interrelated, and very similar to each other, although not completely identical.

– What do you mean by that?

– Well, for instance, you may be faced with a course of action in the material world, and find that in the other realm a similar scenario obtains. However, the difference between the two states in which the action is played out is this. In the material world there is cause and effect, in other words, time and space. In the disembodied realm, however, time and space are neither categorical nor irreversible, so that the action taking place in the material world sometimes precedes the action in the second realm, while at other times it is the other way round. Most individuals, aware of both realms, would describe this awareness as a kind of intuition, an ability, as it were, to see round corners and to anticipate the immediate future. And the reason for this, it seems, is that in those instances the event itself, or some very similar event, has already, in relation to our time-space continuum, taken place. May I put it this way? Have you ever had the experience of thinking about a certain person, or of thinking you actually saw him, only to find out that it wasn't him; then, two minutes later you actually did run into him? Was it all chance that made you think of this person, or imagine him as someone else? I personally don't think so. However, to prove the existence of simultaneous, parallel worlds scientifically, is of course an altogether different matter, requiring diligently applied methods, and, above all, patience.

Wolfmaul, realising that Schröder, in his scientific enthusiasm, might taint the aura of national interest in which Rheinau had invested the project, now used his social rank and senior years to intervene, putting an end to further questioning by proposing another toast to the Fatherland.

– It is all very, very interesting. 'Worlds within worlds', and all that. You see, he added, turning to Rheinau and the terrified Blücher, – Our dear friend and colleague is not only an unusually gifted medical scientist with excellent credentials. He has also convinced us that he fully understands the important mission assigned to national psychiatry at a time when the future of the world has become inseparable from the future of Germany: Heil Hitler! The others dutifully echoed in chorus, – Heil Hitler!

Warm air stirred in the room. Schröder, seeing that Rheinau now drank mineral water only, did not doubt that, no matter how much paternal solicitude Wolfmaul showed towards his protégé, he would remain objective. Schröder had no idea whether or not he had succeeded in gaining his confidence. Only the next days, or weeks even, would tell. Until then he must deal with the euthanasia programme, and the most likely eventuality was that any authority considering offering him the position as head of the new research institute would first test his willingness to carry out government policies. No matter what the result of this evening's conversation, the Nazis were not interested in furthering science as such. Science had to be subservient to the will of the people, figuratively expressed in the idea of the State, and incarnated in the Führer himself. Loyalty was never to be shown in words only; it had to be proven in deeds.

Meanwhile, in the salon, Frau Blücher, given to gossip

and as talkative as ever after the long silence imposed on her at table, had kept any conflict between the two younger women in abeyance. Beatrice was outraged at what she felt to be Laura's incursion into her's and her husband's private territory. In her opinion the discussion on the theoretical ramifications and subtleties of the legal system had been a maladroit attempt on Laura's part to expropriate the attention of everyone at table and to make herself 'interesting'. Sensing that Rheinau regarded her as a pretty but rather wilful girl, and sure of the impression she herself had made on him, she could hardly wait for the moment when she could speak outright. She was not given the opportunity though. While Frau Blücher was still rattling tirelessly on, the study door swung open and the men strolled into the drawing-room. Soon after that the gathering moved to a natural conclusion, and the guests began to drift towards the cloakroom. Laura was the first to reach the door, and held it so that the other guests could pass into the still warm September evening. The red and yellow roses distilled their heavy fragrance into the air, and the gravel path was strewn with early autumn leaves carried there that same afternoon by a vigorous wind. Schröder conducted his guests to the front gate. As Laura passed him, she leaned so close to him that he felt her breath caress his ear.

– As your friend, Hans, I must tell you to beware of Rheinau. He doesn't have good intentions towards you. I think he wants you out of the way. Be careful, won't you?

– Don't worry, Schröder quickly replied, and hurried to settle his guests in their places in the large car Wolfmaul had sent for. The chauffeur was just about to close the last door when Schröder discovered that Laura was not among the passengers. She had hidden behind the chestnut tree beside the gatepost. Schröder made a quick gesture of the head, indicating that she should get into the car.

– I'm not going with that man, she mouthed at him. Schröder made a fierce face at her, leapt to the car door and held it open for her, ostentatiously, so that she would understand that she wasn't going anywhere else. – We are at war, he hissed as she passed him. – Don't make a fuss!

From the window on the second floor of the villa this same scene seemed to Beatrice like a veritable pantomime as she watched the guests take their seats in the car. She saw her husband stare and gesticulate in the direction of a tree. Next, the car backed up. For a moment Hans disappeared. A female shape became visible behind the chestnut tree, and at the same time Hans reappeared. The door closed and the car moved off. Hans stood looking at it. When it was out of view he turned and began to walk back to the house. Beatrice saw him raise his eyes toward the row of second-floor windows, and quickly shrank back behind the curtain. Hans stopped at the flower-beds and inhaled the fragrance of the roses, but he couldn't quite sense it – the hospital smells of antiseptic, chlorine and wax polish still lingered in his nostrils. He shook his head and went into the house. Beatrice had already taken some of the china into the kitchen for Mathilde to wash and dry in the morning. He walked around the house switching off electric lights, and made sure his papers in the study were in order for the morrow. He lit the rest of the tobacco in his pipe and watched the bluish vapours suffuse the moonlight that streamed in through the windows with an iridescent glow. He knocked the smouldering dottle out into the ashtray and left the warm pipe in it. When closing the door he was overcome by the not altogether pleasant feeling of taking farewell of something – a farewell to himself?

Although Schröder was much relieved that he hadn't been obliged to discuss the contents of the new directions in the medical community during the course of this evening, he had an intimation that his troubles were only just beginning. Hope was no more than a faint glimmer in the midst of the masses of clouds looming over the horizon. His immediate concern, however, was deliberately to suppress and conceal for as long as possible the real nature of the menace. Beatrice, on the other hand, had already sensed the danger and the precariousness of their situation. She was determined to let Hans know that whatever he had to do, she would support him. Assessing the situation, she arrived at the conclusion that a man like Rheinau would never have been invited to the house unless there was a very good reason for it. And she could see on Hans' face, in some tension between his eyebrows, that there was something going on in connection with that man which affected him deeply. Still in a pensive mood, and not yet quite able to forgive Laura her earlier transgression, Beatrice undressed, combed her hair and prepared to go to bed. She heard Hans mount the stairs, but he didn't come straight to the bedroom. Instead he entered the children's rooms. The moon, nearly full, shone through the window onto their peaceful features through the intricate pattern of the branches and foliage of the chestnut tree. It was as though the tree was inscribing some dark secret on their blank foreheads, some mysterious runes, selecting the children for an uncommon fate. He went up to their beds, caressed their heads and hair that fell like delicate veils over their marble-like ears. He kissed them. First Renate, his little blonde girl, ten years old, coquettish and angelic like her mother, sleeping with her mouth slightly open, as if swallowing moonshine with each inhalation. Then Peter, his firstborn son, dark-haired like Hans' own father, eight years old, at the age when the world opens out and horizons begin to expand beyond what is next and nearest to reveal a solitary road leading farther and farther away from home. How pale she was, the moon mistress, an ivory conspirator against his love and happiness, and yet innocent, blank, insubstantial. Although her radiance seemed somehow to be transporting the children's souls away from him, there was nobody he could accuse of theft. In the last instance, night itself was the thief stealing away from him. But the night was not just stealing. It gave strength and the courage to live as well. In the morning their little faces would come to life again, their young limbs would long for movement and their minds for excitement. Soon enough the sun would dissipate the fatal kiss of the sinister spirit and make it all seem what it actually was: an obscure dream.

To finish the round, so much dearer to his heart than the one he had regularly to perform in the wax- and chlorine-smelling asylum, he went into the chamber next to their own bedroom where the baby slept. Little Heinz, new to the world six months ago, smiling at everyone, confident and charming. Still, the little boy had big sorrowful eyes that reminded Hans of his own grandmother, the large-eyed woman stoutly defending her husband in the face of calamity. Impregnation by an unspeakable sadness was common to both of them, and they both had a way of gazing outward that seemed to betray superior knowledge.

That an old person may give one such an impression was understandable, but to receive it from a child? It was as though his grandmother's eyes, long since closed forever, had simply changed abode and now lived on, covered by leaf-thin membranes, in the velvety hollow of two small, rosy eye sockets.

As he watched the baby, Hans was overcome by sentiments from the past. He went up to the cradle and slid his finger gently through the thin hair until he arrived at the indentation marking the still-open cranium. Here it is, he thought, the entrance to the parallel worlds. Here the soul enters. Then the traces are effaced and the entrance is sealed off. From that moment the soul is trapped within the material world, although it retains memories of its spiritual past. And in some people, in some brains, this link is never completely severed, so that there is always a possibility of communication, not always an exact and accurate one, more often akin to the messages transmitted along a radio wave subject to atmospheric disturbances and other unpredictable distortions. Consequently, the interpretations vary, but the phenomenon remains essentially the same; a choir of dim voices, a fleeting presence, dark and irrational moods, the sudden illumination brought about by some key words clearly discerned and the ensuing rock-solid conviction: there is someone, something, out there.

Hans finally came to bed. Beatrice pretended to be asleep as her husband's kiss alighted on her forehead. However, after seeing him propped up against the pillows, gazing motionlessly ahead, she turned to him and asked,

– What is it, my love? Is there something you don't want to tell me?

– Oh, it's nothing, dear. Minor problems at the clinic, that's all.

– But they can't be all that minor if they keep you awake like this. Tell me, what is it?

– Unfortunately, there is nothing you can do to help me.

– What do you mean?

– I mean that it was all in vain, the entire evolution from tattooed savage and cannibal to our Biedermeier salons, bourgeois complacency and "Jawohl, Herr Doktor".

– What's got into you?

– I'm telling you how it is. There will soon be a new era, years one, two, three and so on after the advent of the Antichrist. And there is nothing, absolutely nothing, we can do to prevent it from happening.

Beatrice stared into the area of darkness where she assumed the eyes of her husband to be.

– Is it that serious? she asked hesitantly.

– Yes.

– What is it that they want you to do?

– I can't even tell you ...

– No?

– No, absolutely not ...

– Why is that?

– Because it is still a secret, nobody except the medical experts involved are supposed to know ... It is a terrible dilemma ... But then ... All right, I guess it doesn't make much difference. Sooner or later you would probably find out anyway. I may as well tell you the fateful news. They want me to start getting rid of unwanted patients.

– You mean sending them away?

– No, Beatrice, killing them.

– Who are they? Rheinau? Wolfmaul?

– No, Hitler himself, through a certain Dr. Brandt at Tiergarten in Berlin.

– You mean Hitler has specifically ordered you to kill off mental patients?

– Not just me. It's an order issued to doctors throughout the whole country. I am one of the many involved. We haven't received further instructions yet, but they'll no doubt be forthcoming. And I expect them to aim at the elimination of some hopeless cases. The only thing is, they are all more or less hopeless ... It is just terrible.

– And there is nothing you can do to sort of meet the authorities half-way?

– What do you mean?

– I mean, you are not really personally responsible, are you? I assume that there will be more than one medical expert involved in such drastic measures, as well as some kind of ministerial decision-making. Surely, at a time like this, nobody could accuse you of being guilty of wrongdoing, you are just following orders.

– But that's exactly it! Of course I'm responsible – who else is there? We are all responsible if we let this take place. And not just as some form of amorphous amoeba, but each one of us as an individual. Besides, this is probably just the beginning. You'll see, the next step will be to get rid of outlaws, even Gypsies, not to mention Jews. We're in danger, grave danger, Beatrice.

– Is that what Rheinau's and Wolfmaul's visit was all about?

– No, that's our last hope. The government plans to open an institute for paranormal research in the region, and the post of director is still vacant. But there is a lot of secrecy and constant scheming in the wings. I don't even dare to hope for it.

– And if it did happen, who would take over after you at Sankt-Anna Klinik?

– I don't know. They could take someone from outside, or they could promote Uhland.

– And then he would have to do what they are currently ordering you to do?

– I suppose so.

– Well, would you find it easier to live with the fact that he'd be responsible rather than you?

– That's his problem, isn't it? If they decide to offer me another job, then that's it. I can't refuse. It will be an order.

– But isn't what you are expected to do at Sankt-Anna just as much an order, only more unpleasant to carry out?

– What are you saying, Beatrice? That I should start murdering human beings who have absolutely no way of defending or speaking up for themselves? That I should acquiesce in a health-care system which has made it a top priority systematically to kill its patients?

– Oh, Hans, I meant nothing of the sort! I just thought … Maybe it's all just one of those bureaucratic whims, not to be taken literally. You know how they send directions out to everyone, and then nothing comes of it. Hans, I don't want you to get me wrong, especially not at a time like this. I understand your concern. But you know, in the night it is easy to exaggerate things. Sleep on it. Get some rest. You have been working so hard lately. I'm sure that tomorrow you will see it all in perspective. That's when you will be ready to make a decision. Besides, she added while caressing his neck, – If this means that in the end we shall have to leave the house and try to escape abroad, then I shall do everything I can to help us out of here. Who knows, maybe I can influence this, what's his name, Rheinau? He's on the medical board, isn't he?

– Oh, I don't want you to get involved in this dirty business, Beatrice. You just stay out of this, promise me that ... I said, you must promise me that!

– I promise.

Schröder felt somewhat reassured knowing that his wife was now fully aware of the gravity of the situation. At the same time he was surprised. So far it had not occurred to him that a moral imperative was something that could be defined in relative terms. That the Nazis could and indeed did define in any way it pleased them was of course nothing new. He could even see how Uhland, the scientific rationalist, would allow himself in a fit of obstinacy to reason along the same lines. But his wife? "Thou shalt not kill", wasn't that one of the commandments? And what about the Hippocratic Oath? Since when had these things become debatable, not only in the eyes of the Lord, but in the view of a nation's entire medical society and every single person around him? After ten years of marriage and three children ... "Not really personally responsible?" ...

Well into the small hours Schröder kept tossing ideas and plans back and forth in his mind. Eventually everything blurred in chaotic images, and he was haunted by dreams, the one more confused than the other. On waking the next morning, he felt even more desperate than he had the night before, and to the one question at the heart of the problem he had found no satisfactory answer. Or rather, he felt that he had truly found the one and only answer. The problem was that it was also impossible to act upon.

*

In the following weeks, Schröder received a steady stream of communications from the Reich Committee for the Scientific Registration of Serious and Congenital Diseases: information, instructions and orders, as well as a large number of special questionnaires from the Reich Health Ministry. In his reports to this latter authority he had to include details of patients' births, significant events in their family histories, for instance mental illness in other family members and signs of excessive use of drugs such as nicotine, alcohol, morphine and cocaine. In addition, he would be expected to provide further evaluation in each case of the possibility of improvement, estimating life-expectancy, quoting earlier institutional observations and describing the effects of such treatment as had been administered. The Ministry laid special emphasis on the assessment of each subject's capability for work. Schröder did the best he could to accentuate positive aspects wherever possible, underlining the beneficial effects of therapy and treatment, as well as each patient's possible usefulness to whatever community with which he might come into contact. However, to seem over-confident in this regard also involved a risk – it would ring false to any experienced member of the medical profession. To avoid this, Schröder had no other option in certain cases than to describe a patient's chances of recovery and work capacity in negative terms.

For some little time this policy seemed to be working well, and Schröder had the impression that the medical authorities were primarily interested in registering cases of hereditary and clinically defined mental illness, rather than suggesting what was to be done with the patients.

Meanwhile, the position as director of the paranormal research centre remained vacant, and Schröder, by virtue of his compliance and willingness to oblige both the Reich Committee and the Health Ministry, had reason to hope that he might after all be asked to take the job. So it did come as something of a surprise to him when the Chancellery itself, seemingly out of nowhere, sent him a letter asking if Ward-D at Sankt-Anna Klinik, though unused for many years, could be refurbished and turned into a special ward for the criminally insane. The official paraphrases listing the putative aims and functions of the new ward were expressed in terms vague enough to arouse Schröder's suspicions, though in fact nothing was said concerning the future patients as guinea pigs in medical experiments. Nevertheless, it became quite clear to him over the following weeks that this was exactly what the Ministry had in mind. Schröder found himself unable to contact either Wolfmaul or Rheinau, and so realised that he had been fooled and trapped. One morning there was another request from the Ministry on his desk, sharper in tone and turn of phrase than any of its predecessors. Why, the writer asked, had Dr. Schröder not supplied a full answer to the question: could Ward-D, empty and of no practical use at present, be used as a centre for state medical research?

Schröder turned the sheet of paper and weighed it in his

hand. It was printed in heavy black ink and bore two signatures, those of Reichsleiter Bouhler and Dr. Brandt. Having had time to prepare himself for the inevitable, he did not hesitate for long. He went to the telephone and made a call to Berlin confirming to Bouhler's office that Ward-D, provided that the Health Ministry ensured that adequate security measures and sanitation were put in place, and renovations were completed, would indeed be suitable for medical research.

It is possible that Schröder could have postponed the actual decision-making by claiming that the pavilion was in too dilapidated a condition to be of use, and that the Ministry should look elsewhere for more suitable sites for their medical experiments. But he had understood enough of the nature of the game by now to realise that the fact that Ward-D was located near the main buildings of Sankt-Anna, while remaining out of sight of patients, visitors and staff, made it the perfect secret annexe. Even the smoke from the chimneys could easily be confused with that of the charcoal plant further east. This was exactly why the authorities, probably kept up to date by recent topographical surveys, considered it an ideal location. By trying to convince Berlin that this was not the case, Schröder would only make himself more suspect, so he must hope that the plan would turn out to be impracticable. However, in order to underline his willingness to co-operate, he cabled a message to the same effect later that day, following it with a letter of confirmation. In this particular letter he made a last attempt to free himself of responsibility by declaring that in view of the pressure of his current workload, he would find it necessary to decline administrative duties for the new annexe, and to recommend that a separate position be created for the direction of the new department.

The Ministry of Health did not swallow the bait. In the present state of civil emergency, it was out of the question that new administrative directors be appointed solely on the grounds of a hospital's increasing its work capacity. Increased productivity was required from the entire German work-force, and hospital personnel were no exception. On the other hand, in its readiness to support German doctors in their efforts to create a healthy population, the government might be able to put in place measures for the recruitment of reliable medical assistants, and to ensure military surveillance of the area. The document enumerated further practical measures, but although Schröder continued to pore over it, the words could no longer hold his attention.

Absentmindedly, he put the paper away and turned to the high window, opened it and let the deep green and dark blue shadows of the forest enter the room. A bird of prey, perhaps an owl, spread its large wings from a pine tree high up on the Schauinsland. The wind kept the trees climbing the slopes in motion. He rested his eyes on the summit, gradually allowing them to descend into the fertile lands shrouded in autumnal colours. Far to the west, the Rhine valley and its vineyards appeared, enveloped in a haze, reflecting the intense gold and purple of sunset. In its midst, the river meandered in silent silvery coils. Above, the sky grew deeper and deeper, an implacably cold blue, blackening by the minute.

*

According to detailed instructions issued after the conversion of Ward-D, those chosen as suitable subjects for experimentation were to be divided into two main categories: born criminals, and those who had become criminals as a consequence of mental disease. In practice, though, it proved difficult to maintain the distinction. The difference was assumed to be that born criminals enjoyed a higher level of general health even than average citizens, whereas the others, in addition to their psychogenic disorders, usually suffered from various organic diseases as well. The first group, therefore, was considered better-suited to undergo coercive sterilisation procedures, in some cases castration, before being subjected to further experiments, whereas the second should primarily be stimulated to describe or demonstrate their criminal inclinations, if necessary with the aid of addictive drugs which created dependence and were withheld if the patients refused to co-operate.

Another important field of study at the new clinic was the measurement and codification of resistance to serious infectious diseases, in the course of which subjects were to be treated in such a way as to avoid the risk of uncontrolled contamination. When death ensued, bodies had to be incinerated on the premises. Subjects were to be selected from among such criminals as were awaiting execution or had been condemned to life imprisonment. In accordance with Dr. Schröder's ordinances, individuals were chosen and convened at the closed and heavily guarded Ward-D, and then, without the knowledge of other patients, transported to cellars to which only Schröder and certain specified members of the Reich Health Ministry and the Gestapo had access. Together with a carefully selected group of medical colleagues, Schröder was to perform experiments subsumed under the heading "merciful killing". Preparation for this operation began during autumn, and in early January 1940 the special patients began to arrive from criminal institutions and psychiatric wards all over Germany.

For almost two months, Schröder managed to conceal the fact that none of his experiments provided the results expected. There had been some influenza, a case of pneumonia and a few incidences of measles, mumps and eczema, but so far absolutely nothing of scientific value. It soon became apparent that there were no cases of typhus, malaria or yellow fever, and that castrations had not been performed – there was not even one single documented case of enforced sterilisation. Schröder, called to answer for his actions, or rather, his lack of action, managed to defend himself for the time being by claiming that he had not quite understood that the term "to render sexually inactive" should be interpreted as "to castrate". He also argued that the hygienic measures imposed for the staff's protection were still inadequate, and that working on the premises involved significant risk of contamination. It was in all likelihood this last, and by no means irrelevant objection, that saved Schröder from a court martial. Luckily, no one could actually disprove his claim, although it had by now become clear to his superiors that he was not fully motivated in his new position. And Schröder knew that they had found him out. When informed one day that he no longer had to report to the commandant in charge of military security at Ward-D, and could now return to work at Sankt-Anna Klinik, Schröder knew for whom the bell had tolled. Sure of what to expect next, he reassumed his old job and waited all day in his room until the staff on the day shift had gone home. Not until then did he open his desk drawer and take out a heap of papers bearing his handwriting. Rain poured down and streamed along the window panes to fall in cascades to the ground. In a feverish state of mind and eager to finish his writing, he moved the kerosene lamp closer to him. Toward nine o'clock he signed the last document and sealed it with wax before introducing it into the secret compartment of the desk. At the same time, he heard the sound of boots marching over the slippery cobble-stones of the court. He heard an officer shout out orders, and he calmly brought out the gun which had also been kept in the secret compartment. For at least two minutes he kept the muzzle of the pistol pointed at his own head. Then, as the sound of the soldiers' boots grew louder in the hallway, he suddenly removed it, pulled the drawer, and opened the secret compartment once again. He barely had time to close it before the door swung open without warning, and he was formally arrested. Schröder didn't protest. He didn't even ask for what crime he was charged. Accompanied by four Gestapo under their commanding officer, he was led to a waiting car.

The questioning at Gestapo headquarters took place that same evening, and did not take much time. In less than half an hour, Dr. Hans Schröder had been removed as head of Sankt-Anna Klinik, and ordered, in the name of the German people, to serve as an army physician on the eastern front. He was to leave with a contingent of soldiers from Leipzig the following evening, and without further delay to be attached to an army division stationed in eastern Czechoslovakia. No charges or accusations were presented, and Schröder did not ask for any. The only thing he did request was to be allowed to say goodbye to his wife and children. This was granted. At midnight his wife appeared in the doorway of their home, bewildered and seemingly not quite grasping the implications of the situation. In reality Schröder had prepared her in advance.

– This is it, isn't it? she said, holding and kissing his hand.

– Yes. I have to leave you now. I have taken all possible precautions to save you from further harassment, but I can of course not guarantee anything. Please, be cautious and do as I have told you before ... No, don't wake the children up. Tell them tomorrow, and in a way that you think they will best understand. I love you.

They embraced and wept. But in the rain, pouring so heavily over them, not even Hans could tell whether it was the water from above or from within that ran down their cheeks. It was a moment of silent despair. They were both prepared, but it didn't help in the end, no matter how strong and composed Schröder tried to be in the face of the inevitable. They stared at each other for a moment.

– Will you wait for me? he asked.

– I shall always wait for you. Always.

The soldiers closed in on them, telling them that their time was up – Dr. Schröder mustn't be late for the train ... Turning round a last time in the driveway, Hans saw Beatrice enveloped in a curtain of rain. He waved to her, but she couldn't see him. From where she stood he was already gone, as if carried away by darkness itself.

*

The recruits were not to take an ordinary passenger train which would have departed from one of the platforms of Leipzig's main railway station. Instead, they were gathered outside the building and marched across the marshalling yards. There were smells of tar, coke and polluted snow in the air. The night was all-enveloping except for tiny cones of light shed by a few hanging lamps. At a distance they perceived the dim fluorescent lights of the control tower. Here was the back end of a train, its massive iron hook hanging down like a limp member between the bumpers; there was a railway worker, his face hidden beneath a cap or a helmet. To Schröder these workers seemed like mute helpers in a curious operating theatre, where the body to be opened was that of a greasy black giant and the instruments made to fit the incredible thickness of his belly. And there was still another kilometre to march before the sparse light cones clustered around the platform from which the soldiers would finally board the train. Other officers directed them from here. There were windows in the railway carriages, but no seats or bunks. Schröder found himself a corner where he could place his blanket, sink down and rest for a moment. From this remote location, far from the main station, the train, unnoticed, began to move, soon rushing over snow-covered fields. The names of the small stations they passed were mostly unfamiliar to him, though the last station he remembered seeing was Karlsbad. After that the landscape turned pitch-black. He was carried across it together with thousands of other drafted German men – students, workers, fathers, all citizens of the new invincible German Reich. Most seemed to be in good spirits. They shared the little they had brought with them and behaved gently towards one another. Nobody feared a military defeat, except perhaps for one man, who could not shake off the feeling that this imposed nomadic existence was to be theirs for a good deal more than a few days or weeks ... Like blood coagulating in an open wound, dawn rose over the Tatra mountains, bidding the men welcome to the battle, rudely awakening Schröder from a dream in which sunrays, lightning-like, had occasionally succeeded in piercing the massive clouds at the horizon.

Schröder wrote home often, every day if he could. But over time it became more and more difficult. The work burden was overwhelming and endless. His experience of surgery was limited, but since surgery and again surgery was practically the only thing demanded from him, he had no choice other than to become proficient in amputating limbs and removing bullets and shrapnel from open wounds. A few months passed, and Schröder was as full-fledged a surgeon as any other veteran in the field, and went about his business of cutting into flesh with stoic calm. And as long as there were food, blankets, surgical instruments and drugs, the job wasn't too bad. In all events, it was no worse than being out there, constantly exposed to enemy fire.

At the beginning of the campaign there had been relatively few casualties and the patients in the field hospital comprised, in the main, sick soldiers. Then came the massive attack on Russia in the autumn of 1941, Operation Barbarossa, during which German troops began to move into position all over western Russia. However, by October that year, the Wehrmacht faced an opponent that was to prove a hundred times harder to combat than the Red Army itself

– the Russian winter. The Russians would set fire to their own villages as they retreated. The German army became painfully aware that it was sorely under-equipped to deal with the exigencies of an eastern winter. Railway connections were constantly cut. They were rebuilt, but on the whole rarely functioned as they should. Supplies and clothing were delayed or never forthcoming. The oil in trucks and tanks froze, weapons broke. Soon casualties began to take their toll of existing resources, and by the beginning of 1942, as the army was being encircled by the Russians at Stalingrad, there was nothing left of Schröder's field hospital except for a group of moribund men and one sick and exhausted doctor.

There had been rumours that the Russians took no prisoners, that everyone who tried to get out of the pocket of Stalingrad by unauthorised boarding the last transport planes heading back to Germany was shot on the spot, yes, rumours even had it that the General von Paulus himself had already been captured and executed. Schröder knew there was no hope, and he also realised that there was absolutely nothing he could do to help his patients. Those not yet dead soon would be. Feeling that to die in the snow would be better than to be executed by the Russians, he went out into the blizzard. He had the luck to run straight into an army patrol which took him prisoner moments before the suburbian cellar he had just left was blown to pieces.

He was sent to a prison camp at the foot of the Ural mountains. Unlike many of his fellow-prisoners, and although no more than a shadow of his former self, Schröder managed to survive the typhus epidemic raging in the camp. Toward the end of his imprisonment he suffered a serious wound to his right hand. It was infected, and then became gangrenous. There were no doctors to help him, so Schröder himself, with the aid of a bottle of vodka, a scalpel, a knife and bandage, performed the operation and managed to put an end to the infection by amputating two of his fingers. After that he no longer had to perform the same physical labour as the other prisoners, and he lived to see the day when the remaining hundred and fifty prisoners (there had been over two thousand at the beginning) were entrained and in four days transported to the German border. There they changed trains and were told to report to the Russian commandant in Berlin. But the prisoners soon noticed that the train, moving at a leisurely pace through the country-side, in fact had no guards.

The strangest rumours began to spread on board this ghost ship. Some claimed that Germany had actually won the war and forced the Russians to free all prisoners. Others had heard that Hitler had escaped to Paraguay and created a new German state there. Again others held that he was dead, and that a coalition of British, American and French troops had taken over the country. Still others maintained that all Europe had come under Soviet dominion, and that this was the reason why they were no longer under guard – there was simply nowhere to go! Excitement increased to the point where prisoners began to jump from the train and take to walking through the woods. The sight was eerie. It was the month of May. Birds sang while cities and villages still smouldered. Even pastures and fields were burned black, and in the streets people, hollow-eyed, like ghosts, stared at Schröder as he passed. Moving as if physically separate from them, as if lost in an endless maze, he continued to walk, until one day in early summer he reached Freiburg.

It was late in the afternoon when he came to the town, and the intense humidity of the day was about to culminate in a thunderstorm. Just as he turned the corner into the street on which he had lived, a flash of lightning lit up the house – his house. It was unscathed. What a miracle in the midst of so many ruins and hollow facades! His surprise was so great that he didn't at first notice the anomaly of the flash. Lightning had indeed struck, but although it had been close enough for him to discern its sharp smell in the air, it hadn't sounded. And then there was the house itself. In that brief moment of overwhelming light, it had seemed as though it had been slightly out of place, giving an impression that its sides and corners were not forming the same angles to the street and garden as they used to.

At first he attributed this anomaly to the impact of the lightning on his weakened eyes, but even after he had had time to adjust, the house still seemed to be in a slightly different location. Schröder was astonished to witness his own memory playing such a trick on him. Time certainly has a way of changing one's perception, he thought, but then the emotion seizing him practically swept him off his feet, turning his last steps into those of an old mariner struggling to regain his land legs. At the door, as he was reaching for the bell, Schröder discovered that the brass plate no longer carried the familiar inscription, Dr. Hans and Frau Schröder, but had been replaced by one that read Professor Siegfried Rheinau. There was no mention either of a wife or any other family member.

The woman who opened the door did not recognise him. Still, Schröder felt a bolt of joy strike his heart. It was Mathilde, old Mathilde, who for so long had managed his household and looked after his children. He was just about to introduce himself, when she said,

– Neither the Professor nor Madame is at home, nor are the children, but if you wish, you may wait in the hall. Madame will soon be back.

Schröder nodded. Mathilde noticed that the bearded man was pale and weak. She asked him whence he came and who he was, and he answered that he was a relative, a distant cousin of the mistress of the house, and that, in fact, she would be expecting him. Hearing this, Mathilde assumed responsibility for letting him sit and wait in the drawing-room.

With some exceptions, the furniture was still the same. Gradually, he recognised his surroundings. The feeling of disorientation thus receded, only to leave room for a sensation of cold. There was an alien breath in the house, as of a ghost passing through and covering it in rime, inviting death itself to build its nest in a sea of roses. Suddenly he envisaged the other man's meticulously manicured hand, holding a fountain pen, signing one document after another. He saw him rise from the desk after a day's work, saw the soft white, lily-like hand shoot out from the immaculate cuff and alight on his wife's cheek and arched neck.

The reality had become painfully clear to him. That evening some years ago when he had been invited to the house, Schröder had inadvertently given Rheinau all the evidence he needed to justify his decision not to offer him the job. That same night a folder containing confidential documents had mysteriously disappeared from Schröder's office at the hospital. He had been incautious enough to leave it on his desk. The door to his office had been locked, but someone had managed to break into it and steal the folder. Only a few days elapsed after this before he was asked to become head of Ward-D ...

The feeling of giddiness was caused not only by his complete physical and mental exhaustion. In the garden, sudden rain, pouring down into the flowers, had forced the jasmine to transpire an almost tangible scent. In wave after wave it rolled in through the open window, soporific, nauseating as hemlock. Seized by the impulse to get out before he fell fatally asleep, Schröder threw a quick glance into the garden and along the path. At the same moment the gate at the far end swung open, and his wife appeared, lit by a ray of sunshine that pierced the purple cloud. Schröder's retreat had been cut off. He had no choice other than to return to the drawing-room. During the minute which elapsed before she entered the room, he had reconstructed in his mind what must have happened since his arrest. She had never been forced to leave the house, had never been arrested nor sent to a camp. A gracious offer from someone who seemed to be a gentleman had enabled her to marry the henchman, dutifully administering government policies and pondering on solutions in the same detached meticulous way as he polished his nails, pedantically attentive to every unwanted roughness in their texture.

Nobody could have expected that Schröder would come back, least of all himself. And now his return was inevitably destined to become a burden to everyone. At times, on the immense Russian plain, he had hallucinated the diminutive yet sharp voice of the propaganda minister ringing like a miniature bell. The voice of the German ministry had persecuted him in his dreams, the little bell ringing over the door to heaven and hell. It was the minute Goebbels, a thin voice demanding that the door be opened, announced the names of fallen warriors to the Führer in the foresworn knights' chapter. But Schröder had not died, and had no reason to heed the minister's passing bell. Somewhere in the interior of the continent, he had been smiling straight into the starry sky while hearing the bell persistently call out for him. The peals grew more piercing, but louder they couldn't get, could never be more than the sound of a little bell. Thus the propaganda minister disappeared, angrily stamping, into the ringing of his own impotent eternity. The oil in the trucks froze. The drivers hung dead over their wheels. The remainders of the medical transports had been tipped into a ditch outside a burning village. Again he smiled into the starry sky. He saw his wife Beatrice, dressed in white, a bride at her wedding. She gave him her hand and with his two hands he reached out for it; the blinding snow-white hand with the diamond ring and the beautiful nails. Instantly he was appalled at the sight of his own right hand, wrapped in filthy cloth, burning as if his flesh were a piece of charcoal in the Siberian night.

– Who are you? What do you want? Schröder turned and stared into the face of his wife.

– I? My name is Müller ... Heinz Müller. Please excuse me for intruding, but I lived in this house many years ago.

– I see, Beatrice said hesitantly. Tentatively she continued, – Was this your childhood home?

– No, not quite. I wasn't born here, but one could perhaps say that in a sense I died here.

– I beg your pardon?

– Oh, just a clumsy joke. He coughed. – The past winter was not so good for me.

– It wasn't easy for anyone, Herr Müller.

– No, no, of course not. Not easy for anyone ...

Beatrice looked as though she expected him to continue. But then her eyes fell on the mutilated fingers of his right hand, and she involuntarily took one step back. She winced repeatedly, as if trying to shake off a persistent feeling of discomfort.

– What can I do for you? she asked in a low voice.

– I was just wondering ... Perhaps you would understand my odd request. My family is no longer around. I so much wanted to see where I once lived.

Beatrice moved forward again and rang the bell. A moment later Mathilde appeared in the doorway.

– Mathilde, would you be so kind as to show this gentleman the house. He once lived here and wishes to bid his memories farewell.

Mathilde, surprised at the impersonal and formal tone of voice, couldn't help saying, – But this gentleman is Madame's own cousin. I heard him say so himself ... Beatrice's sudden bewilderment terrified her.

– What have I done? she exclaimed.

Beatrice didn't bother to answer her. Instead she turned straight to Schröder saying,

– To my knowledge I have no male cousins, and certainly no one by the name of Heinz Müller. Would you be so good as to empty the contents of your pockets on this table, show me the lining of your jacket, and then immediately leave this house. Otherwise I shall not hesitate to call the police. My husband has important connections, and he can make life difficult for you if you ...

– I have no doubt about that. By the way, who is this man that I should fear, if you'll excuse me asking?

– I don't excuse you anything, and I order you to get out of here.

– You don't have to worry. I haven't taken anything that wasn't mine. I did lie about our blood ties, but it is also true that at one time in my life, I actually lived here ...

– Please leave us now.

Schröder nodded.

– Goodbye. Maybe we shall see each other again, maybe not, he said on his way out, hat respectfully in hand, leaving a shaken Beatrice behind.

Schröder headed towards the letterbox at the far end of the path. Suddenly he felt himself losing consciousness. A deep, pulsating, infinite darkness embraced him. As he collided headlong with the gatepost, he had an intense premonition of how wonderful it must be to die. The state of unconsciousness could not have lasted more than a few seconds, but during these few seconds he felt very far removed from the world. In the fall he hurt his head, and blood began to trickle down his forehead. He dabbed at it with the back of his hand, and found that the wound, luckily, was not very deep. His legs still refused to carry him though. Slithering, he found himself embracing the letterbox on which the name Rheinau appeared in strangely meandering patterns. The name alone was like an ominous inscription, a code to be deciphered, like entwined serpents on some bizarre apocalyptic altar-piece. It gave rise to a vision of a last judgement; carnivorous devils, lofty angels, and the image of man set against the background of imminent doom. Coming to his senses at last, he felt a bitter regret that he hadn't been taken away. All he could think, all he managed to whisper, was, – Even you, Beatrice ...

*

As Schröder gradually recovered from his initial shock, the feeling of giddiness turned into jealousy, hatred and a burning desire for revenge. On second and third thoughts he could hardly blame Beatrice for having remarried – in hers and in the eyes of the world he was dead, reported missing at the battle of Stalingrad three long years ago. Who knew, perhaps desperate circumstances had forced her to take this drastic decision? He had indeed expected on his return to find both her and the children dead. Miraculously, they were all alive. In the days that followed, Schröder often went back to Fürstenbergstraße and watched the children on their way to and from school. Renate led her youngest brother by the hand, while Peter twirled around them playing practical jokes. In the afternoon, Mathilde would bring the boys home, while Renate, now a young lady who carried her load of school books with dignity and pride, returned alone later during the day. She was beautiful to watch, her movements harmonious and graceful. Yet, in her eyes Schröder could even from the distance of his hide-out detect an expression of unspeakable sorrow, and on many occasions he felt the overwhelming impulse to make himself known, to walk up to her and take her into his arms.

It took all of his remaining willpower to prevent himself from doing so.

It had also by now become painfully clear to Schröder, that, if he were to defeat Rheinau, there could be no premature action. Rheinau had not only survived the war, he was still, as far as Schröder knew, quite free of suspicion of participation in the euthanasia programme. At the beginning of the war he had been thought of simply as the head of the thorax clinic at the University. Schröder's search for evidence of later, more sinister activities, had so far led nowhere. Most probably any documents that could in any way have compromised Rheinau had long since been destroyed. Schröder would have a great deal of difficulty in finding evidence to prove his suspicions.

While he was still pondering on how he might best proceed to gain access to reports and documents from Sankt-Anna and the Universitätsklinik, there was a knock at the door of his simple hotel room. An American military police officer asked him to identify himself and then handed over a receipt, which Schröder had to sign and acknowledge. He was thereby formally called to present himself at the Wentzinger Palace, and this counter-move, seemingly out of the blue, and from an enemy apparently well aware that Schröder was still alive, temporarily brought his own investigations to a halt.

The Canadian major in charge of interrogation politely assured Schröder that he was not at present suspected of any criminal activity, and would not be held in custody. On the other hand, the allied authorities would very much like to know if Schröder had knowledge of what had been going on at Sankt-Anna Klinik in the period from March

1940 to April 1945. Schröder truthfully answered that he had been conscripted in late February 1940. From that moment onwards he had had no contact with the clinic, nor had he heard anything about what went on there. Asked if he knew of the existence of a letter bearing Hitler's signature and those of Reichsleiter Bouhler and Dr. Brandt outlining the obligation of medical wards to facilitate the deaths of terminally ill patients, Schröder answered that he had had a copy of it in his writing desk. His former colleague, Dr. Claus Uhland, could verify this, since they had had an animated discussion about the ethical consequences of such procedures.

– Dr. Uhland, Schröder said, can also testify that during the time in question I was…

– Dr. Uhland is no longer with us, the major interrupted.

– Not with us?

– As far as we know, he was run over by a car. He was found in a ditch beside the road about one kilometre north of Sankt-Anna Klinik.

– Any trace of the car that killed him?

– None … Excuse me? … When it happened … The major looked through his papers, and then glanced up at Schröder.

– The body of Dr. Claus Uhland was found on the morning of November 22, 1942. He had at that time been dead for more than twenty-four hours.

– And how do you know that the body wasn't dumped there to give the impression of a road accident?

– We don't, and that is one of the reasons why we asked you to call in here today.

– But I have absolutely no idea what happened at the clinic after I left.

– Then let me fill you in on the details. On Reichsleiter Bouhler's order, Dr. Claus Uhland succeeded you as head of Sankt-Anna Klinik in February 1940. Until his death in November 1942, he conducted experiments on human subjects. Among these experiments we typically find the inoculation of convicts with the sera of highly contagious and possibly fatal diseases, the elimination of old, terminally ill and mentally ill patients, as well as the systematic sterilisation by means of x-ray and surgical castration of racially inferior elements. As a matter of fact, I am reading straight from the hospital's own records, the major added, glancing at Schröder over the top of his reading glasses.

– Uhland? But Uhland was no murderer. It is impossible …

– Until it has been proved otherwise, we have regretfully no other alternative than to assume that that is precisely what he was. There is one small piece of evidence, however, which could indicate that Uhland wasn't, after all, entirely in charge of these operations. You see, the strange thing is that although he was the head of the clinic, responsible for the experiments being conducted in the way prescribed by the Berlin chancellery, by various medical authorities, or by himself, he never signed the reports himself.

– So who did sign them?

The major produced a sheaf of folders filled with documents. This he gave to an officer who then handed the first paper to Schröder.

– Do you recognise the signature, Dr. Schröder?

– It looks … like … like mine, he said in astonishment,

and looked up at his interrogators. The representatives of two foreign occupying military powers stared back at him.

– It looks like mine, he repeated mechanically, and looked around, as though expecting someone to step forward and explain the conundrum.

– We had several graphological experts, independently of each other, examining these documents – there are in all about one thousand, two hundred of them – and the experts are unanimously of the opinion that the signatures, the earliest dating from March 1940 and the latest from April 1945, and these – your regular reports from Sankt-Anna from September 1939 to February 1940 – are almost certainly by the same hand.

– It goes without saying that they must be forgeries.

– Very well, Dr. Schröder, but how would you explain the fact that even the early confidential reports from September 1939 to February 1940 confirm that euthanasia was being practised during that time?

– Again, it is impossible. I never signed any such documents.

The major said nothing but brought out more sheaves of documents. To his dismay Schröder saw that report after report bore his signature.

– I don't understand any of this. The reason I was removed from my position was that I did not carry out the experiments as required of me. It is correct though that we did simulate some innocuous treatments, which were recorded as other than they were in our reports. My problem was that in the end I could never prove that the patients had died or suffered permanent injury as a consequence of the contagious material to which they supposedly had been exposed.

Even though these signatures were so skilfully copied that I probably can't distinguish them from my own handwriting at that time, I nevertheless know them to be forgeries. Not even these last reports are the ones I signed at the time when I was still in charge of the clinic. First of all, the forms themselves are forgeries. You see, in practice, it was never just the one doctor that signed them. In order to ease possible individual feelings of guilt, and to diffuse the matter of responsibility, there had to be at least three different experts' signatures on each one of these reports. The forms were therefore designed to reflect this, in other words, there were three places on the documents which were to bear the signatures of different people. In addition, the actual cause of death was never given. Plausible ones had to be invented, and that was not always the job of the physician in charge. There was a standard list from which appropriate causes of death could be picked and applied to individual cases so as to avoid arousing the suspicion of relatives. But I never had to do this either. Besides, so far as the later signatures are concerned – look at my right hand! In 1942 I had to remove two fingers from it. I can hardly hold a pen today! You must see that all this must be a set-up, designed to harm me, by someone who has good reason to keep himself hidden.

– As a matter of fact, the major said, – We have suspected that the forms themselves might not be authentic, the reason being that all other reports pertaining to euthanasia within the Reich which have come to our notice have been exactly of the kind you just described. Furthermore, as long as we can't disprove your claim that you served in the Wehrmacht and were subsequently a prisoner of war, we have difficulty in understanding how you could possibly have signed and sent hundreds of documents back and forth between Germany and Russia while simultaneously working in field hospitals. You are consequently allowed to remain free, but must report regularly to these headquarters. If you wish to leave town, you must notify this committee at least twenty-four hours in advance, giving details of the route you will be taking, and providing us with a contact address where you can be reached at all times. And by the way, yes, the reports were found in a sealed storage bunker right under the principal building of Sankt-Anna Klinik. Does that ring a bell?

– No, not at all. I didn't even know such a bunker existed. It must have been built after my time.

– Very well. Thank you for coming, Doktor.

Schröder went out into the cobbled square, and as he walked he began to see the situation in a new light. Uhland was the only member of the staff at Sankt-Anna who knew where the army had sent him. Perhaps he had discovered the forgeries and started to ask questions – dangerous questions. So Rheinau had had him silenced, thinking that the trail ended with his death. It was a singularly dirty business. That aside, what he needed to do now in order to clear his own name, was to find the official documents that would prove that he really had been conscripted and sent to the Russian front.

He telephoned Major Beaufort and explained the situation as he saw it. Beaufort promised to get back to him within the next two days, which he did. Schröder was called to a second interview, during the course of which Beaufort informed him that the committee had been unable thus far to find any records in the former Wehrmacht's local registry, which could corroborate his account. His existence as a former soldier and subsequent prisoner of war could therefore be regarded merely as the unsubstantiated declaration of an interrogated party.

– But that's ridiculous! Schröder exclaimed. – Luckily there is one person in this city who knows that what I say is the simple truth. That's my wife Beatrice. She thought I had been killed at the front, and she remarried. She can testify. And by the way, if I don't really exist, however did you find me?

Beaufort answered that the committee would be happy to hear Beatrice's testimony as long as solid evidence was forthcoming that she had actually been married to Schröder. However, Hans received no answer to the question as to how the committee knew that he was alive, and was so sure of his identity. This puzzled and frightened him. Beaufort might have had Rheinau brought in for questioning, and on that occasion either deliberately or inadvertently let slip Schröder's name, including the fact that he was still alive. If this information had been revealed to Rheinau, his life was in danger, and he must protect himself from attempts at murder. It was to be hoped that neither Beaufort nor any other committee member knew anything about Rheinau. But once he had mentioned his wife's name to them, it might be only a matter of days before curiosity got the better of them. Then they would seek her out ... Were they just pretending not to know anything about his family, or were they hoping that he would somehow compromise himself?

Pressed for time, and nervous about the unexpected turn of events, Schröder decided to go and check on the clinic. Early the following morning, he borrowed a bicycle from outside the railway station, and set off in the direction of Kirchzarten. About an hour later he arrived at his destination. The gates to the drive were chained shut. The paint on the letters running in a half circle above the gate had scaled off, and in some places the letters themselves were missing. Over the walls sprawled vine and ivy. Here and there the walls had collapsed, their stones scattered on the ground. Gaping holes had been plugged with balls of barbed wire, and there were warning signs forbidding entry to the grounds. He stood still for a moment, listening to the wind sighing through the cracks in the walls, then looked round to make sure he was not being observed. With the aid of a stick he lifted the wire high enough to enable him to crawl under it. Once past the wire, he decided to keep his way of retreat open and let the hole remain.

The garden, like everything else at the former Sankt-Anna Klinik, was overgrown and unkempt. Above a tangle of overgrown shrubs the linden trees still rose majestically, and from the surrounding hills the wind brought the familiar scents of pine-needles and resin. Far away, between the fallen branches of the trees, he discerned the long white stretch of the main building. He advanced slowly until he reached the large courtyard at the end of the driveway. From here the great gate was out of sight.

Like the wings and other annexes, the principal building was thoroughly barricaded, all the basement windows shielded by the thick planks nailed across them. An oppressive silence hung over the entire complex; the big clock above the main entrance had stopped at five minutes past four. He walked around the building trying the doors, attempting to peep inside, here and there managing to get a glimpse of empty wards. At last he stood right under the window on the third floor where his office had been. He remembered how – it now seemed so many years ago – he had been standing there, looking westward to the mountains, the forest and the plains beneath, seized by anxiety for what the future might hold in store.

He caught himself in the act: "I mustn't let myself be blinded by emotions … think … think clearly …" he said to himself. While repeating this mantra he stumbled on a storage door curiously flush with the ground. He recognised the construction – it was used in other places in the hospital grounds – but he had never noticed that such a door existed right under his office. The door was divided down the middle and closed with a padlock running through two iron hoops. As he attacked it with a branch he saw that the entire locking device was rusty and he redoubled his efforts, finally managing to wedge a small stone into the space between the doors. Then he forced the branch in as well and put all his weight on it until one hoop gave away and the doors opened. A cool, subterranean current of air rose towards him from an inclined shaft in the interior. It was wet and slippery, and fitted with a narrow iron ladder, on which he tried his weight. It seemed solid enough, and he descended into the dark. The shaft led back toward the main building. At its farthest point it connected with an aisle, the end of which he could not distinguish in the dim light. He pulled out his torch and groped his way along the moist walls. Ten or twelve metres farther in he came to a wall blocking the way forward. In the middle of this there was a solid iron door. It was locked, locked so securely that a branch, no matter how thick, could not damage it. He pounded on the door. Judging from the subdued echo, it had to be very thick. What was behind it? He didn't know, because he had never seen more of the cellar regions in the main building than the hospital laundry. And he could not recall ever seeing a door of this kind. But if the door led to other rooms in the basement, what could these be?

The alleged human experiments had not been conducted in the cellars of the main complex, but in a well-guarded annexe two kilometres out into the forest. He wanted to find these buildings immediately. He turned, retraced his steps, climbed the ladder and came out in the open, where he closed the doors and covered them with leaves and branches. He returned the same way he had come and found the bicycle hidden in the ditch. He continued east and came to the little road leading up to the annexe. The sentry-boxes and barriers were no longer there, and when he arrived at the end of the road, his suspicions were confirmed. The buildings were gone. Not one brick, not a flake of plaster, not as much as a nail. Shrubs and even quite high trees grew here now. A peaceful glade in the forest, where the sun wove patterns in the foliage and birds sang. "They certainly haven't spared any effort," he thought. "But why? If Rheinau had gone so far as to falsify his signature on thousands of documents, why not let him, Schröder, take the blame for the death-wards as well? They must have dug out the entire area, filled it with earth, and planted trees," he concluded. "It must have happened a long time ago, perhaps straight after I was sent to the front."

Perplexed, he mounted his bicycle and set off to find the place where Uhland had supposedly been found. The area consisted of meadows with short grass at the sides of the road. There were two drainage ditches, one at each side. Uhland's body must have been dumped at the first convenient place. Perhaps he was on his way home when the murderer struck? The body could of course have been thrown from a passing car. At any event, it did not seem to have bothered the murderer that the corpse could have been discovered by anyone passing on that side of the road. Yet it had taken over twenty-four hours before anybody found the body. In the circumstances it was very strange – if indeed it was fact. Major Beaufort had his information from the report of the German military police at the time, but the police may very well have been implicated in the murder. Yes, Uhland could easily have been killed down in the catacombs of Sankt-Anna and then thrown into the ditch. The story of Uhland's death could also have been pure invention, intended to deter Schröder from trying to contact his former colleague, the only person who at present could prove his innocence. Until the murder had been incontrovertibly proved, he therefore decided to assume that Uhland was still alive, that the committee had based their evidence on hearsay, and that it was his duty to find out what had really happened.

Back in the city, Schröder received a visit in his hotel room from a military orderly who handed him a letter from Major Beaufort. This stated that the investigation committee could now finally confirm that Dr. Hans Schröder, born in 1899 in Tübingen, had, after preparatory studies at the Friedrich Gauss Gymnasium in Berlin, passed his medical examinations in Göttingen under Professor Gottfried Ewald, and there received highest distinction. He had then worked at different German hospitals, specialising in psychiatry at Eglfing-Haar. In 1933, he had been appointed to the post of chief of staff at Sankt-Anna Klinik, Schwarzwaldt. In 1928, Hans Schröder married Beatrice, born Rohde. In 1939, they were registered as having three children, two boys and a girl. Dr. Schröder was called to military service as a field physician in the Wehrmacht in February 1940 and had been stationed in numerous locations along the moving front lines, until reported missing in action at the battle of Stalingrad.

The reason why it had taken such time to find this confirmation on Schröder's dispatch to the eastern front was that the information, strangely enough, had not been found in the Wehrmacht register, but in the files of the SS. There was also a note in the Gestapo files about a Dr. Hans Schröder, who had been the subject of police enquiries, and until further notice removed from his post as chief psychiatrist at Sankt-Anna Klinik.

"Consequently," the letter ended, "the commission sees no reason to assume that the above-mentioned Hans Schröder could have been in Freiburg at any time between January 1940 and May 1945. However, the question of who in his place, and in his hand-writing, signed one thousand, two hundred documents recording inhuman treatment, including executions of prisoners, mentally ill and debilitated subjects, has still not received a satisfactory answer. The committee will therefore now concentrate on finding witnesses who during the period in question have worked at, or in some other significant way had a connection to the clinic. For this purpose, the committee counts on the full and willing cooperation of Dr. Hans Schröder, especially since it ought to be in his utmost interest to have his name cleared. The earlier restrictions on Dr. Schröder's freedom to move are hereby rescinded. Dr. Schröder is nevertheless urged to keep the committee informed both of his whereabouts and current contact address." It was signed, "Major H. Beaufort, Chairman of the Allied Committee for the Persecution of War Criminals."

Schröder had no idea where to turn next. According to allegedly official documents, Dr. Uhland's activities before he met his end could not be traced beyond that ditch. Surely this must be a cover-up. On second thoughts it was quite incredible that the investigation committee should so suddenly dismiss all previous allegations against him, simply because they had found his name in the Gestapo and SS registers. Back in 1939, he clearly remembered, he had been drafted by the Wehrmacht. He had never come in contact with the SS troops operating in the Soviet Union at the same time. So how could they have any record of him? That the Gestapo had held files on him was more obvious, since someone at the hospital, or someone knowing what was going on there, must have denounced him to the secret police. The Gestapo had interrogated him before he was sent to the front. And it was the local head of the police department who spared him a trial, which at that time could only have resulted in a death sentence for refusal to obey the Führer's orders in time of war. His behaviour would have been considered treason pure and simple, but he wasn't charged with that. Instead, he had been given the opportunity to say goodbye to his family.

The children were not to know. Father was going on a trip and would soon be back. But there was no way he could keep the truth from Beatrice. At first he had tried to tell her that he was just temporarily changing station, just another assignment. But she had cut right to the heart of the matter. "Thank God they didn't kill you right away," she had said, showering him with kisses. "If I don't come back, if you hear me reported dead, or missing," he had told her in the pouring rain, "you must do whatever you judge necessary to save yourself and the children. Remember that you are Jewish, my heart, and that you and our children run great risk of being exposed to all kinds of dangers. You must be very prudent and very brave. It is too late to run away. But we mustn't lose heart. Perhaps the war will be over just as quickly as it began. Perhaps I will soon be back, and we'll move for good – to Switzerland, to Sweden, somewhere where they will receive us and where our children will have a future. Oh, don't cry so much, my darling, you will make me cry too …"

"I love you. I shall always love you," she had said. "Even if you had stayed at the hospital and done what they wanted you to do, I would have loved you, because I know that you would have done it for me and the children – for us, not for yourself. I shall wait and put each night's love aside for your return. I'm so proud of you. May God be with you, dearest Hans …"

Those were her last words, and they were true and sincere when spoken. There was no doubt that she had obeyed his instructions. He could still win everything back. All it took was foresight and prudence on his part. She had chosen security for herself and the children according to his wishes. It was all calculated on her part – of course she couldn't love that awful man. Now, since the war was over, her only wish must be to get rid of him. Schröder was going to help her, but not by shocking her. It had to be the right way. And his name must, on account of his innocence, be cleared of all guilt.

Surprisingly, this was about to happen, only a little too easily. Although the Allied Forces had no other immediate suspect, they had, much as the Gestapo had many years earlier, given him the benefit of the doubt. It was a kind of chivalrous behaviour which rang strangely out of tune with the times, almost as if they had expected and accepted a man's word for what it purported to be, namely the truth.

Perhaps, for some mysterious reason, things had happened in the same way at Gestapo headquarters. Someone there must also have concluded that he could still be of service to the Fatherland. It was an inexplicable act of grace that his life was spared. This fact once established, however, there was also a concrete and understandable plan to put him to good use: they expected him to make up for his disobedience. And it was true. With three children and a beautiful wife back home, he was at their mercy.

Schröder was not inclined to believe that the Allies had any reason to have the same confidence in him. After all, of what use could he possibly be to them? Unless of course this was another set-up, a ploy by means of which the foreign authorities pretended to set him free, so that he could lead them to a place where they would find incontrovertible evidence against him, and thereby unravel the coils of a death industry. Or was it perhaps Uhland they were really after? Schröder had to be very careful now, if he wanted to succeed. And he must stay always one step ahead of his persecutors ...

For almost two weeks Schröder stayed put, with the exception of the two days when, duly reporting his temporary absence to the committee, he went to Switzerland, and to his satisfaction found that the emergency account he held at UBS had remained untouched during the war. With identity papers issued by the new German government, he had no problem in gaining access to his money, and he was able to return to Freiburg and pay for his hotel room in much-coveted American dollars. The rest of the time Schröder spent trying to regain his stamina and physical strength. He was constantly on the look-out for spies and assassins, and for this reason kept to himself as much as possible. At the end of the second week, though, he began to feel safer. He had seen nothing that indicated that he was being followed, although he couldn't be sure of that either. Nevertheless, he decided to take a gamble.

One of the ideas that haunted him during these days was that the circumstances surrounding Uhland's death seemed vague to the point of being a deliberate smokescreen. But he could not turn to the police, since they were his prime suspects. On the other hand, he had absolutely no evidence that could substantiate his suspicions. Only a feeling, a deep-seated feeling, telling him that he must find out what had really happened to his former colleague.

Schröder went to the door of his hotel room and put his ear to it. Hearing nothing, he opened it and peered into the corridor. There was nobody in sight. He went back into the room. Hidden behind the curtain, he scrutinised the street below, but couldn't determine whether or not he was being watched. On the other side of the street was an office building. At this late hour its windows were darkened.

He decided to take no risks, and dismantled the telephone to make sure it wasn't bugged. He drew the curtains and arranged his bed so that from a distance it would look as though he was sleeping in it. He turned on the bedside lamp and left.

To avoid leaving the hotel by the front, he slipped through the kitchen door. At the far end of the empty kitchen was another door leading to a courtyard. A wall separated the courtyard from its neighbour's. It was not very high. Schröder managed to climb it, and to take refuge in the sheltering obscurity on the other side. A door standing ajar in the next building led to a hallway which itself led to another door, offering Schröder the opportunity to emerge into the street at the other end of the block. He left the building unseen, save by a black cat, which quickly took to the flight of stairs as he moved through the hallway. Letting the door close behind him, he could still see the cat's two wide open, circular lights pierce the darkness.

He moved on quickly down the narrow streets and alleys, intent on reaching the railway station to check the timetable in case he would have to make a quick escape. But even before he got there he realised the station would still be crowded with military. Identity papers in the name of Dr. Hans Schröder were not exactly the best currency. He went into a bar to give himself time to think, letting a beer and a schnapps decide for him. Reassuringly, the liquid agents instructed him to visit the building where Uhland had lived before the war. Schröder seemed to remember that Uhland had had his whereabouts in the Günterstal area, but he had never been to his house. Uhland had been a bachelor. Schröder thought he would remember the name if only he saw it written ... Yes, and this. Uhland, who had come to Sankt-Anna Klinik from a research post at the university in Halle, had on some occasion made a remark about his new home that it was like falling out of the frying-pan into the fire. The building in which he lived had been a criminal ward in the previous century, which had only later been converted into quite handsome flats. The original iron gates with their heavy locks and the cells in the basement were nonetheless still intact. Sometimes he would fantasise about what might have occurred over the centuries in these vaults. "It seems to me," he had said, "that the poor souls of thieves, wayfarers, bohemians and prostitutes still haunt the place, and I must admit that I don't think I would very much like to go down there after dark."

Schröder remembered these words primarily because of his own reaction to them. It came as a surprise to him that Uhland, usually as rational as a scalpel, entertained such Gothic fantasies. He never knew if he should take these professed anxieties seriously. Maybe Uhland had just wanted to tell a good ghost story. In any case, as long as the opposite hadn't been proved, Uhland himself was a ghost rattling his chains in a dark cavern somewhere.

Schröder left the bar, crossed the square and boarded a tram. Two French soldiers stood talking to each other at the rear, but didn't look in his direction. Their obvious indifference helped to convince him that he wasn't being followed. At Günterstal, the end of the line, he descended and walked around somewhat haphazardly. Dusk was imminent, but the hot humidity of the day still hung oppressively in the air. He felt his shirt tighten against his skin. He unbuttoned his collar but the folds still clung to him. Finally, he had to alleviate his discomfort by rolling up his sleeves, in this way looking as though he were about to do some heavy work, although the only thing he did expect was to walk the streets, ask a question here and there, and stay attentive in general. Why not begin by trying the telephone directory?

It was a good idea, but getting hold of one proved more difficult than he had imagined. He went into a few shops and a café, but none could provide him with a phone book because during the final stages of Allied bombardment all the telephone lines had been destroyed. There were in fact very few people still in possession of their original telephone numbers, so the directories were useless. It had become an almost hopeless task to contact anybody by telephone. Schröder explained that he was looking for an address not a telephone number. Still, they didn't have a phone book.

At the end of a street from which a small footpath continued on into the woods, he caught sight of an inn sign. Coming closer he discerned a black pig adorned by a wrought-iron criss-cross pattern of vines. The sign above read Zum Schwarzen Ferkel. "Amazing," he thought, "how many bars and restaurants in Germany are traditionally associated with some animal, or with people hunting and killing them." As he walked in he saw a few men sitting quietly over their beers. Nobody seemed to take much notice of him. One man, with a beard so long that it disappeared under the table, was staring empty-eyed into his companion's face that seemed hewn out of wood and waxed. Between them stood two enormous steins with pewter lids, decorated in local fashion. Another man had fallen asleep in a corner and was snoring loudly. At the far end of the room, an indistinct group of men in hunting dress was playing cards.

Schröder approached the counter. A woman with arms as thick as the thighs of a full-grown man stood firmly planted behind it, reaching up to some wooden rods above her, on which she was hanging clean beer steins, each one of which seemed more fantastically decorated than the last. He asked her the usual question. She didn't care to answer verbally, and simply shook her head discouragingly. For a moment Schröder suspected that everyone in the room was deaf and dumb, but then someone shouted from the card table, and after a guttural conversation, a new round of beers was ordered by one of the men, probably the loser in the last game. Schröder himself was only too happy to be on his way out, when a dark-haired girl in a tight revealing dress descended the stairs leading from the upper floor. He remained transfixed long enough to allow her to walk straight up to him. Inadvertently, Schröder took a step back. She stopped close to him, letting one of her legs slightly touch his.

– Who are you looking for, soldier?

– A man, a doctor, or he used to be. His name is Uhland, Dr. Claus Uhland.

– He used to be? she asked, and widened her eyes.

– Well, yes. He's dead now.

– But if he's dead, why are you looking for him?

– I need to find out where he once lived, his former address. Do you have a clue? I would be most grateful if anybody …

– Do you have a cigarette? she interjected while applying lipstick.

– Of course. Here you are.

– Will you buy me a drink?

– Yes, what would you like?

– A glass of Müller-Thurgau. They still have some left, last year's vintage, the war-torn grapes of 1944, made by French prisoners of war. They were allowed three barrels of it themselves to celebrate surviving three years of captivity in the prison camps around Kaiserstuhl. Ah, the French know how to make a wine. They are good customers, too – the ones left around here, that is.

She perched on a bar stool, took a sip, inhaled the smoke of her cigarette, pressed her bosom against the counter and exhaled in Schröder's face. In the faint light of the bar the smoke enveloped his head in a bluish halo.

– Yeah, I knew him, she said. – He used to come here quite a lot. In fact, all the girls knew him, but they're all gone now. I'm the only one left.

– Do you have his address?

– Not exactly, but I know the building when I see it. It is somewhere quite near here, that much I do remember.

– Yes, I know, that's why I'm here myself. Would you mind taking me to the building?

– Do you mind letting me finish the wine first?

– Of course. I'm not in a hurry.

– Good. That makes two of us.

– What do you mean?

– Two of us who aren't in a hurry. I mean, people just rush through life, so they don't have time to appreciate what they already have. They all want more and more, and then they usually end up with less than when they started. They're almost lucky to be sent out to fight. At least then they can blame the failure of their existence on somebody else. Poor bastards …

– Shall we? Schröder gestured towards the door.

– Let me just get my coat.

– It's very warm outside.

– Oh yes, I forgot it's still some kind of summer out there.

The men grouped at the tables didn't seem to notice Schröder's leaving with the girl any more than they had noticed his coming in alone. The landlady silently accepted the money he gave her. In the next instant they were out in the street. She wore red high heels and tripped ahead of him like a deer struggling to master the cobble-stones.

– Where does that footpath behind us lead? Schröder asked.

– Oh, somewhere into the woods. The man you're looking for, I mean, the man who once lived at the address that you are looking for, used to walk up there in the morning and come back the same way in the evening.

– Really? What's up there?

– I don't know.

– Weren't you ever curious to find out what he was doing up there?

– Why should I? He always came back, didn't he?

– Did he?

– Until the day they found him dead, of course. Then he was gone for good. It was right here, in the cellar of the building here. Really spooky place to be found dead in, don't you think?

They had stopped at a gate which to Schröder looked like the entrance to a convent. She turned and said,

– It used to be a nunnery, but then the nuns went away, and they turned the whole place into some kind of police station. I remember some of the older girls telling us that they spent some rather unlucky nights there.

– Why?

– Come on now, where have you been all your life?

– Pretty far away lately.

– Sounds like it to me.

– Did you say that they found Dr. Uhland dead in this building?

– That's right. I saw him myself.

– You saw him?

– Sure.

– When was this?

– About two months ago. Of course, they had wrapped him in a white sheet, but I and my friend happened to be passing when they came to collect him. When they were getting the body into the ambulance, the sheet fell back, and you could see his face. It was Dr. Uhland all right, but deader than a doornail. Shot straight through the head. Is that worth something?

– Excuse me?

– I have to go now, but I brought you to the right address, didn't I? And I told you the story, didn't I? Well, is that worth anything? She looked at him with dark eyes, at once melancholy and motionless.

– Oh, I see. You mean... Schröder searched his pocket and found a few bills.

She shrugged when she saw the amount, then casually took the money and turned away. A few steps ahead she stopped and turned around again. – I'll be at the Ferkel if there is anything more you want from me.

– I'll let you know, Schröder said, watching her hips roll

as she trotted down the street on her high heels.

The gate was locked, but there was a bell next to it and a sign for the concierge. He rang the bell. An elderly woman appeared from within the entrance hall of the building.

– Who are you looking for? she shouted.

– Dr. Claus Uhland.

– He ain't here!

– I know. He's dead. I am his colleague from Sankt-Anna Klinik. No, no: Sankt ... Anna ... Klinik. I have come to collect those of his papers that are hospital property.

She had moved up to the gate while he was speaking.

– Do you have a search warrant? she asked.

– Listen Madame, I am not from the police. I am a doctor, just like Claus Uhland used to be, and a very close colleague of his.

– So you are the same kind as him, are you?

– Yes. Why?

– Well, people around here thought he was peculiar.

– Peculiar? In what way?

– Well, he was always correct with me, even at five o'clock in the morning when he used to return from work.

– Five o'clock in the morning? Return from work?

– That's what he said. But I could see that he must have had a few drinks somewhere before he got home. And he must have made himself enemies somewhere, I mean real, nasty enemies. I think they must have been foreigners, secret agents, perhaps. I found him with a bullet in his head, you know. Anyway, even if I did let you in, there would be nothing to see. The police took everything there was.

– Where in this building was he murdered?

– In his flat, Herr Doktor.

– But if you always have the entrance under surveillance, how do you think the murderer managed to get inside and then escape unnoticed?

– The gate is always open in the daytime. Anyone can walk in or out without being seen.

– Although they would have to go past your door?

– Listen, Herr Doktor, I am just a poor old woman. My husband used to be the concierge, but he died, and now I'm the concierge.

– Did you hear anything? I mean, the shot must have been pretty loud.

– No. And I've told the police everything I know.

– Can I see the flat?

– There's nothing to see.

– I should like to see it all the same, you know, homage to an old friend and colleague.

– But I told you, there's nothing to see.

– I'd really like to anyway ... Please.

She sighed heavily.

– Well, if you insist.

The concierge opened the gate and let him in. She walked ahead of him along a corridor with a vaulted ceiling. At the end of it was a wide spiral staircase. They climbed two floors and came to a door. She brought out her key-ring, and opened the door. She turned on the electric light for him. He moved apprehensively into the room. Once inside the spacious living-room he saw that the police had not after all taken everything. The furniture, for one thing, was still in place.

– I thought you said that the flat was empty? Schröder said, turning to the concierge.

– Oh, please don't judge me too harshly. Nobody came to claim Dr. Uhland's belongings. He didn't have no relatives. People are desperate for flats nowadays, there are so many who no longer have a home. A furnished apartment is worth good money, Dr.?

– Excuse me. I am Doktor Rheinau, Dr. Siegfried Rheinau.

– Dr. Rheinau … please understand. I'm just trying to survive. She paused briefly, then continued, suddenly in anguish, – Don't denounce me to the police. I didn't mean to steal them. It's just that nobody asked about them, and …

– Don't worry, Schröder said, now feeling that he had unexpectedly gained the upper hand. – I won't tell anybody, and as far as I am concerned it's perfectly all right that you've kept Dr. Uhland's furniture. You just go back to your apartment, and I'll give you the key when I leave.

She did not protest, and gave him the set of keys.

– Oh, just one more thing. When and where did you say you found his dead body?

– He was in his bed. I hadn't seen him for two days. He didn't say he was going away anywhere, and he always used to inform me if he was, in case somebody wanted him at the hospital. There was mail for him, too. So I decided to go up and check that he was all right. When he didn't answer my knock, I opened the door and went in. I told the police everything. Why do I have to go over this again and again?

– How was he dressed?

– He was in his ordinary clothes, and the shot had gone straight through his forehead. As I said, the police know all about it. You can ask them.

– And what was the day again?
– April 15.
– Thank you. Ah, one last thing. Is it true that this building was once a convent, and later the local police station?

She nodded and her expression became grave.

– There has been a lot of evil in this building, Dr. Rheinau, and I would never stay here if it wasn't that I've no where else to go. The little money I …
– Look. Take this. Get yourself some bread. Butter too, maybe.
– Thank you Herr Doktor, thank you. And God bless your kind heart.

Schröder was left alone. He was surprised at how large the rooms were. Even inside it looked like a typical 19th-century official building, except that here too the ceiling was vaulted and reminded him of the convent it had once been. The police had been there, the woman had said. But according to the same police, at least as quoted by Beaufort, Uhland had not been found dead in his home in April 1945, but in a ditch beside the road one kilometre from Sankt-Anna Klinik on November 22, 1942. So there was not only a discrepancy in time, but of place as well.

Schröder was now even more convinced that he was the victim of a set-up, and that the investigation committee, by lulling him into a false sense of security, was hoping that he would lead them to the truth. Those signatures had been his, there was no doubt about that. The problem was that he had never written them. So how had they appeared on those documents? And how would he ever discover whether or not the man who had been found dead by the concierge really was Dr. Uhland – was he in reality somebody that someone else wanted to look like the murdered man? The address had stirred memories in him, and he was reasonably sure it had been that of his colleague. Besides, it wasn't just the concierge who had seen and identified him. The woman at Zum Schwarzen Ferkel had recognised him too. Schröder didn't know if Uhland, in the days when they worked together, used to frequent her and her like. But he had been a bachelor then and had apparently remained so during the war, so it was by no means inconceivable, although it would of course have been quite easy for him to find suitable company among the pretty nurses at the hospital.

He began to search the place. There were no clothes or shoes in the wardrobes. He smiled as he thought how the concierge must have been scavenging on the extended carcass of Dr. Uhland once she realised that nobody would contest her right to prey on the dead. The bed, which must have been soaked in blood, had been cleaned and stripped of its mattress. He opened the drawers of Uhland's writing desk, but found nothing inside them. There were no papers, no receipts, no documents. Only the barren remains of a bourgeois household, inherited from a parental home which had long since ceased to exist. No sisters, no brothers? Had Uhland been an only child?

He went into the kitchen. It was a large room, its walls lined with cupboards. A gas stove stood in one corner and there was a sink with running water. There was also a large empty pantry. He went back into the study and opened the drawers of the writing desk again. After searching the middle drawer carefully, Schröder found what he was looking for. He knew there was a possibility that a secret inner drawer existed, for he remembered that his father had kept a gun in his own desk, which had been strikingly similar in appearance to Uhland's. And, stunningly, the drawer which one could only access by sliding a wooden bar to the side and then pulling the underside of the drawer straight back, contained, exactly as his father's desk had done, an automatic pistol. It was loaded, save for one bullet. Schröder took the gun and put it in his pocket, put the panel back in place, walked out of the apartment and locked the door.

In the corridor, the lights were out and he groped for the switch. At the bottom of the staircase he now noticed that the stairs actually led down another half-storey, the staircase itself forming a half circle ending at a wrought iron door. This opened into a large rectangular elevator, also of wrought-iron. Schröder, assuming this to be the lift descending to the former cells where prisoners had been kept in custody awaiting trial or further questioning, stepped into it. On the indicator panel the numbers corresponding to the levels were marked with minus signs to indicate that they were below ground level. He pressed buttons but there was no response. He discovered a keyhole down at the bottom of the panel, and tried one of the four keys he had in his hand. It was too big. The second entered but got stuck. The third turned. The elevator began to move downward in what to Schröder seemed an endless shaft dimly lit by the faint glimmer of its lights, here and there revealing the harsh stone walls of vaults and cellars.

Eventually the elevator stopped. As far as the light from the elevator shone, he saw a long corridor vanishing in darkness. Not that he was afraid of the dark, but he was unable to find a light switch by which he might extend his field of vision. He also heard a rat squeak nearby, and made up his mind to come back with a torch – some other day. He pressed the button for the ground floor, but the elevator did not move. Schröder heard himself breathe heavily. Soaked in cold perspiration he fumbled with the key. The elevator jerked. Then, slowly rising from this realm of shadows, it began to ascend. Dr. Schröder, leaning against the iron lattice, felt his knees weaken as he slithered farther and farther down it. When the elevator stopped at last, he found himself sitting on the floor, seized by an inexplicable fatigue, excruciating flashes of light running through his head.

The night was still hot and humid. Schröder was perspiring profusely but had regained some self-control as he stumbled out into the street. Having reached the corner of the block he picked up a piece of cloth and dried his face, then patted his pocket to make sure the keys and gun were still there. He hadn't bothered to return the keys to the concierge, guessing she would be too afraid to make a fuss now that he knew she had expropriated Uhland's belongings. Silently he slipped past her apartment, where the radio, hidden behind a gauzy, dimly lit curtain that swung lightly in the open window, played one of those many songs destined to ease the hardships of soldiers, and to convince them that someone they loved faithfully awaited their return.

He felt in need of a drink, and unwittingly found himself returning to Zum Schwarzen Ferkel. Standing at the doorstep of the Gasthaus, he realised what kind of trick he had played on himself. But it was too late for regrets. Unsurprised, he found her at the bar.

– I knew you would come back for more, she said with a lascivious smile.

– Why didn't you tell me everything from the beginning? he asked. – It would have made things a lot easier.

– For you, perhaps. For me it is easier this way.

– What do you mean?

She didn't answer directly, but slipped from her stool, closing in on him like a reptile on its defenceless prey.

He tried to avoid the physical contact, but she was already up against him. He felt her hand and finger-nails coil around his crotch, felt her firm young bust press against his ribs and her strong, sweet perfume envelop him.

– I came to ask you a few more questions, he said.

– It's going to cost you, she whispered and let her tongue play in his ear. – What do you say about stepping upstairs to discuss it?

He looked around and emptied his glass of schnapps. The men at the tables did not seem to be taking any notice of him this time either. He felt as if he was watching them through the wrong end of binoculars, perceiving them as distant, diminutive figures, inseparably merged with their beer steins. From the bottom of his entrails he felt a gush of heat breaking through the crust of years of loneliness, privation, frustration and – desire.

– I'm doing it for you, only for you, he whispered to Beatrice in his own mind, but the image of her waned as he tried to envisage her, and he could not even recall how it had once been to make love to her. Instead, the only woman in his life was there, right before him. She had swung her arm around his waist and as they mounted the staircase he could feel her hips move rhythmically from one side to the other.

A faint red light lit up the room. It had a wash-basin, a screen with peacocks on it, and a brass double bed. There was a window and a big mirror with a carved frame. She lit the candles in two wall sconces and began, slowly, to undress. Then she moved to the mirror, taking her time to comb her long black hair, before she turned round. He watched her naked shoulders emerge from the intricately woven crimson corset. Her breasts protruded, spilling over the top. He reached out for her body and felt his entire hand fill with warm, rounded flesh. Her nipples hardened at the first touch of his tongue and he heard her sigh, a sigh so deep that he had the feeling that it was she who hadn't been touched in a very, very long time. In the next instant he was already carried beyond such peripheral considerations. She went down on him. When her hot red mouth and tongue finally closed around his shaft, he felt as though time itself was coming to an end.

Had he been screaming? At first he was utterly unable to recognise the room, still convinced that he was held captive in a subterranean cave, where the ceiling would not allow him to stand up, and the walls were closing in on him. A voice had announced that they, at last, had caught him, and that it was time for him to die, to be crushed like an insect between the solid walls slowly but inexorably closing in from both sides. He was too deep into the nightmare to be able to rid himself of the impression that the room actually had become smaller. He was still looking for an opening, a glimmer of light, a ray of hope, a way out. It struck him then that there would be no other light in his life than the ultimate, blinding blast to his brain as he was sucked into the giant fan rotating at the end of a tunnel, solidly sealed off at the other end by an iron door. He must have screamed, surely? There was something lingering in the room, a presence, a silent echo.

When he regained awareness of time and space, he realised that he was still in bed. Driven by an instinctive urge, he reached out with his hand. She was no longer there. The room was dark, but a faint glimmer showed through the shutters. He stumbled across the room, trying to find the light switch, but before he could reach the opposite wall he floundered into a chair and only saved himself from falling by holding on to the armoire. He found the wall sconces next to it and fished some matches out of his pocket. In the sudden light the room assumed its old appearance, except that the woman was gone. He emptied his pockets. Of course, his money was gone with her. It hadn't been much. And she had left everything except the money untouched inside the wallet; his little collections of dim, yellowish, singed photographs and his identity papers. There were even some cigarettes left in the packet. He brought one out, lit it and blew the smoke in a blue cloud across the room.

Seized by an impulse, he reached for the watch in his pocket. It was still there, and showed that it was four o'clock. He couldn't recall how many times they had made it, but a good many rounds it must have been. And then, exhaustion, oblivion, the nightmare and the feeling of the tongue attached like a piece of parchment to the roof of his mouth. He desperately needed water, and hurriedly began to collect his clothes, pulling his trousers up with some difficulty, finding his socks and shoes.

While getting dressed, Schröder observed how the intense heat instantly turned his shirt into a soaked cloth. He opened the window to allow some air to enter the room, but was surprised to feel that the temperature outside was no cooler than it was inside. Suddenly he remembered her remark. The words rang strangely out of tune with reality. When they had been about to leave and look for Uhland's dwelling, she had asked him to wait so that she could fetch her coat. But she must have known just as well as he did that the town was going through one of the fiercest heat waves in decades. Even at night the temperature remained at around 30°C, and it was almost impossible to wear a coat in that weather – "Oh yes, it's still some kind of summer outside, isn't it." Some kind? It was one of a kind! Still, she had seriously considered wearing a coat …

There was nobody in the corridor, but an electric light bulb lit the staircase. He descended the stairs, coming down into the Gasthaus, where the main room was now dark and silent. The guests had left. He heard someone breathing heavily from a room on the other side of the bar. The door leading out in the street was closed and locked, but there was a latch to pull. As he looked up against the dark sky a raindrop fell on his lip. He reached out for it with his tongue, then for the next. Farther up the street he beheld the old water fountain crowned by a gilded statue of some ancient town guardian dressed in his traditional costume, raising a halberd in his outstretched hand.

Water, streaming water from the Black Forest springs and mountains. He satiated himself under the flow from a gargoyle's mouth, then plunged his head beneath the water. As he raised his dripping head, he heard some drunk soldiers coming nearer, and he quickly withdrew into the obscurity of a narrow lane. When the soldiers entered the square, he noticed that there were women in their company. One of them broke lose from the group and started to dance round the fountain. When she passed through the gleams from the faint streetlight, he recognised her. He would have liked to speak to her about her practice of stealing money from unconscious people, but wisely refrained from getting involved.

– Bloody whore, he muttered as he continued down the lane. He made a turn, waited till the voices and the sounds of high heels and drunken laughter had died out, then came back into the square. He passed in front of Zum Schwarzen Ferkel again, and continued all the way down to the main road, by way of which he eventually reached the town centre. He entered the hotel as the first rays of sun illuminated the cathedral spire.

The next time he woke up it was broad daylight, and still very hot. He rose from his bed and began to wash at the wash basin. He then put on a clean shirt. On his way to the Wentzinger palace he bought two pretzels and got himself a cup of coffee. He began to feel better, and could hardly wait to give Beaufort the staggering news that Dr. Uhland, according to at least two independent witnesses, had not been found dead on the roadside near Sankt-Anna Klinik, but in his own home, years later than the official report stated. How was this to be accounted for, seeing that the local police, supposedly, had identified the corpse on this occasion as well? Did they also have two different reports, and were there in existence two different death certificates? There were a lot of questions, questions which to Schröder seemed more and more in need of unambiguous answers.

The first and most important of these questions was undoubtedly: how on earth did Dr. Uhland manage to die twice? Secondly, had there ever been an autopsy, and if so, at what time? Thirdly, where had he been buried, and by whom?

Schröder did not have time to ponder much further, for as he approached the entrance to the Wentzinger palace he saw Beaufort and some junior officers come out of the building and walk towards a car parked in the square. Schröder caught up with them just as they were about to get in the car. The major gave him a surprised glance, and Schröder, still regaining his breath, began,

– Please, Major, I need to talk to you, I have some very important information. The major made a sign for him to continue. Schröder looked around and said,

– Can I have a word with you in private?

For a moment Beaufort seemed to hesitate, then moved away from the car, following Schröder into the immense shadow of the cathedral.

– Major, I'm sorry to have to inconvenience you in this way, but I really have some most urgent information. You said that my former colleague, Dr. Claus Uhland, had been found dead in a ditch beside the road two kilometres outside Sankt-Anna Klinik in November 1942 – correct?

Beaufort nodded.

– Well, I have some information that may throw new light on all that. According to the concierge of the building where Dr. Uhland rented an apartment, Dr. Uhland was actually found murdered as late as mid-April this year, and not in the vicinity of Sankt-Anna but in his own bed, shot through the head.

The major gave him a puzzled look.

– How do you know? he asked.

– How do I know? Schröder repeated. – Because I talked to the concierge herself, and she said so. She also said that the police had been there and that they had all the information pertaining to the case. She herself was convinced that Uhland was killed by foreign agents.

Beaufort frowned as he scrutinised Schröder.

– I hope you are not wasting our time, he said. – Do you know where this building is?

– Of course, I was there yesterday evening.

The major ushered Schröder to the car and bade him take a seat.

– To Günterstal, he told the chauffeur, who turned round with a surprised look. On seeing the major's expression he immediately turned back and started the engine.

– Any address? he asked, remaining motionless.

– This man will tell you, the major replied.

Fifteen minutes later they arrived at the convent gate. Schröder pressed the doorbell. A good minute passed without any apparent reaction from inside. Schröder became nervous, and began to explain to the rather impatient Beaufort that the woman was a little deaf, and not so fast on her legs either. Suddenly Schröder remembered that he still had the key to the gate in his pocket.

– Oh, I forgot, he said, – she let me have the key yesterday so that I could take a look at Uhland's apartment, and then I simply forgot to return it to her. So if you will just be so kind as to step inside. Just like this. Yes, yes. Please enter.

They walked along the corridor at the end of which the gauze curtain was still to be seen gently moving in the breeze. They could hear that the radio was on. Schröder knocked at the door. There was no sign of life.

– Madame, are you there?

He tried the door handle. The door was open.

– Madame, Madame, please excuse us. Are you there? Hello?

They passed through the dark hallway and entered the living-room. In the draught from the open door behind them, they saw the curtain billow into the room. The radio played on. The concierge was seated in her rocking-chair with a vacant, glazed expression in her eyes. In the middle of her forehead there was a black hole rimmed with coagulated blood. At the top of the rocking chair her brains were spread out like one of those embroidered antimacassars that old ladies use to lean their heads against when resting from their knitting. At this precise moment Dr. Schröder realised that he still carried Dr. Uhland's gun in the pocket of his jacket. A gun loaded, save for one bullet.

*

Dr. Schröder had already gone over his story twice with the local police. His encounter with the young woman was somewhat embarrassing to relate, but he had no other alibi. And she had not been found at the inn. The woman tending the bar, who had seen them both together and must have known that the prostitute received customers in one of the rooms, claimed that she had seen neither him nor the woman he was talking about. Schröder knew she was lying, but Beaufort refused to let Schröder speak to her, seeing that his face had turned first red and then completely white from rage.

– She's lying. She saw us both!

– And what was her name? The major repeated the question once again.

– As I said, I never asked for her name. It could have been anything: Esmeralda, Lulu ...

– Was she French?

– No, she spoke German with a Swabian accent. But that innkeeper, for some reason she wants to nail me for this.

– Or else she is protecting the young woman, Dr. Schröder. We have taken every precaution. We will be questioning her again, and we are still looking for the woman, although we only have your description to go by. It would have been a lot easier if we had at least a name, even a made-up one, since other people in the area might know who we are looking for. But, as I said, it doesn't look too good for you right now. You keep saying that it could not have been Dr. Uhland who was found dead almost three years ago. As things stand at the moment, of the two people that could corroborate your statement, one is a hooker and the other one's dead in her own apartment. According to the coroner the approximate hour of death was two o'clock in the morning. You said you left the building at about ten in the evening, and that you did not return to it. You said that you went straight to Gasthaus Zum Schwarzen Ferkel, where you met the prostitute who earlier that evening had told you that in April she had seen the face of a corpse which she had been able to identify as that of Claus Uhland. You also said that she was gone when you woke up in her room at around four o'clock that same morning, and that she had taken all the money you had on you. You were in possession of the keys to the building where the victim was found, and also of this gun which you said you had taken out of a hidden drawer in what had once been Dr. Uhland's writing desk. You claimed that this was still in his apartment because the concierge, when no one came to claim Uhland's possessions after his death, decided to make some extra money by letting a furnished apartment in the building without informing the landlord. Now, is all that correct?

Schröder confirmed it.

– Well, Beaufort continued, – the landlord of the building is a charity organisation. According to the charity's spokesman, Herr Thomas Weber, the offices and archives therein were destroyed by the Gestapo before the Allied Forces arrived here in Freiburg. No records of previous tenants have therefore been found, and so the owner of the building is unable to certify that Uhland actually lived there. Moreover, yesterday, at the moment of your arrest, you were found to be in possession of a gun, the same as the one you found hidden in a desk in Uhland's apartment. You also stated that you suspected that there might be a secret compartment in the desk because your father used to have a desk of the same type, and that he used to keep his gun in that secret compartment. Finally, you told us that that the gun found in Uhland's drawer was loaded with five out of six bullets. But yesterday, when we took charge of the gun, there were only four bullets in it.

Schröder gave Beaufort a baffled look.

– You don't have to strain yourself to account for the missing bullet. We found it, buried in the woodwork of the rocking chair in which the deceased was sitting at the moment of death. Dr. Schröder, I must inform you that unless further investigations yield facts contradicting those presently at our disposal, I must turn you over to the civil authorities. They will then decide whether you should be tried on suspicion of the murder of the widow Frau Irmgard Kampa during the early morning of August 24.

Schröder was taken completely by surprise.

– What date did you say it was? We're in late July now, aren't we?

– It's August 24 today, Schröder.

– Really?

– Yes, really.

Beaufort looked at Schröder, not quite sure what to make of this attempt at a joke. To him, the moment for such humour seemed singularly ill-chosen. Schröder felt cold perspiration break out all over him, as he realised that for some inexplicable reason he was mentally a whole month behind real time. Not only that, because for one and half months, he simply hadn't noticed that he had been. So when did he in fact arrive in Freiburg? Did he even have the year right? To mistake one day for another, that was one thing. But a whole month? For some reason Schröder was not only reluctant to admit his verbal slip, but also keen to persuade himself that it had in fact never occurred, that he had deliberately deceived himself as well. He had of course always known that it was already August. He must have. The imperative to survive relegated the alarming sensation of being the victim of an enormous illusion to the back of his brain. He then made his leap of faith.

– But it is true that it's 1945, isn't it? he asked, with a smile intended to seem confident.

The major, thankfully glossing over the weird incident, felt it incumbent upon him to inform Schröder that at least he was far from joking.

– Dr. Schröder, this is very serious. I wonder if you are fully aware of the situation in which you find yourself? Otherwise, let me make myself perfectly clear to you: You are under arrest.

Schröder felt panic mounting inside him.

– This is ridiculous. I mean, I even led you to the place myself, didn't I? Why would I do that if I were guilty of such a crime? It doesn't make sense, does it?

– Unfortunately, Dr. Schröder, that's not my problem. If you can convince the court that the gun you carried is not the same as the one that was used to fire a bullet through the victim's head, then I can only say that on the present evidence you'll have to be a verbal Houdini.

– You've got to find her! I am innocent, I swear. I led you to her. I'm innocent, I didn't do it … I'm a doctor. I don't take people's lives, I save them. You must find Dr. Uhland for me! I don't know what's going on here, but someone is setting me up. And if it isn't you, who the hell is it? I have had nothing whatsoever to do with these murders. Please, you've got to believe me …

Schröder was asked to stop his tirade and stand up. He was then taken to a cell where he was to be kept in custody until the investigation committee had determined that the necessary pre-investigation process was complete. In a few days this was accomplished, and Major Beaufort came to inform Schröder of the results of the committee's deliberations. Meanwhile, Schröder had fallen into apathy. He was almost incapable of moving. The guards had frequently found him staring at the wall with a vacant expression in his eyes. The return of the major ignited a hopeful glimmer, but it was soon quenched. The news was not particularly encouraging. Neither the investigation committee nor the local police had been able to find the woman to whom Schröder had referred. Worse still, nothing indicated that Dr. Uhland had either lived in the building which Schröder had pointed out, or had still been alive in April that year.

– I regret to say, Beaufort concluded, – that this ends my task with regard to you. A civil prosecutor will now take over.

– How is it that you didn't find her? And what did the innkeeper say? Did you talk to her? Schröder asked.

– We searched the place inside out, we interviewed the patrons supposed to have been there on that particular evening and we looked through the room which you said you stayed in. There is absolutely no clue as to where this girl is, if indeed she ever existed. I tell you, none whatsoever. On the contrary, everything appears to confirm that the person as described by you either never existed or is dead as well.

There was a moment of oppressive silence in the room. The major sat down opposite Schröder at the table and offered him a cigarette. He lit it for him and could not help noticing Schröder's hand trembling slightly as he received the light. Beaufort was a good soldier, not usually prey to doubts or compassion at moments when his sense of duty was called upon, but he had to admit that he felt a strange kind of sympathy for this man, whose face so clearly bore the signs of privation and suffering. Going beyond mere duty, he felt an urge to ask,

– Dr. Schröder, do you have anything more to tell me before I leave you to your fate? I mean, anything at all? Is there anyone who ought to be notified about your present situation?

Schröder shook his head.

– Are you sure?

– Yes, thank you, and thank you for your consideration, I realise you don't have to ...

– Well then, Dr. Schröder, our ways now part. I know this will probably sound ridiculous, but although your signature was on those documents, and everything points to your killing the old woman, I simply can't get it into my head that you in fact did it.

– I have told you, I'm innocent.

– Yes, you may very well be, but I can't prove it for you ... I am afraid that's it, really. I must leave you now. Goodbye, Dr. Schröder, and may God be with you.

Beaufort shook Schröder's hand, then turned around and made for the door when Schröder exclaimed,

– Major! I do have something to say. My wife, would you be so kind as to notify my wife? She lives in town ... She can explain everything.

– Your wife? Why? And if you are so convinced that she can help you out of this and prove your innocence, why haven't you mentioned her earlier?

– Because she doesn't know that I'm here.

– She doesn't?

– No.

– Why is that?

– Because, because ... I can't tell you.

– If you can't tell me, I can't help you ... I mean, the possibility of my being able to help you is even less if you hold back relevant information ... A little awkward, bringing that hooker into the picture, isn't it? Let me tell you, I think you really do need a lawyer, unless of course your wife is your accomplice, and you have decided to keep her out of this. That is, until now ...

– My wife has nothing to do with all this.

– So why didn't you tell me about her from the beginning?

– I couldn't. He would have had me killed, and destroyed all the evidence.

– Who is this "he", Dr. Schröder?

– His name is Rheinau, Dr. Siegfried Rheinau. He is a Nazi. He collaborated all the way. He took over my post at Sankt-Anna, and ...

– And?

– And he married my wife. As you may recall, I was forcibly removed from my position as head of staff and sent to the eastern front charged with the care of sick and wounded soldiers.

– We have already heard that, and the rest, Doktor. Do I still have to remind you that, in spite of your moving story, the documents purporting to prove that you were drafted and sent to the eastern front are still inconclusive?

– So, why did you let me go? Is Rheinau behind all this? Are you just playing cat and mouse with me before having me executed?

– Calm down! Beaufort freed himself from the grip in which the other held his arm, grabbed his shirt and held his face very close to Schröder's.

– Now, listen very carefully to me, Schröder. I don't know who you think we are, but if you are so naïve as to believe that we are here to protect one war criminal at the expense of another, you're simply out of your mind. I have done everything in my power to get you out of this. We even decided to give you the benefit of the doubt, and let you go rather than hold you responsible for the thousands of victims who must have perished in abominable human experiments, causing excruciating pain, unimaginable humiliation, suffering and long, drawn-out deaths. For all I know I could be sitting in this room with one of the most degenerate, sick animals ever to have walked the surface of the earth. We made the decision to let you go because we felt that our evidence would not hold up in a fair trial, such as your country, for one, has not witnessed in the last fifteen years. Even though you might not deserve anything but a bullet in the head, administered with the same cold precision that brought Frau Kampa's life to an end, you have been given a fair chance. Do you read me? I could have you shot like a rabid dog right in here if I wanted to. But I'll choose to walk out of here and turn you over to civil justice. Adieu.

Schröder had regained some of his composure while the major was talking. He understood that he now had to play his last card.

– Doktor Siegfried Rheinau became head of Sankt-Anna Klinik after me. He also married my wife, and made sure neither she nor my children were harmed during the war. Without him my wife and my children might very well have ended up in a concentration camp. I bear no grudges against him on these grounds. But the man is a murderer. He knows that he needs to clear his name. Ever since 1940, rightly suspecting that Germany would in the end lose the war, he has signed death sentences in my name, in the belief that I must be dead, and that no one would come after him if he used my name instead of his own. The Gestapo must have been in on it too. But although I know this to be the case, just as you do, I lack the evidence to have him convicted. When I came here, realising the situation, I knew that I had to proceed with the utmost caution. Well, I did at first, but then I got carried away. I thought uncovering the circumstances surrounding Uhland's death would lead you closer to Rheinau, the mastermind behind all this. Instead he has outsmarted us both. Somehow he has found out that I am here. From now on he'll have no option other than to make sure that I am found guilty of murder, and executed. You can imagine how inopportune my presence in Freiburg must be to him. I wanted to spare my wife the embarrassment of having to see me again and to become aware of whom she really married. My sole purpose was to nail him in due course, but it appears that I have only succeeded in nailing myself.

– Quite so, Beaufort answered. – You should have told us all this right from the beginning. The only thing I can recommend to you now is to tell the court the same story, and hope that your lawyer will be able to convince the judge of the necessity of bringing this Rheinau in for questioning.

– Will you tell my wife I'm here?

The two men looked at each other in silence for a moment.

– I will, but only because I am a man of my word. Where does she live?

– Fürstenbergstraße 18.

– And her name?

– Rheinau, Beatrice Rheinau.

– What am I to tell her?

– Tell her that I love her, and that she is the only one in the whole world who can save me now. And please, don't call her on the telephone. You'll have to go there in the daytime, but avoid the lunch hour. If her husband suspects that I have contacted her, he might murder her and the children as well. I can't risk that.

– I see … Very well, Herr Doktor. I'll go there as soon as I can.

Although the major had maintained his professional impassivity in front of Schröder, he was disturbed by this new development. And it wasn't just because he was a man of honour that he decided to visit Schröder's wife. He really wanted to find out, first of all if she existed, secondly, if there was truth to any part of Schröder's explanation. The case was no longer in his hands, but Beaufort felt that there might just be an extraordinary injustice in the making here. If he chose to forget everything about Schröder now, there was a distinct possibility that the latter would in fact face the death penalty for another's crime. Admittedly, not much spoke in favour of Schröder, but to Beaufort it was not so much words and arguments which prompted him to action, but something akin to a scream of despair, silently emitted through the man's eyes.

The next day, at about two o'clock in the afternoon, Beaufort set out unaccompanied to find Fürstenbergstraße. To avoid attention he had decided not to engage his chauffeur but to go there on foot. After all, Freiburg was not very large, and Fürstenbergstraße, according to the map, was located close to the city centre.

The early September sun, although hidden behind giant cumulus clouds, was hot, and the woods, still lush and green, seemed like a steamy jungle spreading its fragrances into the narrow lanes and passage-ways of the town. Beaufort, not usually of a romantic turn, had to resist the temptation to buy a bouquet of late summer flowers, and to remind himself that he was keeping his word to a prisoner, not wooing a woman.

He found the villa answering Schröder's description, although he couldn't see the name Rheinau marked anywhere. He rang the bell and waited almost a minute before the door was opened. Schröder had cautioned him to be discreet in his investigations, and the major intended to oblige him in this at least. So he had prepared an excuse in case Dr. Rheinau himself was at home. Although it took a while before the door was opened, it did not take Beaufort long to realise that it was Frau Schröder herself who stood in the doorway. He had suspected that she might prove to be a beautiful woman. But this woman was beyond all his expectations: she was stunning. It was possible that hard years had turned her once olive-tinged skin paler, that her face and figure had matured, still …

As soon as Major Beaufort saw her he realised that she was the kind of woman one simply cannot leave on her own, for if one were to, admirers without number would gather in the hallway. Not that she didn't seem proud or faithful, but there was something in her bearing which made a man long to protect and care for her, not to say, to worship her. Beaufort, who had expected no more than to keep his word to Schröder, found himself gasping for air.

– Frau Rheinau, I assume.
– Rheinau? Who are you?

– Oh, please excuse me. I am looking for a Captain Stevenson who supposedly has his lodging here at Fürstenbergstraße, number 10, I believe, in the house of a Dr. Siegfried Rheinau.

– I am afraid you must be mistaken. There is neither a Captain Stevenson nor a Dr. Rheinau in this house. And as a matter of fact this is not number 10 but number 18. Number 10 is farther down the street. And I still didn't catch your name. You are an American soldier, are you not?

– Canadian, in fact. But in this situation that amounts to much the same thing. And please excuse me again for intruding upon your privacy. I am Major Beaufort. And as a matter of fact, I am not precisely looking for an army captain, but for a lady. Beatrice, the wife of Dr. Hans Schröder. Does that mean anything to you, Madame?

– He was my husband, Major.

– He was?

– Yes, he was sent to the eastern front, and died there three years ago.

– Wasn't he only reported missing?

– How do you know?

– What would you say if I told you that your husband is still alive?

– I would say that you are lying, and that I don't know what you are up to.

– Frau Schröder, this is no joke. Your husband is back in Freiburg.

– Nonsense. If he were, why hasn't he come to see me and the children?

– He says he has, but that you didn't recognise him and that his coming back here could prove most inopportune in view of the fact that you had remarried.

– Remarried?

– Yes, according to Hans Schröder you are today married to Dr. Siegfried Rheinau, who he thinks is a war criminal ...

– Major Beaufort, would you mind stepping inside and explaining to me what this is all about?

Beatrice ushered Beaufort through the tall doors of the drawing-room and asked him to be seated. He noticed some framed photographs on a bureau, one of them depicting a man who he assumed must have been Schröder in earlier days. But the man in the picture had no beard, so it was hard to say for sure if it was the same person. Another photograph showed the same figure in the garden together with three young children, the youngest, a baby, sitting in his lap.

– Well, Frau – ?

– Schröder, it's still Schröder. It has never been anything other than Schröder.

– Frau Schröder, your husband is alive.

– But it's impossible ... I mean, where is he?

– Here, in town.

– No, no, I simply refuse to believe it. Why are you doing this to me?

– Please, Frau Schröder. You really have to listen carefully to me now. This is no time to deceive you or to play a cruel trick upon you. Hans Schröder is here but he's not a free man. He's in custody, soon to be tried for murder.

– Murder?

– Yes. And before I pass on his message to you I have to ask you to answer this question truthfully. Has he visited you here during the summer?

– No.

– That is indeed strange, because he says that he has been here, and that he was invited by the maid to sit down, but that you, not realising who he really was, asked him to leave the house. He said that he gained access to the house by pretending to the maid that he was a cousin of yours. He also mentioned that during your brief conversation with him you referred to your husband as a Dr. Rheinau. This is someone Schröder not only loathes from the bottom of his heart, but holds responsible for all the misfortunes that have come upon him since he was dismissed from his post at Sankt-Anna Klinik. In fact, to Hans Schröder this man is the Devil himself. And, as I said, he is absolutely convinced that you are married to him. Now, do you have anything to tell me?

Frau Schröder had become as pale as marble, and at first could only move her lips without producing any sound. The words then came, hesitatingly,

– So that man was Hans ... I thought he was a burglar ... I was terribly afraid ... I told Mathilde, our old maid, that the master of the house ... He must have thought there really was a man in the house ...

– Not just any man, Frau Schröder, but specifically Dr. Siegfried Rheinau. Were you ever married to him?

– No, no.

– Has he ever lived here?

– No.

– Do you know any person at all answering to that name?

– Yes, I remember him. He was a colleague of Hans', who never liked him. Hans suspected Rheinau of wanting him out of the way. He was even invited to our home one evening. I remember it all very well. He complimented me in his way.

– This man Rheinau. Would you say that he was in any way interested in you?

– Yes, I think so. You see, after Hans left for the front he called on me and asked if there was anything he could do for us. I said no, but he kept on insisting.

– But you never obliged him?

– No. Never.

– But how is it then that your husband claims to have seen this man's name on the door-plate when he was here?

– I don't know ...

– You don't know ... Think, Frau Schröder, think. Your husband's life is at stake. Please swallow your pride now, and tell me.

Beatrice looked across the room beyond the major and fastened her gaze on the photographs standing on the bureau. For a while she remained transfixed in what seemed to him a reverie. Then with unexpected energy she turned and stared straight into his eyes, exclaiming,

– Please don't judge me! We had agreed that I should not hesitate to accept protection for myself and the children. Hans wanted me to accept it, and he could foresee from what direction such protection was likely to come. But it wasn't as if Rheinau was here – well, he was, but just visiting, never staying overnight. It was during one of those visits of his that he said that he too was called away on duty elsewhere in Germany. He said that we would all be safer if I agreed to his name being on the door-plate, so as to give the impression that he was actually living here, in other words, to make people think we were married. After all, he was a very influential man. Considering all the horrible things that were happening to Jews, even here in Freiburg, I really didn't think I had a choice. It wasn't for my own sake, but for the children's. It was their only guarantee of protection. The children – do you have children, Major?

– Yes, I do. What happened?

– We put his name up and it worked. Throughout the entire war I was never questioned by the Gestapo, nor taken to a camp.

– And Rheinau, what happened to him?

– He became ill, so I heard. He died of a brain tumour. It all happened very quickly. But we kept the name on the door, just in case. And we were spared. After Stalingrad, the neighbours came to know of Hans' death, so they didn't think it strange that I had accepted Rheinau's protection. They may even have thought that we were in fact married. I would never tell, and it was of course a common event during these last years that men were absent from their families fighting for the Fatherland somewhere.

– But isn't it true that you accepted Rheinau's protection before your husband was reported missing?

– Yes, Major, it is true. But we had an agreement. Hans didn't believe that the Nazis would ever let him come back to Germany, and that he had been sent on an outright suicide mission to Russia.

– Frau Schröder, I am afraid that he might just as well still be on that mission. And for all he knows, you are in fact married to Dr. Rheinau, who he thinks is responsible for forging his signature on thousands of papers recording experiments on retarded, mentally deranged and convicted subjects. Most of these experiments resulted in death, mutilation and unspeakable suffering. You see, just after your husband's return from Russia, archive material was discovered that had a bearing on the work carried out at Sankt-Anna Klinik after your husband's removal from his post. For a while we had reason to believe that he was in fact the victim of a plot against him. However, only a week ago, he himself led us to a crime scene where a woman, the concierge of an apartment block, had been shot in the head. Your husband seemed as surprised as we were, but the problem is that we found the bullet that killed the old lady. It just so happened that the striations on it perfectly matched those produced by the 9 mm pistol your husband was carrying. The bullet was found in the wooden frame of the old lady's rocking chair. The sight of her brains spread all over it wasn't pretty.

– But what was he doing in that building in the first place? Who was she?

– That's another thing I was hoping that you would be able to help us with. He said he was looking for a man named Claus Uhland. Have you ever heard of him?

– Yes, he was my husband's closest associate at the clinic. My husband did mention him quite a few times.

– Did you ever meet this man?

– No, never.

– Are you positive?

– Yes.

– Well, then, that concludes my task. Your husband has asked me to tell you that he loves you and that you are the only person in the entire world who can help him now. In a few days he will be transferred into civil custody. As head of the military investigation committee, I can assure you that on the present evidence, or lack of it, we will not be bringing charges against your husband for the crimes perpetrated at the clinic during his absence. As for the accusation of murder, however, circumstantial evidence weighs heavily against him. I can arrange for you to meet him before he is moved to the prison where he is to be held until his trial, but once he's moved I will no longer be able to grant you permission to visit. It will be out of my hands. I assume that you do want to see him?

– Yes, Major, I want to see him. And thank you for everything you have done for Hans, for me, for all of us. You can't know this, of course, but Hans would never kill anybody. He's the finest person I have ever met in my life, and I just can't believe that he is back, alive. I have missed and mourned for him so long. How could I … not recognise … my own beloved husband …

Her voice began to break and the last phrase was swallowed by the emotion mounting inside her. Her bosom rose and fell, and her dark eyes, filling with tears, assumed the aspect of two mysterious wells. The thought crossed Beaufort's mind that there was nothing as moving as the sight of a beautiful woman giving full expression to the deepest feelings of her heart.

*

The meeting between Schröder and his wife took place the following day. After sending the children to school, taking pains to conceal the news of their father's return, Beatrice went into her bedroom and began searching through her wardrobe. After a while she found what she was looking for, an old dress that she had kept as a memento of their happy days together. He had always particularly liked it. It had a yellowish tinge, with folds in which stylised oriental irises made up the pattern. She also tried some hats on, but then decided to go without, realising that it was another of those hot and humid days typical of the region in late summer. Her shoes were dark purple. She took her time perfecting her make-up, carefully deepening the red of her lips, turned round in front of the mirror and was at last satisfied with her appearance. She instructed Mathilde not to let anyone in and walked out of the door into the hazy yet glistening light. Arriving right on time at the Wentzinger palace, she presented herself to the officer at the front desk, and was received by Major Beaufort. The major made sure that she was brought down to the cellar, and into the same green room in which he had conducted his last interrogation of her husband. Once she was inside, the door was closed behind her. Schröder was already seated at the end of the table. She stopped midway between it and the door.

– Is it really you? she said. She moved slowly towards him, fell to her knees and embraced him. Schröder was still in his chair and silently leant his head against her.

– Major Beaufort told me everything. Oh, Hans, this is too much for me. I still can't believe it's true. It is a miracle. How is it possible that I didn't recognise you the first time? Well, you have changed a bit, and with the beard and the glasses ... I don't think I ever saw you with a beard, not even a two-day stubble, but it looks good on you ... Why on earth did you remain ... Oh, look at that (her eyes had fallen on his right hand with the two fingers missing). You must have suffered atrociously, my poor, brave Hans. But why did you want to remain incognito for so long? Why didn't you give me a sign? You know I didn't recognise you.

– Didn't you?

While speaking she had kept touching her eyes with a handkerchief. Suddenly she stopped trying to dry the tears from her face, and stared at him in large-eyed bewilderment.

– What do you mean? she asked.

– I said, are you sure that you didn't recognise me when I came to visit you?

– Hans, what are you talking about?

– Maybe you just chose not to recognise me ...

– Hans, what is all this about? Did they brainwash you in Russia? Beaufort said you were all right ... basically ...

– But you seemed so afraid of something.

– Yes, I was afraid, I thought you might be a burglar. You had pretended to be my cousin. Remember?

– Yes, I remember, and I would accept that explanation if it weren't for something in your eyes that told me that you weren't sure. I wondered if you sensed something familiar, in spite of my speaking in an altogether different voice. Something held you back, not from realising, but from wanting to realise who I really was.

– And what would that be?

– Rheinau, my dear. Dr. Siegfried Rheinau. You don't have to explain. As soon as I saw his name on the name-plate of our house, I understood that everything had happened exactly the way I had foreseen. It was part of our plan that it could very well turn out this way. I do understand that you had no other choice once I was gone. I have accepted it. You have my word. But now, listen, we don't have much time. In ten minutes the guards are going to tell us time is up. I have to speak briefly, and you must believe what I will tell you. Then, if you still love me, you must do as I say in order to get me out of this. Rheinau has taken good care of you and the children, hasn't he?

– Hans, I think you've got all this ...

– Beatrice, there is no time for discussion. The man may be a good provider, a stepfather whom the children have come to accept. The problem is that he is a mass murderer, and he wants me out of the way. This whole trial is the consequence of a set-up which he has arranged for me. He even killed the old woman and tricked me into leading the military police straight to her, so that I would be executed or at least put away for life. You've got to believe me, Beatrice! The man is ruthless, and the fact is that you will have to choose between him and me now, because there is no way that both of us can walk away from this as winners. If he stays on top, I go down. And vice versa. Now, you decide, and you must decide very quickly on whose side you are going to be, now that you know the truth. What do you say?

Beatrice had tried to stem the torrent of words which came gushing out of him. Finally, resignedly, motionlessly, she stared at him, her eye-sockets darkened by the eye-liner that had run and smeared them.

– Hans, she said in a muffled voice, – Hans, dearest, there is no Dr. Rheinau.

– What do you mean, there is no Dr. Rheinau? You're married to him, aren't you?

– No, Hans. I was never married to him.

– Was? He's still in the house, isn't he?

– No, he isn't. He never was.

– So you neither married him, nor lived with him in the house?

– That's the truth.

– But there is a name-plate, my dear. I have seen it. Beaufort has seen it. All of Freiburg has seen it. How can you deny it?

– In 1942 you were reported missing in action. Rheinau, knowing that I am a Jewess, offered to marry me formally so that we would be protected from the Nazis. His name was to guarantee that the Gestapo would not come for us, whereas your name – our name, I am afraid to say – had fallen into terrible disrepute. Hans, it would have been a matter of days before they would have come and taken us away.

– Yes, yes, I know, but where is he now, if not in our house?

– He's dead.

– Dead? He can't be dead. Or do you think he's arranging all this from the other side of the grave?

– He had a brain tumour, and he died only a couple of months after the papers were signed that declared us man and wife. He never lived in the house. He said he was called on duty to another part of the Reich.

– Of course. He was called on duty – and you believed him?

– Yes. Why shouldn't I?

– Because, as the secret head of Sankt-Anna Klinik, he was signing medical papers with my name from February 1940 to April 1945. Because he had Uhland murdered. Because he set a trap for me, paying some people off so that they would tell me that Uhland was found dead in his apartment in April this year and not, as the police report states, in a roadside ditch near the clinic in November 1942. Because he killed the witnesses as well, and tightened the rope round my neck. And here I am, waiting for him to strangle me. And you are not going to do anything to prevent him, are you? Are you? Answer me!

Beatrice crouched in her chair and remained silent, but her body betrayed her weeping. Schröder, his mouth foaming, stared madly at her. The guards, who had heard the shouting, entered the room. They went straight to Beatrice to make sure she wasn't hurt. She made a sign to them to wait outside, and summoned her strength to give an answer.

– Dr. Rheinau was never behind the plot you think you have detected. He died many years ago.

– How? Did you ever see his corpse?

– No, but I am ... Oh, Hans if you only knew how I have hoped for you to return. How can you say these things to me? I don't know who is behind all the terrible things you are going through, but it isn't me and it isn't Rheinau. Whatever Siegfried might have wanted to do to harm you, he can't have, simply because he is dead. I'll do anything to get you out of here so that we can live together as husband and wife again.

– You are protecting him, aren't you?

– How could I when he's not alive?

– Then you must be protecting somebody else. Who is it?

– For God's sake believe me. There is nobody, nobody! God, I think I'm going insane!

– You think you are going insane? Well then, look at me. I am accused of having deliberately killed or mutilated one thousand, two hundred patients during the war as well as having murdered an old widow out in Günterstal.

– What were you doing out there?

– I was looking for Uhland.

– Ulrich Uhland? Don't you know that he was murdered many years ago?

– His name was Claus Uhland. Anyway, that is what they have told me, but my own investigations have shown that Uhland was seen alive by several witnesses long after the time of his supposed death, but now these witnesses have apparently disappeared. And even you, who used to be my wife, refuse to believe me when I say that I have seen and met them. You are with him, eh? You have always been with him!

– Hans! She heard her own voice cut through the room, but he remained motionless, his face pale as death itself.

It was intended as a security device for the benefit of visitors, but it was Schröder himself who sprang from his chair and pulled the cord which alerted the guards. When they entered the room they found Frau Schröder unconscious on the floor. Terrified by her husband's allegations and the shock he had put her through, she had fainted and fallen from her chair. There was a moment before she lost consciousness in which she saw his face recede farther and farther away until it merged completely with the pale green wall behind him. Then everything went black.

Regaining consciousness, she found herself lying on a bench in the hallway of the Wentzinger palace. The nurse attending her was relieved that she was now capable of communicating again. She inquired about her health. Frau Schröder assured her that she was all right now. Two soldiers then helped her out in the open. After having made sure that she was quite steady again, they drove her home.

Meanwhile, Schröder was taken back to his cell, where he sat motionless on his bunk, staring at the wall opposite. He remained in this position all night, smoking one cigarette after another, stubbing them out on the floor. About midday the following day he swept the worn blanket around his body, fell asleep and slept through the rest of the day and the entire night following. He was reawakened by the noise of guards, jingling keys and loud voices, and had but little time to make himself ready to face another visitor.

– Who is it? Schröder asked in bewilderment.

– Your defence counsel, came the answer.

– I didn't know I had asked for one, Schröder replied.

– Neither did we … Well, are you going to see her or not? the guard asked.

– Her? Schröder asked, now even more perplexed.

That the defence lawyer he hadn't called for was not only not expected but also a woman was most intriguing to him. Although he had made up his mind not to accept any further visitors, and had decided to represent himself in court, he nonetheless agreed to be brought to the interrogation room again. When he entered, the smartly dressed woman – she wore a grey skirt with matching jacket and high-heeled shoes, and had her lustrous brown hair tied in a knot – turned and faced him. She was smoking a cigarette. He recognised her curly hair, small brown eyes and pretty face, and exclaimed, as if he couldn't actually believe what he was seeing, – What are you doing here?

– I heard you were back in town, and that you were in trouble, so I came to offer my services.

– Whom did you hear that from?

– You are front-page news, you know. She handed him the Freiburger Nachrichten. The headline ran, "Famous Psychiatrist Faces Trial for Murder". He gave it a quick glance and returned the paper to her.

– Don't you want to read it? she asked, her eyes widening a little.

– Why should I? They know even less than I do. Anyhow, in what way do you think you can help me?

– One of the things that happened during the years of your absence is that I graduated from law school and …

– I didn't know the Nazis had any law necessitating studies, Schröder snapped at her.

– I went to university in Strasbourg. After taking my final examinations, I spent a year working for the civil court in Mulhouse, and then became an assistant with a law firm in Paris. It was only two months ago that I got my licence to practice here in Germany. Normally such a quick advance from law student to certified lawyer would have been impossible. But I guess the French and the Allied Authorities saw some advantage in helping people trained in their own law schools to practice within the German legal system as quickly as possible, not least because there is hardly a civil court in the whole country that hasn't compromised itself irretrievably during the war.

– So how many murder cases have you worked on up until now?

– None. In fact, if you accept me as your attorney, you will be my second case ever.

– And what was your first?

– A prostitute accused of having stolen money from a client while he was asleep.

– Did you win?

– Yes.

– How?

– The defence took the line that since prostitution is in itself an illegal activity, for which a person could indeed be tried and sentenced, the accused must therefore first be brought up on that charge. Otherwise there is no way to prove that the woman in question was not just the man's mistress, and that he had given her the money.

– So you persuaded the woman to plead not guilty as charged, although you knew of course that she had stolen the money?

– Yes, of course. She told me that she had stolen it, but I advised her to stick to the story that they had met as lovers, and that the man had given her the money. In this way she could innocently say that she would be happy to pay him back, now that she realised there had been a misunderstanding between them.

– And what happened?

– The judge felt that the evidence against the woman was inconclusive, and said she was to be freed unless the prosecution thought they had reason, time, resources and evidence to back up the allegation that the woman was in fact a prostitute.

– So, they just swallowed the bait you fed them?
– I guess you could put it that way.
– And she didn't have to pay anything?
– No. Well, she paid me a little.
– You took stolen money?
– What are you implying? If the court says the woman is innocent, then she hasn't stolen the money, no matter how many times she tells a different story to the other girls on the street.

There was a moment's pause, in which Schröder searched for words. Laura kept her eyes on his, trying to convince him of the sincerity of her proposal. Schröder was the first to break the silence.

– Laura, he said slowly, – The last time I met you was at that informal evening party my wife and I arranged a couple of months before I was sent to the front. One of the things that stand out in my recollection of that evening is that you gave Attorney Blücher a hell of a time. You cross-examined him, as if you were in a court-room, on this specific question: would he be prepared to defend a serial child-killer even if he knew that person was the actual perpetrator of the crimes. I seem to remember how he was struck by your remarks as if they were physical blows. He began to stutter and perspire and lose control of himself. Considering the alleged informality of the situation, I don't know why he should have felt that way, but if this evening was indeed ominous for me and my family, it may very well have been so for others as well. Rheinau decided to put an end to the discussion by stating that an official of the law (which attorneys are, regardless of whether they deserve to be or not) has an objective mission to complete, which mustn't in any way be interfered with by his personal convictions and opinions. A lawyer, in order to become one, has taken an oath of silence, meaning that he has sworn never to divulge a client's confidence unless that client gives the attorney explicit permission to do so. As a consequence, a lawyer is always and invariably expected to present his client in the best light possible. Do we, today, six years later, agree that this was approximately the way the arguments were presented? ... Well then, Laura, would you have the kindness to explain why I should believe a woman, who six years ago seemed willing to tear the eyes out of an attorney because he couldn't give a coherent answer to a highly hypothetical question, has begun her professional career by herself doing exactly what she previously pretended to loathe?

– Let me tell you, she said, while still searching for another cigarette in her handbag. – First of all, Dr. Schröder, you seem to believe that just because I am a woman, my reasons for pressing Herr Blücher so hard must have been of an emotional nature. I have the gallantry to grant you this prejudice, but in fact this was not the case. You see, at that time I had already made up my mind to become a criminal lawyer eventually, so these questions were actually part of my own considerations, questions that I felt I had to ask myself rather than anyone else. And I guess I did answer one crucial question for myself that same evening. After having heard Rheinau speaking, I realised that he was right. You see, the tremendous advantage of the liberal court system over the German system – especially in the perverted form we have experienced in recent years – is this. Any suspected person is formally considered innocent as long as evidence has not been submitted that proves "beyond any reasonable doubt" that he is in fact guilty of all or some of the offences with which he has been charged. This means that the defendant can only be found guilty or not guilty in relation to the crimes of which he has been charged, not for crimes for which he has not been charged. In other words, if someone has murdered two thousand people in cold blood, but is being tried only for murder number two thousand and one, the defence has no need to worry about what to come up with if the trial were about all the other people's deaths as well. The two thousand and first murder is the only one under consideration, and the attorney may think the evidence suggesting the defendant's guilt is inconclusive. If he thinks that there is a chance that the accused may be acquitted, he should inform his client what he believes the odds to be. He should also – if the circumstances allow of such a gamble – go so far as to encourage his client to plead not guilty, even though he knows him to be guilty. And to answer your question: yes, we do agree completely that this was the subject of the discussion in your house at that time.

– And now you seem to suggest that although I might be guilty of murdering two thousand people, you would be happy to act as my defence lawyer for the one crime I have been accused of committing, the one in Günterstal, right? Your aim is to test your skills again, to demolish the evidence of the prosecutor and see if your rhetoric can persuade the judge and jury to let me go, or at least, in the case of there being extenuating circumstances, to have my punishment reduced. Well, you may think that right and wrong, innocent and guilty, are clear-cut opposites, and that there would be no way that the court could remain indecisive in this matter, so you see the chance of getting some further experience at law, while at the same time fighting for truth and justice ...

— Who said anything about truth? You are rambling, Schröder, and you delude yourself. If you had listened to what I said, you would have understood that I'm willing to defend you, even if you *are* guilty of this murder.

Schröder was taken aback.

— I don't care if you did it or not, Schröder, but if it ever came to your accepting me as your defence lawyer, it might be useful for me to know the facts, since it will give me a better chance of deciding what course of action to take. I have already gone through your files, and come to the conclusion that, as things stand, you're finished. However, the situation can be altered, especially if there is any chance of contacting the woman you said could give you an alibi for the time of the murder.

— You don't care! Schröder exclaimed in exasperation.

— You don't care, so why have you come here? To use another guinea-pig for your forensic laboratory? Who are you working for? Who hired you?

— To speak of truth for once, Schröder, your wife did. She thinks you're innocent, and she's been begging me to try to get you out of this.

— My wife? The woman who married Dr. Rheinau, who is also your hero as I understand it? The Rheinau who set all this up ... Is he sending me a lawyer now as well?

— Calm yourself, Schröder. Your wife is on the brink of a mental breakdown. She managed to explain to me that you think that Dr. Rheinau is still alive, and that he's the mastermind behind some sort of conspiracy. There is none such, believe me. I know that Rheinau died three years ago, at least I haven't seen him around your wife in that time. And he wasn't a Nazi either. He protected your wife and children. Without him they would have been sent to a concentration camp long ago.

– What do you mean, he was not a Nazi? I knew him. He worked for them.

– It seemed that way, yes, but if he were, he could not have said what he did about the legal system, simply because the Nazis didn't believe in the necessity of evidence to convict anyone they wanted out of the way.

– And how do you know that he wasn't telling us that simply so that we would conclude that he must be a man of honour and principle after all?

– I don't. But I have seen what he did for your family, and that was not the doing of a confirmed Nazi, Schröder. You have wronged your wife by not accepting her love and believing in her sincerity. Whatever she did, she did it for the children.

– She already told me that.

– Yes, and can't you just get a grip, Hans Schröder? She loves you, and you have both survived. Why can't you give yourself the chance to find her again?

– What about the children? Has she told them about me?

– No, she doesn't want to worry them. You can understand how all this is affecting her, or did you lose your soul at Stalingrad?

– But Rheinau …

– There is no Rheinau, Schröder. He is dead. Whoever signed those reports, it wasn't him!

She watched him intently as he hid his face in his hands.

A torrent of thoughts and feelings rushed through his head. Images from another lifetime, childhood scenes, his first meeting with Beatrice, their first vacation together, their marriage, the birth of their children, his graduation as a doctor of medicine. In seconds the pattern of conspiracy, the tower of accusations, came tumbling down and overwhelmed him. He struggled as if for his life, trying to reach something to hold on to, to make it to shore. If everything until now had been one huge illusion, what was left of reality except that he was going to be charged for an inexplicable murder? And there was no Rheinau? There was no such person? Who then was behind it all? Slowly, as if reluctantly awakening from a dream, he removed his hands from his face. He told Laura Emming that he was ready to accept her assistance, and that he wished his wife would forgive him for suspecting her. He wanted to tell her that he loved her, and would do whatever it took to set things right again.

– Do you think there is any hope whatsoever for me? he asked. He waited for Laura to answer, but the word hope had suddenly become long and diffuse, as though vanishing into a whirlpool of opaque, constantly rotating emotions. When she didn't answer, he opened his eyes, experiencing a shock as the glare in the room collided with his own inner carousel. And what he saw in those last moments of a dissipating dream was not the intense brown eyes and pleasing features of Laura Emming, but the fearful face of the prison guard trying to wake him up.

– Schröder, Schröder, the guard cried out, – Are you dead?

– With any bit of luck, the other murmured.

– You have slept for nearly eighteen hours. The warder

thought it best to wake you. There's a visitor for you. You better start making yourself ready. Here, eat your breakfast.

It wasn't until the guard had left that Schröder noticed that the coffee he had been brought was already cold. Who could this unexpected visitor be? He did not have to wonder for very long. Even before he had time to finish dressing, he saw the Judas window in the door open to reveal the Cyclops' eye of the warder. Then the keys rattled, and an unshaven, bespectacled man, wearing a worn suit and a tie that bore traces of his breakfast entered the cell. He held a shabby briefcase under his right arm.

– Herr Schröder, he said, sneezing into a handkerchief that had probably once been white. Without excusing himself for the unannounced intrusion he rapidly continued,

– I am your lawyer, and I must ask you …

– Your fly is open, Schröder replied in a low voice.

– What?

– I said, your fly is open. Why don't you begin by buttoning it and then wipe your spectacles so that you don't address my night commode when you wish to talk to me?

– Oh, er, quite. Er, Dr. Schröder, we don't have very much time …

– I'm sorry. I didn't get your name, sir.

– As I said, I'm your lawyer and my name …

– I didn't know I had appointed a lawyer.

– That's right, and that is also the reason why the court, at state expense, is providing you with one – after all, we are not Nazis.

He ended his phrase with a nervous laugh, unfavourably revealing two rather dingy rows of teeth between pale and protruding lips. As Schröder showed no sign of amusement, the man grew even more nervous. He sat down on the only chair in the room and began to fumble with the file he took from his briefcase. Schröder, still leaning against his bunk, waited for him to make his next move.

– As I said, we haven't got much time and I must press on with the task at hand.

– I'm sorry, Schröder once again interjected. – I still don't have your name. Who are you and why are you here if you haven't got the time?

– Oh, yes of course. Quite … I mean, absolutely. My name is Göbel, Dieter Göbel, and I'm here today because you have a legal right to defence counsel. Since you have not expressed a wish for any particular lawyer to represent you, I have been appointed to assume that responsibility.

– And what makes you think that I would like you to represent me?

– Well, you'll need someone, won't you?

– Why? Is it going to make any difference?

– What do you mean?

– Is it going to make my case better or worse?

Göbel assumed an expression that might well have been one of genuine indignation, except he couldn't prevent himself from sneezing at the same time. Schröder waved his hand in the air as the other continued.

– To be quite frank with you, Schröder …

– Dr. Schröder, actually.

– Dr. Schröder. To be quite frank with you, I fail to see how circumstances could presently be much worse for you. But it will of course be entirely up to you to accept my assistance or to reject it. In the latter instance I shall of course cease to bother you. Shall I?

– Shall you what?

– Leave you right now? Göbel blushed with anger and frustration as he realised that Schröder was playing cat and mouse with him.

– That would considerably relieve you, wouldn't it?

Schröder stared across the room at his singularly amorphous adversary. In a deceptively low tone of voice he continued,

– I know that's what you would prefer. Not having anything to do with other people's dirty laundry, since you have your hands full of your own stinking underwear. But as long as obscure defendants pay for you to turn up at court and most obligingly lose one case after another, you don't mind, do you?

– Dr. Schröder, first of all I must say that I am not used to being addressed this way, neither by the court, nor by my clients. I have thirty years of experience in this profession. Before the war I had my own much-respected law firm in Munich.

– In Munich?

– Yes, why?

– I don't think it remains a secret how justice has been done in the state of Bavaria for the last thirty years. I happen to know how the völkisch trials were set up and conducted. You were all in on it together – prosecutors, judges and lawyers – making deals beforehand and splitting the money, preferably American dollars or Swiss francs, among you. But not before having each contributed ten to twenty per cent of your fees to the NSDAP that was protecting and enforcing *your* law. Your own part in these ludicrous pseudo-legal proceedings would have been to coerce your client into pleading guilty so that, with a standard formulation or two, you could obtain the miracle of reduction of sentence. Naturally, this procedure only applied in the case of certified Germans and good patriots. If someone had molested a Jew or cheated a Czech in business, he didn't even need a defence lawyer, since such actions were considered as being committed in the interest of national resurrection. In cases like that it was an honour to be accused!

– Thank you, Doktor. Considering how well versed you already seem to be in the ways of the law, I have no alternative other than to recommend that you take over your own defence. I wish you good luck in court, and please forgive me for having trespassed on your valuable time.

Göbel was just about to rise from his chair when he was brusquely forced back into it by Schröder.

– Listen, you sharp Bavarian practitioner, you are going to represent me, and you are going to do exactly as I tell you.

Göbel did not answer. Schröder continued,

– You would prefer that I pleaded guilty, wouldn't you?

– That would undoubtedly be the simplest solution, Göbel replied unenthusiastically.

– Yes, it would, for you, for the prosecutor, the judge, the newspapers, the Allies, the mob, in fact, for everyone except me! And the difference between all these others and me is that while they need no more than a scapegoat, I must arrive at the truth. Because once the truth – meaning in this case the uncovering of the true circumstances surrounding the death of Frau Irmgard Kampa – has been established, a much more important criminal issue will be brought to light.

– Let me point out, Schröder, that one murder, however insignificant it may seem in comparison with the millions of victims of systematised killing, is considered enough of a crime to send its perpetrator to the gallows.

– But what about the truth? Can it really be that nobody wants the truth to be discovered?

Because of the unintended naïveté of this last question, Schröder, who until this point had seemed to be gaining the better of his opponent, began to lose some of the ground he had made. Seeing the precise nature of Schröder's vulnerability and weakness, Göbel did not hesitate to strike back.

– If there is one thing that living through years of dictatorship and censorship has taught me, it is that the question of guilt or innocence is not so much a matter of truth as of persuasion. Truth itself never wins on its own merits – there is no innate sense in us either of justice or truth – and that is why a court case is always open to debate. The ancient Jews came to the very sensible conclusion that the notions of God and Law are nothing but subjects of perpetual debate and discussion. Although the law says what it says, it is first and foremost in need of interpretation. Thus, truth and justice can be negotiated and thereby attained. They can also be lost without recompense – that's the risk.

"You devious fox," Schröder thought. He was thoroughly surprised, however, that the man seemed to be so much more intelligent than his shabby exterior had given reason to assume. Somewhat more intrigued now than before by the man's appearance, he looked at his profile. He was suddenly seized by a suspicion.

– Your name hasn't always been Göbel, has it?

– How did you know?

– What was it then? Steinhardt, Mandelbaum, Goldmann?

– Even worse, Schröder. Once upon a time, in the dreaded east, whence came the horrors of the Golem and Ghenghis Khan, in a land more recently contaminated by Bolsheviks and curious men in long black caftans and corkscrew curls, my name was quite simply Ashkenazy, Yehudi Ashkenazy. But my mother was German. So I changed my name to her maiden name. Without actually adopting another name, simply by using my existing ones differently, I tampered with my papers. And I survived. In other words, the truth is – as you yourself said – that nobody cares about the truth. They need to frame someone for this, and they need to do it quickly. It's a matter of making a pre-emptive strike. Just imagine how all the widows, all the elderly women who have recently lost husbands and sons during the war, are placed. They are grievously alone, but still may have money – life savings hidden in mattresses, Swiss bank accounts, gold, silver, jewellery, diamonds and antiques. Some of them may even have villas somewhere, undamaged during the war, at a time when half the nation is homeless and desperate for shelter and security. It would be easy for a professional confidence trickster to make these women happy, and so grateful that they would readily give away everything they possess. Now, since here in the south of Baden we are under French occupation, the French legal system is used in civil court cases. In French law there is a clause that allows a householder to sell his house yet remain in it until the end of his days. Such a system may work in France, I suppose, but in Germany now it's tantamount to inciting desperate and unscrupulous adventurers to start arranging fatal accidents for little old ladies – accidents, or discreet suicides … Your case, being one of the first of its kind here, could establish a precedent. If your sentence is severe enough, it may be regarded as a deterrent.

– But what about the truth?

– To hell with the truth! How many times do I have to explain this to you? What we are talking about here is your neck! As far as the future is concerned, I see the following options. Either we find the woman who can provide you with an alibi for that night, or we introduce the interesting hypothesis of suicide – which cannot be entirely discounted as a possibility – or you confess.

– But I didn't do it!

– They usually "didn't do it".

– What do you mean, "they"?

– Murderers. They usually claim they never did it.

– I don't care about them. The only thing I want to say is that I am innocent.

– Sure. And if we repeat that phrase a couple of thousand times, waiting for the propaganda effect to kick in, we might in the end even sway the jury by such eloquence. The question is not what you in reality did or didn't do, but what can be proved that you did or didn't do. Bismarck insisted on the definition of politics as the art of the possible. He could have included the law in that possibility. In short, your innocence is worth nothing if there is absolutely no evidence to prove it.

– But isn't it the court's task to prove me guilty, not for me to prove my innocence?

– Correct, but in what direction do you think that your

carrying a gun, the bullets of which match the one that was buried in the rocking-chair behind the victim's head, will lead the court? Towards finding you guilty? Or innocent? Even if I'm willing to believe in your innocence, and take your word for it, the single fact that your eyes are blue won't get us very far ahead in court, Herr Doktor.

Schröder was just about to fire off another sarcastic remark. But he pulled himself together and said,

– So what would your plan of action be if I did decide to plead guilty?

– We could possibly have the charge commuted from murder to manslaughter.

– I can see that! The suspect came into the room, pointing a gun at the victim. The victim started to scream, and he told her to shut up. When she didn't stop, the gun he held in his hand went off all by itself, and it just so happened that the bullet ricocheted and hit the woman right in the forehead. Her death was instantaneous. Maybe we could use that as a defence, that she didn't suffer. Mr. Mastermind, if you had taken the time to study the coroner's report, you would have found that the bullet was fired from within a range of two metres, by a gun aimed straight at her. There can be absolutely no doubt that the murder was intended and carried out in cold blood. It's first-degree murder all right. So, what next? Suicide? But where was the weapon? No, the only way out of this is to prove that the gun I was carrying, although apparently identical to the one used in the woman's murder, was not in fact the murder weapon. And the only way to prove that is to find the gun that really killed her. But wait a second ... Strange as it may sound, I never thought of this before. I was asleep in that bed when the murder was committed. When I woke up the gun was in my pocket, but it could have been taken by that prostitute, who also took the gate key from my pocket. She took both gun and key with her, and went to the building, found the door open, entered the room where the woman was sitting in her rocking-chair, killed her, and went back to Zum Schwarzen Ferkel. There she put the gun and the key back in my pocket and disappeared into thin air. But why was it so important for her to get the old woman out of the way? Yes, of course! The old lady was probably the only non-official person beside herself who had seen Uhland, or whoever that person was, dead. She wanted to stop the woman from talking, as she knew I would be back asking questions, questions that could become just a bit too dangerous for her.

– So, maybe she had a thing with this Uhland, Göbel said. – Maybe she killed him, too.

– Yes, Schröder replied heavily. – Yes. If there is no Rheinau, then there must be someone else behind it all. Who is he? Who is she? Who the hell is this devil-woman?

– We've got to play this by the rules, Schröder. And since the rules are those handed down by the notoriously unpredictable French (thus allowing for the unexpected to happen) we do have a possible last recourse. It will take your full cooperation, though. Are you willing to listen?

*

At ten o'clock on the morning of November 6, 1945, Dr. Hans Schröder was brought into court, and directed to swear on oath that he would speak the truth and nothing but the truth. He was asked to place his hand on the court Bible and to repeat what the police sergeant dictated to him. He was then told to be seated, and the proceedings began. These were conducted in the German language under the supervision of the Right Honourable Heinz Giessen, appointed to his office by the likewise recently appointed Minister President for Baden-Württemberg, Dr. Reinhold Maier. As a consequence of no fewer than three differing national legal systems being used and obliged to work together as one, it was exceedingly difficult to predict the course of the trial, not to mention its outcome. There was no reason to suppose that one single legal system would have absolute supremacy, even though the French code had been imposed by the occupying French military. The Americans controlling the north of the province of Baden bore a grudge against the French for refusing to abide by agreements previously made. They judged it beneficial to their interests to ensure that the court officials were appointed by the president of a county government sanctioned by General Eisenhower himself. The French authorities, surprisingly, had objected as little to this as they had to the previous appointment of Major Beaufort, a French-speaking Canadian from Quebec, as chairman of the military committee that had been responsible for the now-closed martial investigation of Schröder. The prosecutor was an Alsatian, fluent in both German and French. It was he, Daniel Nemese, who now, on this rainy and windy autumn day, when a profusion of red and yellow leaves was falling from the chestnut trees, opened the proceedings against Dr. Hans Michael Schröder. He began by asking the defendant where he had spent the night of August 23, that same year.

– I was at home with my wife.

There were murmurs and whisperings in the court-room as he spoke these words. The room was duly quietened, and the prosecutor continued,

– But it has been established that in both the interrogation report put together by the German police and the protocol resulting from the court-martial proceedings brought against the defendant, that ...

– Objection, Your Honour! Göbel quickly intervened.
– My client has not been brought to trial on charges put forward by the Allied Forces at present upholding law and order in this country. On the contrary, he has been acquitted of every criminal charge. I therefore move that all material pertaining to an investigation terminated long ago be excluded from these proceedings, and be regarded as inadmissible evidence.

The judge scrutinized Göbel. He then gave the prosecutor a quick glance, and added in a perfunctory tone,

– Objection sustained. Prosecutor, in this court-room the defendant may only be quoted as questioned by German civil police. Please continue.

– According to the record of the police interrogation of the defendant on August 26, you, Hans Schröder, stated that you spent the night of August 23 in a first-floor room at Gasthaus Zum Schwarzen Ferkel in Günterstal with a prostitute. Is it correct that you told this to the investigating officer on August 26?

– Yes, I did.

– And why do you now wish to change that statement?

– Because I was not speaking the truth on that occasion.

– May I then ask you what caused you to change your

mind? By this I mean that, if you have an alibi for that particular night, Dr. Schröder, why did you not tell us earlier, so that we could have arranged for your early release from custody? Why have you insisted on telling a lie, which, instead of affording you a possible advantage, brought you under suspicion of committing a horrifying crime, a crime, which you knew all the time that you hadn't committed? Why, Dr. Schröder?

– Because I wanted to protect my wife. I didn't want her to be drawn into this ...

– You mean you didn't want her to prove that you were innocent, that you did not have sex with a prostitute, that you did not shoot an old woman in the head, spreading her brain ...

– Objection, Your Honour! Göbel, whose spectacles were unusually clean this morning, again uttered the word, – Objection! What the defendant has or hasn't said prior to his arrival in this court is irrelevant. The facts should be noted as stated here, not elsewhere.

Again the court-room began to heave like a rising sea. Judge Giessen had to use his gavel several times to calm the crowd. The hall was thronged with people unwilling to remain quiet. When silence had with difficulty been imposed, the judge turned to the prosecuting counsel, and said,

– It is my duty to inform you that trial procedure starts here and now in this room, and that whatever Herr Schröder has or hasn't said earlier shall be dismissed as irrelevant. The jury shall of course not pay any attention to the last remarks by the prosecutor, who will now come to the point, I hope.

– In view of this new development, Daniel Nemese said, I shall have to ask that the court be adjourned for as long as it will take to summon Frau Schröder to the stand as principal witness in this trial.

– Would forty-eight hours be sufficient time for that? the judge asked.

– I should think so.

– I hereby declare that the court be adjourned until November 8, at ten o'clock, Judge Giessen announced, and was about to rise from his chair when a woman's voice made itself heard from the back row.

– There is no need for any delay. I can testify to my husband's innocence here and now. Please, let me step forward.

There she was, fearlessly walking up the aisle leading to the judge's dais. She stopped directly in front of him.

– Do you have identification papers to prove incontrovertibly that you are the person to whom the defendant refers?

– Yes.

– Well then. Would you please be so kind as to register over there?

To all the others gathered in the court-room he added in a louder voice,

– The court will adjourn for twenty minutes.

Hans Schröder looked around as though utterly taken by surprise at this last turn of events. But in fact he was only playing his part in a scene that had been already arranged. The background to it was as follows. Following their conversation in the interrogation room, it had finally been agreed between Göbel and he, though with considerable reluctance on Schröder's part, that Göbel should go to Beatrice and tell her, that if she believed in her husband's innocence of the atrocious deed for which he was now standing trial, she should not hesitate to give him an alibi for that night. This course of action would offer the best prospects of a successful plaidoyer, as any other plea would in all probability lead to his being indicted. Göbel had prepared his words just in case Frau Schröder might be seized by panic at the thought of committing perjury. It proved to be an unnecessary precaution.

Although Göbel had taken pains to make himself more presentable since that day when he first met Schröder, he was still pretty shabby-looking, and the fact that he had had his hair cut was somewhat negated by a three-day growth of beard. Nonetheless, he was warmly welcomed by Frau Schröder once he had told her that he had come straight from prison with a letter from her husband. She bade him enter and make himself comfortable in the drawing-room. As soon as he was seated, she tore the letter open, devouring every word with avid eyes.

Dearest Beatrice,

I am devastated by the feeling of having wronged you. How could I ever have doubted that you were telling me the truth? I beg you to forgive me if you can – if only you knew what I have had to go through for our sake ... There is simply nothing and nobody I can trust any more, not even my own judgement or my own senses. I feel as if the very earth under my feet is giving away and I have fallen into a never-ending abyss. I want this nightmare to stop, but it keeps getting worse, to the point where, in order to save myself now, I must ask you, implore you, beg you on my knees, to do the exact opposite of what I so desperately demanded from you last time, namely to lie for me.

It is perfectly true that I didn't kill the old woman. It is also true that I did spend the night on which she was murdered with a prostitute – only she was gone when I woke up in the middle of the night. That woman, the only one who could have given me an alibi, has been missing ever since. Nobody can find her, and the landlady of Zum Schwarzen Ferkel, where she had a room, denies that she ever knew her; she also says that she has never seen me. No wonder I started to believe in a conspiracy. Or to doubt my own perception of reality ... Did she even exist, or did I dream that as well?

The man who stands before you is my lawyer Dieter Göbel, who, under a hail of protests on my part, has finally convinced me of the necessity of persuading you to testify that I was with you at our house on the night of August 23. Where were you that evening? Is it possible that you were at home alone – except for the children, of course? I know that perjury is a heinous crime and that you could get into serious trouble if they find out – and believe me, they will do their best to break your evidence. But if there is any chance at all that you could insist on it – and I do hope that they never will be able to get the better of you – then if you want to save me from the death penalty, you must try. So I beg you to do this for me. First simply to disregard the fact that I, believing that you had remarried, sought the company of a barfly. Secondly, carefully construct my alibi in collaboration with Herr Göbel. Then, under a storm of cross-questioning, you will have to stick stubbornly and unto the death to your word.

Now that you know the truth and nothing but the truth, I place my destiny in your hands. So help me God.

I love you
Hans

P.S. Please destroy this letter as soon as you have read and understood the contents.

Half-way through reading the letter, tears began to roll down Beatrice's cheeks, but as she neared the end of it there was already, set against the background of consternation, a glimmer of resolution in her eyes.

– But how are we going to put this together? she asked.
– I can't even recall what day that was. And if I were to say that Hans was here that day, where has he been all the other days?

– All the better, Göbel answered. – You were up that night. The children were in bed. There was a tapping at the window. At first you thought it was caused by the branches of the tree outside swaying in the wind, but the noise was repeated, and seemed to you as if it might be caused by someone at ground level throwing a pebble at the window pane. You opened the window and heard your husband whispering to you. You immediately recognised his voice because he had already called you by telephone several times during the summer.

– But why didn't he come to live with us once he was back in town?

– Because at first he thought you were living with Rheinau, so he didn't want either you or the children to come to harm. Realising that Rheinau was no longer around, his attention turned to the mysterious disappearance of Dr. Uhland, because Hans Schröder still felt he had to clear his reputation in the matter of the clinical reports and death certificates signed in his name.

– So when did he find out that it wasn't Rheinau behind all this, and change his mind about what to do?

– Well, only you can tell; you're the witness.

– Wait! Now I remember. There is a major problem here. A week later, by the end of August, Major Beaufort, the head of the military court investigating Hans, came to see me. He knew everything Hans had and hadn't done over the last months, and he specifically asked me if Hans had ever come to see me in our home. I said I had never seen him. Then he said that the unknown man who came here in early summer had been Hans himself. You see, when I returned home one day, there was a man sitting right here in this room. Mathilde had let him in.

– Who is Mathilde?

– She's our housekeeper.

– Does she live in the house?

– No, she comes in the morning and leaves in the afternoon.

– Good. Then at least we do not have to rely on her to corroborate your testimony. Please continue.

– As I said, there was a male person sitting on that chair. It was Hans, but he had changed so much. He had lost weight. There were two fingers missing on his right hand. He had a long beard. I simply didn't recognise him, and he said that he was just visiting because as a child he had lived here. To Mathilde, however, he had said that he was a cousin of mine. Because of this Mathilde had let him in and asked him to wait in this room until my return. When I heard Mathilde say that the man had presented himself to her as my cousin, I immediately became suspicious. I knew of no such cousin, and I suspected he might be a burglar or a tramp. That's what he looked like.

– So you told him to leave?

– Yes.

– And he did?

– Yes.

– And this is what you told Beaufort as well?

– Yes. Then he informed me who the man really was. In other words, Beaufort knows that I didn't know Hans was back, and that the only time I really did see Hans was on that one day when I couldn't recognise him. Herr Göbel, is there any chance that the prosecuting counsel might call Beaufort as a witness?

– It cannot be excluded. I certainly would.

– And he would be obliged to tell the truth?

– As a military officer, and as a man of honour – of course.

– So what are the chances? Is it possible that he would refuse to testify?

– Only if it would mean that he was not risking his own neck by doing so.

– Well, then there is only one solution. We must make him part of the plan as well.

– How do you intend to do that?

– I really don't know, but if I can somehow convince Beaufort of Hans' innocence, then maybe I can buy his silence. It is not a formal criminal offence to refuse to testify in court, is it?

– No, not as such. But it wouldn't put him in a very flattering light either if he were to decline to testify.

– Be that as it may. We haven't very much time to lose. We can't take the risk of letting Beaufort jeopardise my testimony. I'd go to hell and back for Hans. I'd do anything to save him.

– I'm very happy to hear that, Frau Schröder, and believe me, there is someone else who is even more grateful for your support.

She followed him to the door. He had put on his hat, but turned just as he was about to leave.

– Oh, one last thing. Are any of your children aware that their father is back in town?

– No, I don't think so. I haven't told them, and even in the newspapers Hans' name has not been mentioned. He has only been referred to as a "well-known psychiatrist in Baden charged with murder".

– Yes, I know. It is a security measure put in place to prevent public disorder. Since the military investigation of your husband commenced, a veil of secrecy has been cast over him. Well, one must admit that he himself has in no small degree contributed to the mystery now shrouding him. My job, our job, is to tear that veil apart and to clear his name once and for all. You will carefully reconstruct your husband's alibi, and then advise me, so that I can co-ordinate your version with your husband's. That's about all for now. Good afternoon, Frau Schröder.

She stood at the top of the steps and looked at the odd figure of the lawyer as he hobbled, somewhat stiff-legged, down the gravel path. When he was out of sight, she raised her eyes to the grey, impenetrable sky, then lowered her gaze to the flaming trees and the dying garden around her, still in its decay adorned with red and yellow roses. There was moisture in the air, almost a mist, carrying a strong scent of steaming earth and compost. Branches were burning in a nearby garden. The thick smoke rose in a straight column, dissipating in the air. A dog barked and a black cat disappeared behind a dustbin. She took a deep breath and pressed her hands tightly together. There was no time to lose. The children would soon be home.

Beatrice went to the telephone and dialled the number Beaufort had given her.

– May I speak to Major Beaufort, please?

– Speaking, the voice at the other end replied.

The instant connection surprised her, and she had to search for words before she could finally string a phrase together.

– Oh, er, I was ... I thought, if ... at all possible ... Could I ask for ... Will you able to answer ... Oh, I'm so sorry, you must think I'm completely crazy. You see, I feel so grateful for what you have done for me that, as a little sign of my appreciation, I wonder if there is any chance at all that you could come to dinner, as a guest of Hans and mine, of course. Although he can't participate in person, for obvious reasons, I'm sure he otherwise would. Would you come?

– Please, Frau Schröder, you have absolutely nothing to be grateful for, as far as my actions are concerned.

– But you did help my husband, Major.

– I was doing my duty, Madame. And I can assure you that I do not expect to be shown favours just for doing my job.

– Oh, please, Major, do come and join me at dinner, just so that I can thank you properly.

– Madame, I really don't know ...

– And if I were to say it would make me happy if you came, would you not do it for my sake, regardless of your duty?

– Well, you see, in two days' time I'll be going to Heidelberg to deliver my monthly report to the district commander, and I won't be back until ...

– What about tomorrow evening, Major? Would that be too soon?

– Well, let me see ... there is a meeting in the evening, or rather, in the late afternoon ... As a matter of fact, I do happen to be off duty at eight o'clock tomorrow evening, but surely ...

– Please, Major, do me this little favour. I would feel so honoured. Just come when you can tomorrow evening, and I'll prepare a little something to eat and drink ... Yes, yes ... nine o'clock. Perfect.

She hung up with a sigh of relief, knowing all the same that her mission was only about to begin.

*

The roses, yellow and red, brought in fresh from the garden, still had dew clinging to the insides of their petals, enhancing both their colour and fragrance. Beatrice arranged them in a tall vase and placed it on the table, where they formed a beautiful relief against the white lace cloth, the linen napkins, the china and the Bohemian glass. While she was busy setting the table, the declining afternoon sun peeked through the broad windows and painted the entire scene in gold. Beatrice felt herself to be a Midas of sorts; everything she touched instantly changed into the colour of the sun. She could hardly believe her good fortune. And she would need it now more than ever before, for she had taken a solemn vow to make a last attempt to rescue her husband. If he went down now, she would go down with him. It did seem as though he now finally trusted her, or (although this possibility did not present itself in any precise way to her) that he simply didn't have much of a choice. But Beatrice was carried along on a wave of love and compassion, and she was determined not to allow doubt to rear its head during the course of this evening. She had taken every precaution, and had sent the children to stay overnight with a woman friend, herself pretending to go to Basle to visit an aunt. Mathilde had helped to prepare some of the dishes, but she was not told for whom they were intended. Being a discreet and somewhat timorous domestic, Mathilde kept any thoughts she might have had about this sudden culinary interest on her mistress's part to herself, and did not delve deeper into the matter. She had realised that something extraordinary must be in the making, since the children were not at home, and the house had had to be thoroughly dusted, unusually for a weekday, as if it was indeed being prepared to receive a most important visitor.

Mathilde was a German Alsatian from Riquewehr, a small town in the Vosges with an indisputable reputation for delicious white wines, such as the Riesling, Sylvaner and Gewurztraminer. She was asked to go down to the cellar and bring up some of the pre-war vintages kept there. Her mistress knew little about which wines were best for certain regional dishes, and Mathilde took real pride in finding the right ones for her. The wines to be served this evening were therefore not only subtle and elegant, but also particularly suited to accompany the variety of dishes prepared and put aside in the pantry.

Her work finished, Mathilde hung her apron on its hook, washed her hands and went from the kitchen into the dining-room. There she discovered her mistress standing with her back turned to the darker part of the room, absorbing the last rays of the glorious sun as it sank behind trees and roof-tops. Mathilde, who was a religious woman, was overwhelmed by the sight. It was as if she were in the presence of a saint enveloped in a flood of light that formed a golden halo round her head and a strangely intense purple aura round the rest of her body. Involuntarily, she made the sign of the cross, and was silently retreating as Beatrice turned round and said,

– Thank you, Mathilde. That will be all for now. As the children won't be back until tomorrow afternoon, you may take the morning off as well. I shall see to … But what is it Mathilde? You look as though you've seen a ghost!

– It's you, Madame. You look so beautiful in your dress, in the light – like an angel!

– Oh, dear. Well, it's just plain old me, I'm afraid. But

as for the dress, well, it does have a special significance for me. I wore it on the day of my engagement. It's a bit out of fashion now, of course, but the material is of the finest quality. Here, feel it. The finest satin.

– Oh, I couldn't touch it.

– Don't be silly, Mathilde! Come, feel it.

When Mathilde made no sign of wanting to come closer, Beatrice moved towards her and held out her arm, so that she could touch the sleeve. It was as if Mathilde had been right in wanting to avoid contact, for, at her touch, a little static electricity was discharged from the satin. In the obscurity of this part of the room, they could both see it leap across from the cloth to Mathilde's finger in the form of a tiny, bluish flash of lightning. Mathilde was startled, recited a Hail Mary, and again made the sign of the cross. Beatrice began to laugh, not malevolently, but amused by the ignorance of the simple peasant woman. Before she had the chance to say anything though, Mathilde spoke,

– Dear Mistress, I do not know what is going to happen here tonight, but may God, Jesus our Lord and all the angels be with you, for you have been chosen.

– Nonsense, Mathilde! Now, you run along home and have a nice evening. Do make sure that you take some of the food with you.

– Oh no, Madame, I'm not eating that, that's for you. For you and ... she hesitated for a moment, then added,

– For you ... and your guests.

– As a matter of fact, Mathilde, there will only be one guest tonight.

– Yes, I know there is only one. And he will be here soon. Make everything ready and treat him well. You need to convince him of something very important. I can feel it. Good evening, Madame, and God bless you.

– And you, Mathilde.

The silence which entered the room after Mathilde's departure was long and pregnant with meaning. In the drawers of the bureau were all the family photographs, letters and cherished gifts Beatrice had received over the years from her husband and the children. It was as if a scent of the past still lingered there. The invisible presence of these objects prevented her from quite fully experiencing the present time. When she looked about her she saw the world the way it had once been, and her ardent wish was to restore that ancient harmony. With hindsight, the old world, their old world, seemed like a paradise lost, although her reason kept calling her back to reality by reminding her of how precarious in many ways their existence had been. Long before the outbreak of the war, Hans had faced professional difficulties because of his interracial marriage. The children had been branded as Mischlinge, the term used by the Nazis to designate persons with mixed Aryan-Jewish blood. Hans himself had been advised to divorce her. The insecurity of the last years before the war had been constant. And when the war was finally over, when Hans had miraculously returned, and it seemed that their lives could be switched back on to the right track again, he was accused of this absurdity, an impending death sentence, unless ... Oh, my God! There she was, not even fully dressed when the grandfather clock struck the hour. She hurried through the dining-room and went upstairs. The flames of the candles made a sudden bow in the wind of her passing. In her bedroom she found the shawl she was looking for. She wrapped it around her shoulders, adjusted her hair a last time and descended again, only to find that it was still only eight o'clock, another hour before the major might be expected. There was still time to review possible complications. She must let him do the talking, encourage him to talk about himself, gain his confidence, so that he would let slip some information that she could use as a lever against him, if necessary – to compromise him. In the final instance she would have to improvise, do anything it would take to secure Beaufort's unswerving loyalty to her cause ... Deeply enmeshed in the last intricacies of her imaginary game, she heard the clock strike nine. Ten minutes later Major Beaufort was at the door.

– Good evening, Frau Schröder.

– Oh, you made it, Major! Was it hard to find the way here? Please come in ... Let me take your coat.

– Thank you.

He was dressed in uniform, but this time the formality of his dress had not prevented him from bringing flowers for his hostess.

– Quite a place you and your husband have here, he said tentatively as he handed her the bouquet. Luckily, it wasn't roses (considering the array of red and yellow roses already decorating the dining-room, such contribution would have seemed de trop). The main cause, however, of this piece of luck was that Beaufort had purposely taken care to avoid flowers likely to evoke emotional associations. With carnations he thought himself on safe ground; a bouquet of those seemed considerate, respectful and at the same time sufficiently impersonal. Beatrice took her time admiring them and putting them in a vase – by no means did they outshine her own flower arrangements. The carnations were placed at the end of the sideboard. Beaufort himself had taken a seat in one of chairs, a glass of cool *crémant* in his hand.

– I have to thank you once again for coming here at such short notice, Beatrice said, raising her glass. – And you are absolutely right in assuming that I haven't asked you here just to thank you for your kindness to my husband and myself. We both know his life is at stake. My reason for bringing you here was to ask you one last question … May I ask you a personal question?

Beaufort, feeling that it was better to get straight to the heart of the matter than to toss the hot potato back and forth the whole evening, nodded.

– In that case, Beatrice said, – I shall hesitate no longer. Do you personally believe that my husband is guilty of the murder of which he has been accused?

She accompanied her words with a long dark glance that made Beaufort think of a gun-muzzle pointing at him. In the very next instant her ominous expression changed and she hurried to reassure him.

– Oh, please, Major, speak your heart. I promise you that I shall not be surprised or offended if you tell me that you do believe so.

Beaufort, still intently staring into the darkness, was apparently not altogether taken by surprise. After having carefully pondered an opening phrase, he leaned forward in his chair and said,

– Frau Schröder. With all respect, I cannot see what difference my personal opinion could possibly make in relation to your husband's unfortunate personal situation. As a representative of the court-martial of the Allied Occupational Forces in Heidelberg, and by virtue of the judicial authority with which I have been invested in the specific task of detecting and bringing war criminals to stand trial, I have been able to conclude only this. According to existing identity papers, a male person named Hans Schröder, aged 46, was on several occasions this summer taken in for questioning. The subject of his interrogation concerned the so-called mercy killing of mentally deranged and criminal patients under the aegis of the euthanasia programme initiated by Adolf Hitler in September 1939, and brought to bear on all physicians of the Reich. Right from the beginning, Dr. Schröder admitted that the signatures on several documents (mainly on attestations to facilitate the liquidation of unwanted citizens, but also on a number of apparently false death certificates) looked as if they could be his, although at the same time he declared them to be forgeries. In support of this statement he claimed that he had himself been an early victim of Nazi injustice, but also that he had been spared the death penalty for insubordination in wartime. Instead, he had been sent to serve as a field doctor at the eastern front. After the battle of Stalingrad he was captured and imprisoned in a Soviet camp. He was subsequently put on a train somewhere in the Sudetenland in May 1945. During that train journey, he and other German prisoners of war managed to escape. In the month that followed he walked all the way to Freiburg, with the intent on looking for his family. In essence, this was his story.

Beaufort held his breath for a moment, then looked at Beatrice. Her eyes glowed like silent cat eyes in the dimness. When she showed no sign of wanting to interrupt him, he continued,

– With the aid of recruitment lists found in the files of the Gestapo and the SS, we were able to ascertain that a certain Doktor Hans Schröder, the former head of Sankt-Anna Klinik, had been sent to the eastern front as early as the beginning of 1940. Unless these documents turned out to be forgeries as well – and for an investigation into this we had neither the time nor the resources – there was nothing else we could do but call the preliminary proceedings to a halt, and let the man go. In other words, our evidence in support of any possible involvement on the part of your husband in the Nazi euthanasia programme was inconclusive. Consequently it was unanimously decided to let the mystery of the signatures bearing his name remain.

Beaufort stopped again. This time Beatrice's silence had begun to discomfort him. He felt the heat under his collar and feared an imminent outbreak of sweat on his forehead. At that precise moment, Beatrice came to his rescue by finally breaking her silence.

– Oh, it's hot in here, isn't it? Terribly hot … Let me just open the window and get us some water.

At these words the major gave her a thankful glance. Her brief absence and turned back gave him the chance to wipe his face with his table-napkin. Beatrice saw the whole room reflected in the dark glass of the window. Coming back into the salon she casually continued,

– But weren't you in the least curious to know whether or not he could have done it? I mean, for yourself personally, aside from your work?

– No, not really. On the contrary, I felt relieved. And his arrest, following his leading us to the place where the old woman had been killed, was in many ways just as uncomfortable as were the circumstances leading to the first inquiry. But what choice did I have? In this case the evidence was against him. This had to be investigated.

– And so you had no alternative but to turn him over to a civil court?

– That is correct.

– Major, is there any possibility that on this occasion you could have acted differently without violating martial law and your own code of honour?

– You mean by not turning him over to the local authorities?

– Yes.

– I am afraid not.

– Why?

– Because even though your husband seemed to me a trustworthy man, my judgement could be wrong, and I would not …

– But if you really think that my husband is a trustworthy man, then you must somehow believe that he told you the truth?

– Frau Schröder, even if I was absolutely convinced that he was innocent …

– So you aren't?

– I'm what?

– You are not absolutely convinced of his innocence.

– As I said, even if I were, I would have had no option other than to detain him. You see, I was not alone in the room when the weapon and the bullets it had fired were discovered. If I had decided to dismiss such a piece of evidence as immaterial, that negligence on my part would without doubt have been reported to my superiors by the members of my own staff, in fact, it would have been their duty to do so. The possible consequence of this would be my dishonourable discharge from the army. So, although I understand your concern, I am, alas, unable to further your husband's case ... Now ... Now that you have the answer to your question ... you would, perhaps, prefer me to leave, so as not to cause you ... more pain?

– Oh no, please Major, I understand completely. You have to forgive me. I'm just a poor woman unable to find a way through all this. You mustn't take my whims too seriously – really. I understand that you have done everything, everything in your power, to help us. And that was also, apart from my childish wish for a miracle, the reason why I asked you over for dinner. Shall we proceed to table?

– I would be delighted, Beaufort replied, gracefully regaining his composure.

Beatrice went into the kitchen and put the various dishes on a big tray that she brought back to the dining-room. Meanwhile, Beaufort, at Beatrice's request, busied himself with the opening of a bottle of wine, taken straight from its bed of crushed ice in a large silver vessel on the sideboard. The major, being not only fond of good wines but something of a connoisseur, too, was surprised.

– Gewurztraminer. Riquewehr 1938. Pre-war vintage. What do you know!

Beatrice re-entered the room and went over to the sideboard. She turned round with an air of coquettish insouciance.

– Oh yes, amazing, isn't it? I found them in the cellar the other day. I had completely forgotten about them. Hans was, still is I suppose, very fond of Alsatian wines. He sometimes quoted Goethe saying that a bottle of Rhine wine was a daily necessity. So we used to have all these wines in our cellar. I thought we had drunk them all; ah, there were days during that wretched war when you wanted above all to forget the dreadful thing and see reality through rose-coloured glasses. Then Mathilde, our old housekeeper, you know, found a few cases under some old furniture. There were even bottles in the drawers of the writing desk that Hans inherited from his father.

– And you didn't know they were there?

– I had no idea. But it did come as a nice surprise.

– I can understand that. And then, look at all this exquisite food! How on earth do you get such delicacies these days? What do we have here?

– Well, that's home-made duck-liver paté, that's smoked ham, there are cucumbers and salad. There is some blood sausage, if you care for it – I'm not too keen, myself. Here's an Alsatian speciality called choucroûte – lard, sausages, potato and white cabbage cooked in white wine and vinegar. Mathilde does a very good job of it. It's delicious. I'll take it off the stove in a minute. It is to be served with mustard and, Mathilde says most emphatically, a cold Riesling and nothing else, so you'd better hurry up with the Gewurztraminer! And if you're still wondering what conjuror's hat all this was produced from at a time when people have hardly enough bread to eat, the answer is: the black market. You can get anything there, American cigarettes, nylon stockings, paté, brandy, fruit, vegetables, cheese, meat, even fish. You can buy tin-openers, monkey-wrenches, army trucks and motor cycles as well. There is only one problem. You can't pay with the German Reichsmark since everybody knows it is worthless.

– So how do you manage?

– I traded a case of wine and got this food in return, *Voilà! À votre santé, et mille merci d'être venu. Je vous souhaite bon appétit ... Majeur Beaufort.*

Beaufort, a native French-speaker from Quebec, who had nevertheless spent most of his life as an adult in the service of the primarily English-speaking Canadian military forces, was impressed with the ease by which Beatrice switched from one language to the other. Her English alone was most accomplished, and her French betrayed no hint of an accent, which was all the more remarkable considering that her mother tongue, for all Beaufort knew, must be German.

– How is it that you speak foreign languages so well? he asked.

– Our family life between the wars was very cosmopolitan in character. Different languages, even Polish and Yiddish, were constantly being spoken by guests and relatives around us as we grew up. Besides, our father always wanted us to be well educated. He even sent my sisters to university.

– Your sisters? What about you?

– No, unfortunately. I think he felt that I was too pretty to go to university, so he wouldn't let me. He didn't think it was going to be a problem to marry me off successfully.

Beaufort didn't say anything, but he raised his left eyebrow while taking a good sip of the wine. Excellent Gewurztraminer, he thought to himself. And yes indeed, she is too beautiful to go to school ...

– You didn't believe that, did you? I was only joking, of course. The truth is that I didn't want to moulder away in some dusty library. I wanted to do something, something for other people, so I joined the Red Cross and became a nurse. I was taking a course in first aid and emergency rescue in Göttingen when I met Hans, who was there studying to become a doctor. You see, although my family was Jewish, we were privileged. My father was a somewhat distant relative of the Rothschilds. You've heard of them, no doubt.

– You mean the famous 19th-century banking firm and the most important single figures in international finance? Oh, I've heard of them!

– Well, father was the great, great grandson of a cousin of the famous Baron Anselm Rothschild himself, the founder of the house in Frankfurt. We came from Frankfurt, and father was a banker too. Even though he didn't practise Judaism, properly speaking, he taught us Biblical history, and sent us to Rabbinical evening school. We learnt about the Talmud, about the persecution of our people throughout the ages, about the great Maimonides, about Spinoza, about the fraudulent Messiah, about Isaac ben Luriah, and many others. As a matter of fact, father even made us study the cabbalistic tree and the curious practices of the Hasidic Jews in eastern Europe, who, even in the midst of pogroms and misery, sang, danced and clapped their hands on every possible occasion. So we were privileged, and not only insofar as we never had to worry about the necessities of life. During the economic crises of the 1920s, when so many Germans lost their private fortunes in eventually worthless state bonds, father took the precaution of placing his holdings in other countries. After Hitler came to power, he realised that it was high time to move his remaining German assets abroad. Apart from investments that were already frozen in foreign companies, he deposited money, as well as his own collection of precious stones and my mother's jewellery, with a Swiss bank. Although he said they would never dare to do it, I think he knew what to expect. So I don't think that it came as a surprise to him when in 1938, after the Austrian Anschluss, the Nazis simply confiscated our house in Frankfurt. That same year Father emigrated to America with my two elder sisters. But the humiliations he had suffered at the hands of the Nazis, as well as his constant worries about me – as I had refused to go with them and leave my husband behind – proved too much for him, and he died of a stroke shortly after his arrival in the United States. My sisters are still safe and sound over there though … married too, Beatrice added with a mischievous smile.

– What about your mother?

– My mother died when I was young. She was a very honest person. Beautiful too …

– Seeing you, that makes sense, Beaufort said, charmed by her straightforwardness and candour. Feeling a bit more daring, he said,

– And what about the money, if you don't mind my asking?

– Oh, not at all. Nobody could get access to it during the war, of course, but my father had given us permission to draw upon the account after his death. How this was to be done was stipulated in his last will and testament, deposited in the safe with all his other papers. We three sisters agreed that, in accordance with our dear father's will, we would divide the money, the collection of stones and my mother's jewellery among us, if anything still remained.

– Does it?

– Surprisingly, it is all there. A Swiss lawyer, a friend of the family, helped me to execute the will. The inheritance was divided into three more or less equal portions – yes, more or less. You see, I kept my mother's wedding ring without asking for Sarah's or Rebeccas's consent – wicked, wasn't I?

– No, I'm sure your mother would have given it to you herself if she could.

– Do you know what? I think so too. And I'm also sure that, apart from that, the Swiss lawyer executed my father's will down to the most minute detail – father was a very conscientious man who thought about almost everything and everyone except himself – he would have had no idea as to which finger that ring should be on. For him there was only one finger for that ring, and that finger was no more. Anyway, my sisters seem happy. As for me, apart from my concern for Hans, that awful big dark cloud in the sky, I am very glad to be able to entertain you correctly as a dinner guest in our house.

The responsibility of choosing a suitable subject of conversation thus swung back to Beaufort, who understood that he was expected to tell a little about himself, now that Frau Schröder had been so gracious as to share some rather private matters with him. He may have wished that he also had a fortune hidden away somewhere. Alas, this was not the case. Nonetheless, he considered himself rich in experience. He was a happy family man whose only complaint was that he hadn't had enough time to see his children grow up. It had been easier when the kids were small. Even after a prolonged absence from home they would soon adopt him again as their father, but in later years he had felt more and more estranged. It was as if they talked between themselves, over his head, or behind his back, albeit with no malicious intent; still, he had the feeling that whatever the family talked about, he would not be around to see it happen, and so they simply spared him the task of bothering. Yet he wanted to bother. And his children were luckily old enough to understand that he couldn't just pull out of a war at a moment that pleased him or them. Being perfectly bilingual, he was an important interpreter and communicator between the French and the other Allies. All the same, his wife Françoise, the good woman, was not too happy to see his overseas assignment prolonged indefinitely, and Beaufort had made the decision to ask for a transfer back home by the end of the year. Whether his request would be granted was another matter. As long as people suspected of war crimes were being brought before him, he had his hands full. Dr. Schröder was only one of many that he would prefer to see no more of. "Let the dead bury the dead." Was that a saying from the Bible? Anyway, he and Francoise would have the money to send the children to college, and apart from love and affection, what more could you really expect from a parent? They had a home, he still had a life, a good life, to go back to. Oh God, it was so long since he had last been with a woman ... And here she was, a perfect specimen of the gender as well. What a pity he couldn't touch her ... But what is this? You're dreaming soldier boy! "Always obey your superiors and never fall asleep on guard." Those were the first rules ingrained in him at the military academy, and they suddenly sounded, a call from the enemy within. The words were jangling like alarm bells in his head. This was definitely a danger zone. Opposite him sat a charming woman, who at times demonstratively and seductively hid her face behind a mountain of red and yellow roses. "Don't forget," Beaufort told himself, "that she might very well hate you for not having helped her husband out of the trouble he was in, since you could have looked the other way and obtained bail or release on parole for Schröder." But it was also probable that members of his own staff would have reported him if he had attempted such a thing. The longer this encounter continued, the more he succeeded in convincing himself that the rich, beautiful and almost uncannily intelligent Beatrice Schröder wouldn't be inviting him to a dinner party *à deux*, wouldn't be flirting with him this way, if she didn't have a secret agenda. There was most definitely something she wanted from him. What it was he did not quite understand, since it must be very clear to her, that once the case had been taken out of his hands, there was nothing he could to do to influence it, except to find the real murderer, or to help Schröder to an alibi …

Here the major was interrupted in his thoughts by Beatrice's smooth, melodious voice, which insidiously seemed to whisper something in his ear while simultaneously carrying on another conversation, aloud. It was only now that Beaufort became aware of a scent in the room other than those of the roses, the wine and the food. It was rather like the saturated sweet smell of white lilies, and he realised that the heavy fragrance of funeral flowers was diffused with her perfume, turning its wearer into something like a giant night fly camouflaged as a tropical vampire, with a double pair of inscrutable, dark, yet glistening eyes staring at him from over its unfolded wings. Beaufort took a deep and not altogether steady look into his wine glass, and became aware that Beatrice, although speaking most of the time, had also constantly invited him to pour more wine into their glasses. He had naturally tried to keep up with her, and now discovered that they were already approaching the end of their third bottle. Beatrice kept giggling, and the major himself had already half forgotten the crucial point at which his inner monologue had stopped.

– Oh, dear, now you really must tell me something more about yourself, I mean, if there is anything at all that you can tell me without compromising yourself in the eyes of your *superiors*. How about your lovely wife, and your children? What are their names? Do you have any pictures of them? Where do you live? Is it right in the city of Quebec?

– Frau Schröder ...

– Oh please, call me Beatrice. Everyone does.

– Well, my name is Henry. Nice to meet you, Beatrice.

– That's much better. Now, tell me.

– I have a past, that's true. A family that I love. But it wasn't really until I came here to Europe that I realised what it means to have what I have, and what a tragedy it must be for all these people over here to see their loved ones disappear one after another. There was a moment on the dunes of Normandy when the senselessness of this war became apparent to me. Do you want to hear?

– I'm all ears, Henry.

– I took part in the D-Day action in Normandy. Fortunately, for me anyway, our battalion was not among the very first to storm the German defences. The first lines, for the most part made up of Irish and English units, were just simply machine-gunned down as they tried the approach. Eventually, and thanks to our vast superiority in numbers, we managed to entrench ourselves and finally, step by step, close in on the German artillery, which by then had been completely encircled by our forces. In short, they were trapped. We let them understand that they didn't stand a chance, and we ordered them to surrender. Their answer was to shoot at anyone or anything they could see. So we had to crush them, and this we did. We annihilated them. Suddenly the gunfire ceased and nothing could be heard except the wind, which swept in from the English Channel and cleared the sky of its clouds of smoke. We moved in and found every German soldier dead on the ground, in the bunkers or inside the few remaining tanks. As we turned the badly mutilated bodies over, we saw only adolescent faces, on those bodies that still possessed heads, that is. Some of those boys can't have been older than fifteen years of age. There were hundreds, thousands of them scattered over the dunes. On some of them the birds had already started to feed. Although we had orders to relentlessly pursue the enemy, nobody did. The sight in front of us was too gruesome – we had defeated and killed to the last individual an army of children ... I remember stopping by one of them. As I turned him on his back I saw that his chest had been completely ripped open by a grenade. But his face was undamaged. He was a blond boy with clean-cut features, an Aryan to be proud of, a beautiful son and brother. He could have been sixteen or perhaps seventeen years old. I found his torn jacket next to him. There wasn't much left of it, but, as if by a miracle, an intact letter was sticking out of his pocket. I opened it and read.

Dear parents, dear sister,

I don't think you will ever receive this message from me. But I write it all the same. I know I shall die today. We are waiting for the English and American dogs to attack us. Our commander has said that we will not surrender, that the Führer expects each one of us to stay at his post and defend his beloved Fatherland. I know the Führer is still alive, but when I see the number of ships, planes and guns that the enemy has, I realise that he too will soon be dead. But I shall still fight for him, as I shall fight for you, and for the future and glory of Germany. Goodbye, dear parents, goodbye, dear sister. May God always be with you and remember that I have always loved you.

Your Heinz

And there he was – dead. I doubt that he did very much more for the Fatherland than sparing it another mouth to feed. Apart from that it was all completely senseless. Far away from there, in his Berlin bunker, a crazy dictator, little by little understanding that his bloody farce was drawing to a close, kept sending the children of the nation out to die. All that this would have achieved is another fading photograph on a bedside table somewhere, another mother weeping herself to sleep for years to come, another father deprived of a hand in his workshop. There might be another sister, hoping in vain that the telegram saying "missing in action" might mean that her brother is alive somewhere, that he was wounded, then healed, and now has two kids with a French woman in Honfleur. And the photograph yellows over the years, and the mother and father become old, grey and bent, and the sister eventually marries and has children of her own. The photograph of the young man, with hair the colour of the sun, clean-cut features and a shy smile, stands in the light of the bedside lamp, surrounded by nothing but silence and the fateful ticking of an untiring clock. How many letters like this have been written never to find their way home? How many letters like this have been buried within the skull that composed them? I don't know, but I do know this, that while wars have always been fought, and always will be as long as there are men on earth, all that will remain to tell the ultimate truth about us, is the grave of the giant unknown soldier, who died for something infinitely smaller and more insignificant than himself.

Beatrice, visibly moved, was trying to say something. It took her some time to find the words, then she said,

– Did the family ever get his letter?

– No, there were no identity papers, no bracelet, nothing to tell who he was. But I took the letter. I still have it, and I still read it sometimes.

– But you just did, without even having it before your eyes – you know it by heart, don't you?

– Yes, I know it by heart, but sometimes I feel that I have to look at it to convince myself that the whole thing wasn't just a dream.

– You have a heart of gold, do you know that? Beatrice said, a tear glistening at the corner of her eye.

– No, it's only that I've seen too much. And the only way to go on from here is either to become a complete cynic, or try to make whatever remains of life and hope worth fighting for. No matter what I have seen, I shall always remain a soldier at heart. And soldiers don't have hearts of gold. They have red, vulnerable, fleshy, egoistic hearts, like everybody else. All we think about in the moment of danger is: Oh my God, I'm so scared. Will I ever survive this? And that's the moment when the bullet hits you – or it doesn't.

– And life goes on, Beatrice said.

– And life goes on. Life will always go on. And don't read me wrong. If a gun is pointed at you, it doesn't matter if it's held by a child or a woman. The bullet is still deadly. In a life-and-death situation you shoot first if you still have a chance to do so. The day you think otherwise in combat, you're dead. I find it deeply regrettable that these kids were killed, but I cannot regret that we did it. We had to. You know, there are moments in a man's life when he has to do what no other man can do for him. And if my children, and one day perhaps my grandchildren, ask me what I did in the war, I shall have to tell them that I was sent there to massacre youngsters just like themselves, young people who had not had time to do harm, even if they wanted to. And I will tell them to think hard about the reality of war, so that they can appreciate to the full what they have been spared. They were born and brought up in a democratic society, a society in which no leader will ever have the right or authority to send children to their deaths. It is absolutely just that those who assumed that right or authority should be brought to face the consequences of their perverse actions. So, yes, my family, so far, leads a tranquil suburban life in the suburbs of the city of Quebec. I have two sons and a daughter, she's the youngest …

– And she wraps her father around her little finger, I'm quite sure!

– Oh yes, of course. After many weeks, sometimes months away from your loved ones, you may experience a strange sense of guilt, as if you are somehow neglecting them. And although both they and you know that this is an inevitable concomitant of your profession, it still gnaws at your guts. So you tend to spoil them when at last you are home, trying to make up for lost time.

– Why did you want to become a military man in the first place? Does it run in the family?

– I didn't, actually, and there is no family tradition. I studied law, and went on to Oxford, England, hoping to become an attorney, but after I arrived there and had studied one term, the first world war broke out. Many of my fellow students volunteered, and their enthusiasm was infectious to someone as young and gullible as I was. When I heard a Canadian unit was preparing to march with the British army, I volunteered too, completely ignorant of what lay ahead of me. We thought it would be some kind of party. You go out there and shoot a bit and then the Krauts have to call it a day, pack their things and go back home, and you've won the game and have something to brag about back home. Needless to add, the prolonged war in the trenches came as a shock to every one of us. We had left London poets and kings; the ones that made it back home returned in rags and ashes. And God knows why I was spared. It must have seemed like a miracle to everyone. I was even decorated for having survived.

– Really, did they give you a medal for that?

– Well, officially it was for bravery, but really it's just a little piece of metal invested with a prestige that is utterly out of proportion to what you have been willing to sacrifice for it, namely your own life. And even though I saw through the entire humbug, I was still strangely attracted to it. So when I was offered a place at Sandhurst Military Academy, I accepted. After graduation, thanks to my contacts and, to a lesser degree, to my insight into the game of the European balance of power, I was offered a job in Intelligence. But I was still interested in law, and kept it up. I was lucky to be able to use it in my daily work. So when this war was finally over I was seen as the ideal senior officer to lead judicial investigations in the occupied zone, which is the reason I'm still here.

– Do you miss your wife?

– I would be lying if I said I didn't.

– Why express it so cautiously? I won't hold it against you! Beatrice cried out, and threw her hair back over her chair while opening her mouth in generous laughter.

– Hmm. Well, yes, I miss her. Very much.

Major Beaufort was on the verge of suggesting to Beatrice that she must really know how it is to miss somebody, but then held himself back as he realised that it would only bring the conversation back to Hans Schröder. Beatrice, thankfully, did not revert to that topic. Instead she said,

– I can imagine. How did you meet?

– At a Light Infantry ball.

– Oh, how romantic!

– It wasn't romantic at all. I got into a fight with a guy because he was behaving disrespectfully to the ladies. I was solidly drunk myself, and before I knew what was happening, the other guy punched me. I flew over the floor, came up again and we started to try out our fists on each other. Other officers came along, holding us apart, but not without trying to arrange a fight. In the heat of the moment, we both agreed, but the colonel of our regiment happened to be near, luckily for us both. He saw what had happened, and put us both under house arrest for having brought the name of the regiment into disrepute. I had to spend three days in the cells, and on the last day my future wife came to visit me. She had been to the ball herself, and had been sitting near where the argument started. I had thought she was the prettiest girl I ever saw. I was thinking about a way to approach her. Maybe the whole show was in reality all for her. I think she understood it was, one of those macho-man things, you know: prove to your woman that you're willing to fight for her love and to defend her. But the time we really met was during my arrest. I was ashamed, but she was charming, no, she was adorable, and we started to date. Well, that's how it all happened. *In vino veritas*, I guess. Cheers to you ... The major raised his glass, soon realising that there was nothing in it. Bemused, he looked for the bottle. It was empty too.

– Oh goodness me, the Riesling! Beatrice exclaimed. Mathilde says we're to have Riesling with the choucroûte. I can see that I didn't bring up enough. Of course, there simply wasn't enough room in the ice bowl. Anyway, they keep quite cool in the cellar. While I bring the food in from the kitchen, would you be so kind as to go and fetch a couple of bottles ... Where? You go down the stairs, through the hallway and on through the door on your left ... yes, they'll be down there. I brought them out earlier today. They'll be standing on the writing desk I told you about. You can't miss it.

At first he didn't think her request in any way strange. But then a warning-bell rang in his head. As his vague suspicions kept mounting, Beatrice's words spoken earlier that evening reverberated in his mind: "... we even found some of the bottles in the drawers of the writing desk that Hans inherited from his father." The drawers of the desk? Beaufort now recalled that Schröder had claimed that the gun in his pocket wasn't his, and that he had found it in a secret compartment in the writing desk in Uhland's apartment. This desk not only looked like the one his father had made use of during his lifetime, but also contained exactly the same type of gun in exactly the same type of secret compartment. The coincidence, if ever there was one, was too striking to be ignored.

Beaufort grew cold and analytic. Years of service in Intelligence told him to follow up all clues and coincidences. This one could be decisive. Chance had placed this trump card in his hand, and he was determined to seize whatever opportunity it offered. He would have to work fast though, so as not to raise Beatrice's suspicions. He found the cellar door and the switch lighting up the circular staircase. At the bottom was a corridor and a door, beyond which a larger room opened. At its far end stood the desk with the wine cases on it. He tried the centre drawer. It was locked. He tried his penknife on it, but the lock wouldn't yield. There were tools hanging on the wall though. A screwdriver proved strong enough to break the lock and force the drawer open.

Beaufort fumbled inside it in an attempt to find the mechanism that would reveal the hidden compartment. In vain. He had been down there for quite some time now.

His absence would soon be noticed by Beatrice. Damn it! Where was it? He shook the drawer, then impatiently opened and closed it twice. To no avail. He couldn't find it. What a pity. Guided by an impulse, he slowly pulled out the drawer one last time. Then the miracle happened. The bottom of the drawer had receded and beneath that level was a gun, identical to the one that had been found in Schröder's pocket. He took a quick look at the cartridge. The same. Two bullets missing. Like a mirrored image of Schröder's reality. He weighed the four bullets in his hand: "An eye for an eye, a tooth for a tooth", he murmured to himself.

– Put the gun down on the table, turn around, and place your hands on your head, she said, and her voice had a stern calmness which made it sound all the more threatening. She stood about four metres away pointing his own automatic, which he had carried in a holster under his coat and left hanging in the hallway, straight at him.

– Move over here, she ordered. He obeyed.

– Exactly what we needed. You walked straight into the trap, Mr. Intelligence. Now we have your fingerprints on a gun matching the one that killed Frau Irmgard Kampa during the night of August 23, and that means you're under suspicion, and Hans will have his alibi. If that's not killing two birds with one stone, I don't know what is.

Still pointing the gun at him, she picked up the other weapon, her hand covered with a piece of cloth, and with remarkable swiftness threw it inside the safe right under the desk itself. In his hurry, Beaufort hadn't even noticed it.

– Beatrice, will you please tell me what kind of cat-and-mouse game this is? he asked with a nervous smile.

– Don't come any closer, or I'll shoot. Do you hear me?

– Give me the gun, he said, and moved closer, his smile broadening.

– I'll shoot you dead, I promise!

– Give it to me, he repeated, and took another step towards her. In that same moment she pulled the trigger. There was no more than a click. She had time to pull it another three times before the major, six feet two inches tall and athletically built, wrenched it out of her hand as easily as if he were taking a dangerous toy away from a child.

– So, you really would have killed me? You would have stained your beautiful hands with blood to protect him. I say, that's admirable. You must really love him. To go through all these minute preparations just to secure his alibi. And how do think you would have got away with it? Do you know how soon the military would be here looking for me?

– Let me tell you something, Major Beaufort. Maybe I'm not quite the sweet Red Cross angel you perhaps believed I am, or the hysterical woman forging a pathetic plan to get her husband out of jail. How can you be so sure that I even want the man out of there? For me he has been dead for three long years, and I didn't believe that he had miraculously survived and married some Mongolian woman in Yekaterinburg. Perhaps Hans' return was in reality most inopportune for me. Perhaps I'm not Frau Schröder. Perhaps I don't have any children. Perhaps I do have the means and the accomplices to be very far from here indeed when they finally find your body, like so many other bodies in this intricate story, in a ditch somewhere.

Beaufort took a backward step back, and began to laugh at the top of his voice.

– You? You, who can't even make sure a gun is loaded before you use it? You're really too much, Beatrice. You should have been a *comedienne*. I took them out of the magazine before I arrived here, you silly woman. Just as a little precautionary measure, in case seeing an unguarded gun might prove too great a temptation for you. In this way, I figured, I would know whether or not you were capable of killing another human being. And you proved it yourself, didn't you? Would you like a cigarette?

– Why not? But then, Henry, you must promise to come over here and play with me.

– What?

– Oh, Mr. Know-it-all, I want you to make love to me. Here, on this very table.

– Oh yeah, and what makes you think that I would be in the slightest inclined to make love to a woman who has not only threatened to kill me, but in fact would have sent four bullets straight through my body? Beatrice, come on, let's go upstairs, talk this over and behave like sensible people. I know what you want. And for you, for your determination, for your charm and for the love you feel for your husband, I want you to know that I shall not be contesting your testimony that Hans Schröder spent the nights of August 23 and 24 here with you in this house. The only thing I want in return is that gun you put in the safe. You have my word, on my honour, as an officer and a gentleman.

– You seem to think very highly of yourself, Henry. You believe you're really smart, don't you? Contrary to what you think, I'm quite willing to pay the price, if there is something I really want. But the thing is, Henry, that I'm a bit proud myself, so I do pay, but only when I want to. You see, you could have been as dead as an entire army of sixteen-year-old German soldiers if I had wanted it. Because the gun that was going to kill you wasn't your impotent weapon, Henry, but – this!

From the back of her satin dress Beatrice quickly produced another gun, and before Beaufort had time to react she aimed above his head and pulled the trigger. The sound of the explosion in the small room was deafening. Beaufort instinctively crouched on the floor, his hearing numbed and his mind in shock.

– Now, be a gentleman, Henry, and come over here and kiss me. Don't be afraid, I'll put the gun aside. Look, I'm throwing it away! You see, I trust you … A promise is a promise, and now you must make love to me. It's my way of paying you.

– I'm not seeking payment, Beatrice.

– Oh yes you are, Henry. You have just entered the black market, where everything can be bought and sold and everything has its price.

– Nonsense …

She didn't care to respond in words any longer, but let her shawl fall down to reveal her alabaster shoulders. She pulled down the sleeves of her dress, letting a breast shine in the light of the swaying light bulb. She approached him, slowly caressing herself while staring him in the eye. She stopped in front of him and, as if in slow motion, moved her lips closer to his, and dragged him down onto her while hungrily searching for the piece of winged lead which soared from his crotch. Henry now knew that he could not resist her. She had outsmarted him. It was not the other way round. He had an obligation to her.

– You and I, she breathed in his ear,– are two of a kind. Lulu, Esmeralda or Beatrice, what does it matter? Even my husband sleeps with prostitutes, I have heard. And if he can do that, and be so cruel as to leave me alone here in this house for so long, then I might as well from time to time buy myself something I really like. Don't you think so, Henry? ... Darling ... Ah, oui, Henry, ... You're so big ... so strong ... Oh yes, right there ... Oh yes, keep going ... Oh yes ... *Ach, mein Gott!*

Beaufort, pumping into her, made a quick decision. "If I'm already dead, I might as well enjoy it. This is payback time, Schröder. I'll go along with you, and in order to seal our pact, you will have to let me possess your woman. In this way we become brothers for life – brothers in blood and crime. Oh, Jesus, is this wild beast your woman, Schröder? And if she is, who the hell are you?" He kept going, relishing her cries as they echoed from the walls, not caring whether or not they were also part of her game. Whatever they were meant to be, they seemed like the moaning and groaning of a hungry animal locked in a cage, and her movements like the battering of a vampire struggling to get loose from the fangs of a cat. At the end of his powers, Beaufort felt it coming, as if out of the entrails of the earth, mounting through his toes, his legs, all along his spine. His brain turned spongy, as if melting away inside his cranium. He pulled Beatrice's legs over his shoulders, forced himself one notch deeper into her, and nailed her there as if she had been a giant butterfly, anaesthetized and pinned down by a needle as the rarest sample in the entire collection, with four dark eyes for a pattern and a ferocious bat's head at the centre. It was like opening a faucet with hot liquid at full blast. It kept gushing out of him, like a geyser, an ejaculation of the kind that for a moment would seduce any man into believing himself a god, whose act of creation is at once devoid of purpose and endless.

*

The court-room began to fill up again. There was the same murmuring expectation and tension in the air as there is in a theatre before the premiere of a play rumoured to be scandalous. The solid, polished wooden doors, with their inlaid scenes depicting old tribunes and antique trials – Socrates, Catalina, the two women before Solomon – were closed, separating the multitude of curious eyes outside from the privileged individuals who had been able to procure seats for themselves, and thereby of exclusive places at the drama. Everybody who had been in the room before Frau Schröder made her sensational announcement had been given special badges as they went out to show if they wished to re-enter. Apparently everyone did. The hall was again packed to the last seat. Regardless of the formal prohibition, people were standing behind the benches at the back of the room. Schröder assumed they were officials, although there was nothing to distinguish them from other spectators. Seen through the ornate Gothic windows, the silhouette of the cathedral rose majestically. The sky, impenetrably grey, was interspersed with yellow and red leaves, like giant butterflies dancing in the air. At the top of distant hills the trees swayed heavily in the strong gusts of an impetuous autumn storm. The judge's gavel pounded three times, and was then laid to rest. The floor was given to defence-attorney Dieter Göbel.

– I call to the witness stand Frau Beatrice Schröder.

Pale, dignified and impressive, she rose from her chair. As she moved along the seats to get out in the aisle, Schröder noticed with astonishment that one of the persons who got up to give her free passage was Major Beaufort. Through Göbel, Beatrice had given Hans to understand that Beaufort would present no threat to their story. Schröder could only imagine how this certitude had been obtained. Even if a promise had been made, could the major's word be trusted as the pressure mounted? What if the prosecutor called him as a witness; how on earth could he possibly fail to comply?

Beaufort's presence in the room made Schröder fear the worst. As he listened to the judge's advising Beatrice that perjury was a serious crime that could entail severe consequences, he almost got up in an attempt to stop the proceedings and relieve Beatrice of a task which could very well bring about her downfall. But Göbel was alert and sent Schröder a quick glance which hurled him back into the chair before anybody else had noticed his profound feeling of unease.

– So help me God.

She had reached the end of the preliminaries. There was no return. Göbel continued,

– Frau Schröder, do you remember when you met your husband for the first time after the war?

– Yes, on June 4.

– Where was this?

– In our home.

– Did you recognise him right away?
– Of course.
– Were you happy to see him?
– It was a miracle come true. Beatrice gave her husband a long, deep look across the room.
– Is it also true, that, although you were both so happy to see each other, and although the children would naturally be thrilled to meet their father, whom they had believed to be dead for so long, it was decided between you that your husband should not move in directly. Instead he was to remain incognito and hidden for some time?
– That's correct.
– Why was this?
– Because Hans feared there was a conspiracy against him, that too many people here in Freiburg, people who may still be alive, and may even be sitting in this courtroom, wanted him out of the way. He was afraid that his knowing too much about them and their actions during the war could expose all of us to tremendous danger if he didn't proceed with the utmost caution. He was especially worried that something would happen to the children if they began to spread the word that he was back.
– So what happened?
– Hans and I decided that our best course of action was to try to attract public attention, and by extension, official protection for him. In this way it would be more difficult for anyone to harm him. To this end Hans agreed to let suspicion point in his direction. He even admitted that he had taken part initially in the Nazi euthanasia programme. Little by little, though, it was made clear to the investigating committee that there was something fishy about Hans'

trying to establish only a certain amount of guilt, only just enough for the Allies to keep a close eye on him. Finally the committee realised that Hans had made the whole thing up, and that his real aim was to lead the Allies to the actual perpetrators of these abominable crimes.

– And during all this time you were seeing each other regularly?

– Yes, but in great secrecy.

– And on the evening of August 23, your husband came to see you in your house, and stayed overnight?

– Yes.

– Are you absolutely sure about that?

– Positive.

– How is it that you remember it so clearly?

– Because August 23 is a very special day for all of us. It is the birthday of our son. We celebrated him in his absence. Hans was annoyed that he couldn't personally give him his birthday present, a bicycle. We had to pretend that it came from me only. Hans said that evening that he was right on the trail of the suspect, and that he must try to see a representative of the investigating committee so as to lead him to what he believed to be the dragon's den. You see, the doctor who succeeded my husband at Sankt-Anna Klinik was a certain Dr. Claus Uhland. He had reportedly died, and Hans thought that whatever had happened to him was part of a cover-up. That's the reason he went straight to the martial investigation committee; to tell them about Dr. Uhland's death.

– But wasn't it also true that your husband on this occasion was carrying a weapon of the same type as the one that killed Irmgard Kampa?

– Yes, it is true. He always kept a gun of that type in the secret compartment of his writing desk. The reason he carried it that day was simply that he wanted to be able to defend himself in case he was attacked.

– So, in other words, the fact that the gun appears to have fired the bullet which killed the victim is pure coincidence?

– I can't see how it could possibly be otherwise, unless of course someone already knew what kind of gun he was carrying, and used that knowledge to scheme against him.

– Thank you, Frau Schröder.

Göbel now addressed the jury.

– I can see doubt written on your faces. I don't blame you, and I would not be standing here before you with such confidence – confidence in my client, in you the jury and in justice – I would not be standing here today, I say, and have the witness hypothesising about a mysterious weapon, if I weren't absolutely sure that by the end of the day you would come to the same conclusion as I have. Regardless of the perfectly sound alibi the witness has given the defendant, which in itself suffices to clear the defendant once and for all, I can assure you, that during the course of this afternoon we shall also have incontrovertible proof that the gun which Dr. Schröder carried that day is not in fact the one with which the victim was killed. For the moment, I shall have to keep you in suspense. But not for long, ladies and gentlemen of the jury, not for long!

Visibly satisfied with his performance, he turned to the judge.

– No further questions, Your Honour.

The prosecutor now rose to examine the witness.

Schröder did not doubt that his interrogation would be of greater severity than the lawyer's, which to Schröder had seemed unbearably self-assured. Beatrice remained sitting, her face betraying no emotion.

– Frau Schröder. Where were you and what were you doing during the day of August 23 this year?

– I spent most of it in our garden, raking, picking fruit and trimming the roses.

– You say our garden, Frau Schröder. To what persons do you refer?

– To myself and my husband, and to our three children and our housekeeper, Mathilde.

– Were any of these individuals at any time present with you in the garden that day?

– Yes, Mathilde was helping me.

– What about the children?

– The children, who were on vacation from school, had gone to visit an aunt of mine who lives in Switzerland.

– What about your husband?

– He came later.

– Did Mathilde see him coming?

– No, she had left by the time he arrived.

– We have heard you tell the defence that you saw the defendant at different times this summer. The first of these encounters would have occurred on June 4. After that you saw each other on various occasions throughout the summer. You also stated that the reason why Hans Schröder did not immediately disclose himself to anybody other than yourself was that he feared a conspiracy against him.

– Yes.

– Very well. But isn't it also true that he believed that

this conspiracy had its origin in his own home, that it had been initiated during his long and involuntary absence? Indeed, that it was actually as a direct consequence of the fact that you, in his absence, had remarried?

– Objection!

– Overruled. Please answer the question, Frau Schröder.

– Yes, for some time my husband believed that I really had remarried.

– Was there anything to substantiate this? Was there any reason at all for him to suspect you of having betrayed him?

– Objection! I object to the prosecutor trying to establish a case based on conjecture pure and simple.

– Sustained. The prosecution will please abstain from insinuation, and stick to factual investigation.

– Frau Schröder. Did you marry another man while your husband was serving his country in the line of duty?

– It wasn't like that!

– It is a very simple question, Frau Schröder. Either you did or you didn't. Please answer yes or no.

For the first time Beatrice flinched. The spectators couldn't help noticing it; the jury itself moved like sea anemones swaying on a reef in some invisible current.

– Whom are you actually trying to protect, Frau Schröder?

– I'm trying to protect my heart, she answered, her eyes growing even darker.

– Frau Schröder, would you now please answer the question. Did you marry another man while your husband was in Russia? ... Frau Schröder? Would you please tell us more about the circumstances surrounding this bigamous marriage of yours?

– It wasn't a bigamous marriage.

– I'm afraid that in legal terms to have two husbands simultaneously is called bigamy, and is actually not permitted by law.

– But it was nothing of the sort, I have done nothing wrong. What am I accused of? What do you know about the background …

– I'm trying to establish …

– Establish your perfidious insinuations as truths, that's what you're trying to do! But you have no idea how it was to live here at that time. You have no idea of the menace from society. You, how can you judge!

Beatrice was talking to the prosecutor, but inadvertently looking at her husband.

– I'm not the judge, Madame. I am the district attorney.

Beatrice finally turned to him and lashed out,

– Well, keep to your district then, and …

– Order in the court, order … in … the … court!

The judge swung his gavel like the hammer of Thor, and Beatrice involuntarily cowered when she saw the fire in his eyes.

– The witness will comply with the requirements deemed necessary to establish law and justice. Being under oath, and obliged to answer all questions put to her, the witness will be told this for the very last time. One more failure to conform with the procedure of this court, and I shall have a warrant issued for the witness's detention in custody, accused of conspiring to pervert the course of justice!

– But it wasn't a real marriage! God, is there nobody in the whole world who even wants to hear or understand? You all talk as if you already knew all the facts. Take me, then.

Take me to your prison! Take me away!

She had worked herself up to something resembling genuine hysteria. The jury, concerned, exchanged hurried confidences. Some spectators expressed their heartfelt feelings: "Let her speak up!", "Is this how justice is done in America?" "How much have they paid you?" The entire court-room had become a stormy sea.

– Order in court! Session adjourned for ten minutes to give the witness time to compose herself.

The judge's words had the effect of a cracking whip, and released the tension in the room. Schröder, who had been clenching his fists so hard under the table that they were white, slowly opened his palms, shaking and covered in sweat.

Beatrice, having carefully calculated in advance the intensity, duration and culmination of her passionate outbreak, leaned back in her chair feigning exasperation. She knew that her first goal of creating confusion and hysteria had been attained. Now she must move on to a simulation of remorse. She shut her eyes, taking advantage of the pause. An irrational feeling seized her all the same. This was not exactly the kind of image she wanted to project. She would have much preferred to see Hans fill out the entire frame of her desires and hopes, but the image which she involuntarily conjured from the depths of her heated imagination was that of Siegfried Rheinau on the evening when they first met. That he had made himself indispensable to her in her husband's absence by virtue of his contacts and paternal protection, was undeniable. It could both be seen and excused as a necessary concession. But that wasn't all. On the evening that Hans had left them alone together for a few moments in order to attend to some unfinished business, Beatrice had felt paradoxically attracted to Rheinau. Although she still thought of him as their enemy, she had fallen under the spell of his determination all the same. In comparison to Rheinau's single-mindedness, Hans had suddenly seemed timid, ridden by doubts, and prey to the vacillations of an over-sensitive conscience. In Rheinau, on the other hand, there was something of the predator, of the superior man of vision and willpower, who takes what he wants and leaves behind what he can no longer use. It was his particular kind of spiritual ruthlessness that had made such a strong impression on her. In combination with his not unattractive manly exterior, it had indeed given rise to some erotic fantasies within her. And over some days and nights to come, she envisaged herself in intimate situations with him, that were all but compromising. At the time, though, Beatrice thought very little of them, not considering these fleeting sensations as anything more than a sign that her commitment to Hans was real and fulfilling. Although there had in some sense been temptation, she had never let Rheinau or Hans know. She knew that it was ultimately her love for Hans that really mattered to her, and that her feelings towards Siegfried Rheinau were in the last instance no more than the frozen fascination of a paralysed prey in the power of its imminent killer. No wonder, then, that once Hans was gone, Beatrice resolutely shut out all possibility of emotional involvement with Rheinau. The game she had begun playing by accepting his protection was of course utterly dangerous, and would probably have ended in eventual catastrophe for her and the children, had not destiny itself come to her rescue.

Having finished her glass of water and brushed the last lingering tear from the corner of her eye, she answered the judge's question if she was again ready to take the witness stand, with a compliant nod and a discreet, – Yes, Your Honour.

The proceedings continued. Nemese picked up the thread where it had been dropped.

– Frau Schröder, how did it happen that you married another man while your husband was serving at the Russian front?

Her voice was now pleasantly poised, and carried easily to the far end of the room. – Let me take this opportunity to set the record straight. Allow me to tell you how I felt. Please let me try to make amends, to make everything right again ... I do not blame my husband for coming to the conclusion that another man had entered my life and was living in our house. The circumstances were these. When Hans was reported missing after the siege of Stalingrad in the winter 1941-42, I did indeed pretend to marry Professor Siegfried Rheinau, who had declared himself willing to shield us from Nazis by offering his name as protection against possible persecution. The actual wedding ceremony, which was followed by no reception or celebration, was conducted in the Town Hall. The following day, Professor Rheinau left for duties in the region of Nordrhein-Westfalen.

– And what date would that have been?

– We were married on March 8, 1942. On March 9, Siegfried Rheinau left on a journey to the north, at least that's what he told me, and we never met again.

– Why?

– Because according to what I have heard, Dr. Rheinau

was suffering from a brain tumour, and he died no more than a couple of months later.

– Who told you this?

– The news was sent to me in the form of a letter of regret. A card accompanying the letter informed me that Theodore and Waltraude Rheinau had the painful duty of announcing the death of their son.

– Was there any mention of the cause of death?

– No.

– How did you come to know how he died?

– We received the news from the Universitätsklinik in Freiburg, in the form of a certificate, stating that Siegfried Rheinau had suffered death as a fatal consequence of a surgical incision in his brain.

– And from this, you drew the conclusion that he must have suffered from a brain tumour?

– Yes, that's what I thought. And then someone called from the hospital who confirmed this.

– Was this all you ever heard of him?

– Yes.

– Did you believe what you had been told?

– I had no reason to disbelieve it.

– Meanwhile, you kept his name on your door plate throughout the war as a sort of talisman, hoping no doubt that it would protect you and your children from being harassed by the Nazis?

– That's what we hoped for.

– And were you in fact spared intrusion from these authorities?

– So it seems.

– Would you mind clarifying for the jury why you had

reason to believe that you and your children would otherwise have suffered persecution, humiliation and possible arrest by the Nazis?

At this point Göbel hurried to support Frau Schröder by taking over the question.

– As instructed by my client, I am authorised to clarify to the jury why this was thought to be the case. First, because Hans Schröder had refused to co-operate in the euthanasia programme known under the title "Life-Unworthy-of-Life". In those early days of the war this was also known as the T4 programme, the code-name simply denoting the Berlin chancellery address on Tiergarten 4. It was from here that orders were issued to the Reich Group of Sanatoria and Nursing Homes, of which Sankt-Anna Klinik was one. Secondly, and perhaps no less importantly, because the witness is of Jewish birth, and her children were consequently what the Nazis contemptuously called half-blood.

– Is that correct, Frau Schröder?

– Yes.

– Given that you accepted Rheinau's proposal, because the man seemed to you a decent Nazi, if I may use the expression, why did you think that his name and hand in marriage would guarantee your security once he was dead?

– There were of course no guarantees. But what choice did I have? Do you suggest I should have married a third time once he was gone? Whom then? Heinrich Himmler, perhaps?

The people in the room burst into laughter. It appeared that Beatrice was getting an increasing proportion of the audience, including perhaps the jury themselves, on her side, but the sound of the gavel put a sudden end to the crowd's gaiety.

– I must instruct the witness not to put her own questions, but to leave that to the prosecutor, who will now please continue.

The judge looked menacingly round the room, as though hoping to find someone to have thrown out. The general laughter however had gone, and the stage was left to Nemese.

– Frau Schröder, or shall I say – Rheinau?

– It is Schröder.

– For how long were you acquainted with your second husband before you married him?

– About three years. He was a colleague of Hans, and a well-known bachelor.

– Would you say that he ever showed any interest in you beyond what could be expected and regarded as proper as a colleague of your husband's?

Göbel seized this opportunity.

– Surely, Your Honour, the hypothetical feelings of the said Rheinau toward Frau Schröder at a time when her first husband was not only still alive but still in frequent contact with her, must clearly be irrelevant.

– Objection sustained. Would you please come to the point now, Herr Nemese?

It was by now obvious to everyone that the prosecution was trying to ensnare Beatrice, but so far Nemese's machinations had been easy to detect and the noose too slack. There seemed to be no cause for Beatrice to show any eagerness to explain, or to give the prosecutor more information than he had asked for, or had been allowed to obtain. Nonetheless she continued, unprotesting, to answer his insidious questioning.

– Yes, I believe he took an interest in my person beyond the call of duty. He was definitely interested in me before Hans was reported missing. I have the feeling that Rheinau was convinced that Hans, regardless of the outcome of the war, would never return home.

– So, Professor Rheinau became your admirer and protector long before the defendant was reported missing in action?

– Yes.

– From what time?

– I'd say pretty much immediately from the time Hans left for the front.

The silence following her last statement was so heavy that it almost seemed solid. Schröder felt his face invaded by a nervous tic which he had developed during the Russian campaign. He managed to control it by sheer willpower, and stared ahead with a fixed gaze.

– Frau Schröder, would you say that you and Siegfried Rheinau by then had an intimate relationship?

– What do you mean by an intimate relationship?

– I mean, did you and Rheinau have a relationship of the kind that could and would on occasion result in sexual intercourse?

– No. He never lived in our house.

– Did you perform the act of love elsewhere?

– No.

– Did he ever come to visit you in your home?

– Fairly often.

– But he never stayed overnight?

– No.

– Not even once?

– I have told you.

– So you insist that your relationship was of a, shall we say, platonic nature?

– Actually, I'm neither a philosopher nor a homosexual. Consequently, I have very little experience of what it takes to engage in platonic relationships.

There was a fresh outburst of laughter mixed with murmurs, one of the participants in this being Göbel himself, who couldn't prevent himself from chuckling a little while sardonically muttering something to an imaginary listener.

Although the prosecutor seemed unable to get the better of her, Schröder feared he was only playing for time. Nemese would accept the day's ending in her favour because he would have time to do further background research, check the accuracy of her testimony and return to the next session with his firepower at the ready. Schröder felt disturbed for other reasons as well. Her frivolity, not stopping short of ridiculing the prosecutor himself, was in itself a potential danger. He certainly would have preferred her to be less outgoing. All this about her own subtlety, and the ease with which she had accepted Rheinau's patronage as soon as Schröder had left the scene, was, if nothing else, hurtful. All the same, he knew he had no other choice than to allow her to continue in this role. All he could hope for was that she knew what she was doing. Still, by deliberately scorning her opponent, and in this way exposing him to the laughter of the court, she had chosen to confront him head-on. Schröder's worst fears were confirmed when Herr Nemese, without a trace of indignation in his voice, closed his interrogation by asking,

– Frau Schröder, do you believe that it was Hans Schröder's feelings of uncertainty as to whether you and Siegfried Rheinau had an erotic relationship, rather than this alleged conspiracy, that made him reluctant to come back home for good?

– I believe it may have influenced him in his conspiracy theories. Hans insisted on visiting me only at times when the children were at school, and Mathilde was absent.

– How many times?

– Exactly five times.

– Can you tell us the dates?

– Certainly. As I said, June 4 in the afternoon; then June 18 in the evening; July 10 at night; July 29 in the evening, and August 23 during the evening and night.

– Is there a possibility that anyone could have seen him coming and going on any of these occasions?

– The possibility exists, but I don't think it's likely. He was always anxious to avoid attention and he would use the garden door to enter the house.

– At what time did your husband leave you on August 24?

– Around nine o'clock in the morning.

– Was that about the time you woke up together that morning?

– No.

– When did you wake up? Can you tell us the approximate hour?

– I'm afraid I can't.

– How is that?

– For the simple reason that we stayed up all night talking. We never went to bed.

– Thank you, Frau Schröder. I have no further questions.

With these words Nemese turned to the jury.

– Ladies and gentlemen of the jury. We have heard Frau Schröder bravely justify her own actions in the past. We have heard her talk about necessity and the fear that she has been exposed to, circumstances which ultimately forced her to remarry while still wedded to another man. We have also heard her certify that the defendant, Hans Schröder, was with her the entire night when the murder was committed. So far, Dr. Schröder has an unbreakable alibi. So what could prevent the court from setting him free? Nothing, it seems. But then there are circumstances, still murky circumstances, that must be brought to light. For instance, the witness assumes that no one else saw or could have seen the defendant when he came to visit her that night. Nor was he seen by anyone other than his wife on any of the other occasions when he paid her his secret visits. Isn't that just a bit strange? And how is it that Dr. Schröder, after having visited his wife on five previous occasions, still wasn't convinced that Professor Siegfried Rheinau had died many years ago, that he never lived in the house and that he never had an intimate relationship with the witness? Why all this secrecy? And why didn't Schröder go straight to the local police authorities to inform them of his suspicions of a conspiracy against his life? And why – apart from the mysteriously deceased Professor Rheinau, and the likewise mysteriously absent, probably murdered Dr. Uhland – haven't we heard the defendant give us one single hint as to who the persons responsible for the murder and the alleged conspiracy against him might be? Rheinau was originally his best bet, certainly, but his wife had to sacrifice that story, and, yes, I almost forgot. It might interest the members of the jury to know that we have in fact found Dr. Rheinau's death certificate. Here is the document, which I hereby place in evidence. As the witness said, it was issued at the Universitätsklinik of Freiburg. However, it does not cite as probable cause of death that Rheinau suffered from a brain tumour. The immediate cause of death, according to this certificate, is summed up in a medical Latin that makes little sense, even to the doctors we have consulted. It is reasonable to infer that Siegfried Rheinau could indeed have died of a degenerative brain disease, but what the cause of it was – a tumour, dysfunction of the ganglia, microbes or even a fatally poisonous substance – cannot be determined. Nonetheless, the certificate records that Professor Rheinau, for the benefit of science, gave the medical staff permission to remove his brain *post mortem*. This authorisation on the death certificate itself is quite exceptional; it has never been found elsewhere on documents in the hospitals and morgues of the Third Reich. And as is the case with so many other falsified death certificates in existence during the war, this one typically omits to specify the actual date of death. On the other hand, it does bear three different signatures. The most important of them is obviously the one in red ink at the bottom of the page. It is a bit hard to read, but our graphologists have been able to identify the signature. It has been found on other records as well, and it reads – and this may come as a surprise to some of you – H. Schröder. Now, as we know that Schröder was in Russia during the war ...

– Objection!

— Withdrawn. It could certainly be a counterfeit as well, but who signed it, and for what purpose, we do not know. This means that for the time being it remains a remarkable coincidence that the man whom the defendant feared had taken over his house and was trying to eliminate him, met his death here in Freiburg. Further, that he donated his brain to scientific research, and had his death certificate signed in the name of H. Schröder, the initial H. standing possibly for Heinz, Henning, Helmut, or perhaps ... Hans. As we all know, we are not here today to investigate that question, but to establish whether or not the defendant is guilty of the cold-blooded murder of a senior citizen in Günterstal. The defendant's wife, unsurprisingly, has presented a watertight alibi for him during the night on which this dreadful deed was committed. But it is a fact that neither the judge, nor I, nor you, members of the jury, have been advised in advance that she would take the stand. Considering how absolutely vital it is in establishing the defendant's innocence, isn't it once again remarkable that the defence did not submit the witness' testimony in evidence at the opening of the trial, but preferred to break the news on this very day, in this very room? The suspicion that must arise in all of you is, of course, that the introduction of the key witness was made in this dramatic way in order to take the prosecution by surprise. Luckily, I was aware, as you can see, that something like this might happen. I therefore took the precaution of investigating the circumstances of the witness's alleged marriage to Siegfried Rheinau. It did indeed take place in the Town Hall on March 8, 1942, attested by two witnesses, Laura Emming and a certain Dr. Claus Uhland. This means that whoever this Uhland was – and we know that he was a close associate of the defendant, eventually succeeding him as the head of Sankt-Anna Klinik after the former's dismissal at the beginning of 1940 – he must have known about and approved of this marriage as well. Sadly, Dr. Uhland is no longer with us, and our attempts to find the other witness, Laura Emming, have at this short notice proved unsuccessful. But that which remains as established fact amid this mass of circumstantial evidence, indicates that there is something suspicious, to say the least, about Dr. Schröder's alibi. He was found on the premises where Frau Kampa was killed, and he had a gun in his pocket. Two bullets had been fired, and one bullet found in the woodwork of the chair corresponded, according to ballistic experts, to those remaining in the magazine of that gun. If that is not the gun which was used to kill Frau Kampa, well, then we have another strange coincidence on our hands. But we shall not rely on conjecture only. At least one man in this room will be able to give us the facts leading to the arrest of Hans Schröder.

All eyes now turned to the judge who, after once again letting his gavel speak, announced that the prosecution was ready to call another witness. Imperiously, his voice sounded,

– The prosecution summons Major Henry Beaufort to the stand.

As he saw Major Beaufort rise from his seat and proceed past the spectators, Schröder had the feeling that reality had become a film in slow motion. Although no more than a minute could have elapsed between the time the judge called the witness to the stand and the moment when Beaufort began to take the oath, Schröder had the sensation that he was seeing his entire life in retrospect. It was as if he were separated from the events by a wall of glass, a transparent haze as it were, tinged with purple hues. Dreamlike, his gaze began to wander around the room, shifting focus from one stern official to another, to the wide-open eyes of the public, to the sombre earnestness of the jury, to the authoritative bearing of the judge. His eyes finally fastened on the frescoes depicting scenes from rural Germany – the carnivals of winter, May bonfires, the joys of summer, the harvest, and a sturdy horse making its way through the snow with a load of timber.

Other scenes were from the plains of Prussia, from Berlin and Brandenburg, the moors and dunes of Schleswig Holstein and the Lüneburg Heath, the forest-clad, undulating hills of the Harz, the vineyards of the Rhine, Mosel and Franken, the cities of Nuremberg, Leipzig and Dresden, the Sudetenland, Thuringia, Saxony, Bavaria, and last but not least, Baden-Württemberg and its mysterious Black Forest. One scene in particular captured his interest. It was from the eastern fringes of the old Reich, showing villagers preparing for a feast, a Gypsy fiddler, women in colourful peasant costume, birch trees in their primal green, children and men raising the maypole. It was a scene of rural innocence, a celebration of life, fertility and hope. But what above all caught Schröder's wandering eye, was the portrayal of dark portentous clouds hanging over a distant horizon. It was clearly a landscape from the east – to his feverish mind not unlike Russia – and as soon as the association struck him, he was there again, back in the railway carriage that was to carry him to the front.

The individual voices around him receded and blended into one long, mournful whisper. They became the wind that sweeps over endless snow-covered expanses, where there are no trees, not even a bush, to hide under. The snow swayed like curtains in the wind. It was bitterly cold. All around him were the carcasses of tank machines. Here and there parts of dead, frozen bodies could be seen in the snowdrifts. The remnant of the army had been surrounded by the Russians. The concentration of troops inside Stalingrad was getting denser by the hour as the lethal grip of the Red Army tightened upon it. A group of wounded soldiers and medical staff had been miraculously rescued at the eleventh hour, and brought out of the deadly trap by aircraft – truly a heroic deed. But Schröder himself had been ordered to stay with those injured beyond hope of recovery. He knew himself doomed. There was nothing left for him to do but wait for the enemy to arrive. The 'hospital' was turning into a morgue – indeed it had the temperature of one. He was running out of morphine, which he had used in some abundance to help the most painfully wounded from this world into the next. And when everything had been taken care of, and all the dying knew where they were heading, Schröder shot the last of the morphine into his own veins. Its effect spread like a heat wave through his body and he felt a tremendous relief. He propped himself up against a wall and waited for the end. Then a voice reached him. It came as if out of the winter storm itself, like the little bell of Propaganda Minister Goebbels, like a faint whisper in the enormity of destruction.

– Help me, for God's sake, help me ...

Schröder, halfway into slumber, believed himself to be

hallucinating, when, in the obscurity of the room, he beheld a moaning figure, apparently still alive.

– Help me. I can't feel my legs any longer.

With the greatest of difficulty Schröder managed to stumble the short distance to the wounded man. He lifted the stinking blanket that covered him and saw that both his legs were gone. How he had managed to stay alive and conscious with half his body shot away, Schröder could not understand. But he had little time for wonder. The man, whose feverish whisper so reminded Schröder of a little bell in the midst of a roaring blizzard, repeated his request.

– You are the doctor, help me. Give me morphine. Let me die like the others.

– Listen, there is no morphine left. I took the last myself.

– Then use the pillow.

It took Schröder a moment to realise what the dying man was hinting.

– I can't do that!

– Do it!

– No!

– Kill me now. Otherwise you're a murderer!

With these words, the encounter turned into a farewell scene between two lovers who know they will never see each other again unless in heaven or hell; a slow dance, as it were, the partners intently watching each other as the orchestra slowly fades. During this last waltz the other dancers gradually disappear, and at last the dance floor itself gives away. A rotating wheel remains, a swirling crystal ball in empty space. If one could imagine the eyes of Eurydice as Orpheus turns to look at her, and she is conducted back to Hades by the winged messenger of the gods, one may well imagine the melancholy of eternal departure in this soldier's fixed stare. Schröder laid his hand on his forehead, and said something to the effect of placing the man's soul in God's trust.

– Don't bother about that, the other murmured. – Save yourself, and live my life as well. It is all yours now.

Hearing this, and although long since accustomed to seeing death take its toll, Schröder could no longer hold back his tears. A strange, alien and persistent feeling came over him, not so much of compassion as of simply being at one with another human being, sharing his fate to the full and last.

– Now, the other whispered. – Now, is the bell swinging in the wind. Now is the bell swinging in the dying wind? Now, now, now ... Can't you hear the wind, the snow in the wind, the snow in the wind ... Now ... Snow ... Come snow ...

Schröder picked up the pillow and placed it over the dying man's face. He pressed his hands against it, and then put his entire weight on them until the torso beneath had stopped breathing. He then removed the pillow. It was over. The feverish dark eyes had come to rest and stared glazed at him. Soon he would himself walk into the blizzard, walk deeper and deeper into the land of no return. But although he could feel himself getting closer to the great barrier with every step, he never crossed it, or – he was violently pulled back, since he, the recent expert in bringing about merciful death, had proved incapable of granting eternal oblivion to himself, and the dose administered had failed to produce the intended effect.

The Russians found him, and only he, alive outside the field hospital. He was so weak that he couldn't stand up by himself, but he was conscious. An order to shoot him on the spot was recalled at the last moment when a Russian officer discovered that he was in fact the doctor. There was a permanent shortage of trained medical staff behind the Russian lines as well, and the same dearth of resources, so the difference between being alive in a Russian camp and dead in hell was probably just a difference in degree – hell being, by all accounts, if not actually preferable, at least substantially warmer. "One wouldn't have to amputate limbs because they have been deep frozen," he thought, and smiled sardonically as the prosecutor repeated his question.

– As I have said, I was never there. I was in Russia. I came back to Germany five months ago.

He heard Göbel's voice objecting that what Dr. Schröder had or hadn't done during the war was irrelevant to the present investigation, the aim of which was to establish the truth in the case of the death of Frau Irmgard ... Frau Irmgard Kampa ... Irmgard Kampa ... There was another painted scene which painfully reminded him of his own family. And another in which a piano had been placed in the background of a Swabian inn. A piano ... There had been a prisoner in the camp, a musician, a pianist. He had manufactured a little piano. It had no strings and made no sound, except in the mind of the player. It was a wooden box with white and black keys that spanned three whole octaves, a real little keyboard. And he could play on it. There were elastic bands to make the keys bounce back into position once they had been pressed down. He would sit for hours and enjoy the music he imagined coming out of the silent box. He was practising even, singing the melodies to his mute accompaniment. In this way he obviously kept himself from going insane. Which didn't prevent the Russians from regarding him as such. Eventually they removed him. They never met again, and Schröder, who had seen men suddenly removed, believed that the other had simply been taken to the woods and executed. He had a rather weak constitution, unfit for hard physical labour, Polish too – not the best combination to impress the Bolsheviks. But he had a wonderful expression on his face as he wandered in his world of imaginary sound, and his joy had been a constant reminder to Schröder of the hidden resources summoned up by some men in the face of adversity. It reminded him again that there was something inside him, too, that could not be destroyed, something that not even a unanimous declaration of guilt on the part of the jury could alter. At this moment of internal triumph, he happened to set eyes on his wife, and began compulsively to re-enact the dream he had had about Laura Emming coming to his cell, offering him her services. It wasn't until now that he realised to whom those departing eyes belonged. The man he had helped to die – his eyes, his eyes were the eyes of Beatrice; she was the Eurydice he had turned to see and thus to desert ... Or maybe it was the other way round ... He was the one left behind, he was – Eurydice.

At this point something extraordinary happened in the court-room. As from an enormous distance he heard a multitude of voices, sudden shrieks. He saw guards making across the room to where his wife, assuming superhuman size and stature, rose from her seat and cried out, – Can't you see the man is sick! Get a doctor! Get a doctor! The doors swung open and the call for a doctor continued as the guards took up their posts. In haste both prosecution and defence were summoned to the judge's bench. After having exchanged a few words with each, the judge said,

– This court is adjourned for today. The proceedings will continue at a date still to be determined, but not before the defendant, Dr. Hans Schröder, has undergone a medical examination.

Dr. Schröder, coming to his senses, did not at first realise that he himself had been the cause of the tumult in the room. Victim of a sudden nervous attack, he had been uttering strange and scattered phrases during the time Major Beaufort was about to take the oath. Semi-conscious, finishing his profuse incoherent rambling with a series of exclamations in which the name Eurydice kept recurring, Schröder had risen to his feet, and now stood looking around the room with an expression that showed that he had no idea where he was. Göbel came to his rescue, giving him water, loosening his collar, guiding him back into his chair. Then, as rapidly as the epileptic seizure had come over him, he began to regain his bearings and realise what he had done.

– Did I really stand up and speak? he asked Göbel incredulously.

– The jury is also dismissed.

Hans Schröder, by now clearly realising that the judge was on his way to postpone the trial, was seized with horror. First, they would conduct him back to that dreaded cell. Secondly, they, his enemies – the ones that were perhaps here in this room – might now have more time in which to call medical experts to certify that he had indeed killed the old woman. He would be judged as being unaccountable for his actions, mentally deranged. He might be locked away in a mental asylum for the rest of his life. Göbel nervously hissed in his ear that he must pull himself together, since Beaufort was about to produce evidence that Schröder couldn't have killed Frau Kampa. Before he had time to speak for his client, Göbel saw Schröder hasten to assure the judge that he was quite capable of understanding the proceedings.

– Please, Right Honourable Judge Giessen, I'm fine. Don't adjourn the session because of me. It's really nothing, a little repercussion from some old infection, nothing serious, just a flashback. I'll be fine.

– Are you sure about that, Dr. Schröder?

– Oh yes. Yes.

– Well then. Giessen scrutinised the accused man. – If Dr. Schröder shows no further signs of incapacitating mental disturbance in the next hour, the trial will continue. Until then, this court is adjourned.

The spectators were ushered out of the room to give the defendant a chance to recuperate. Beatrice was full of concern, and most unwilling to leave her husband to the discretion of the guards. But Göbel, looking at her over the rims of his spectacles, shot her a discreet twinkle to reassure her that things were going as they should. The jury, in the manner of an antique choir led by its coryphaeus, marched off to discuss this latest turn in the drama behind closed doors. The entire scene was cleared. Even Göbel, having reassured himself that Schröder was not about to have another attack, decided to try to get his client a cup of coffee, so as to prepare him to receive stage directions for the last act. Schröder remained sitting in his chair, flanked by two mute policemen.

Panes in the Gothic windows had been opened. A strong wind suddenly rushed into the room and put all loose papers in an uproar. For the first time during the proceedings it occurred to Schröder that a court-room with windows through which scenes of daily life could be seen, was something of an anomaly. Justice, normally blindfold, had had her fillet slightly lowered, and she could now see out toward the forest-clad hill beyond the irregular rooftops of the medieval townscape. The woods were on fire, a patchwork of red, ochre, orange and yellow set against the sombre willows of the ponds, so far unwilling to let go of their weeping green and accept the scorching fire. They looked as though they were carrying his entire destiny in their drooping arms, laying him to rest on the marble floor close to the stagnant water overgrown with waterlilies. For the second time since his return, Schröder was overcome with the dreadful sensation that time had made a giant leap forward without bringing him along. Incredulously, he stared at the dying landscape, unable to move himself to the conclusion that it was well into autumn. To Schröder it still had to be summer. It had been only days since he was arrested, and that day had been August 24. And this? This must be ... November? How was that? How come he hadn't seen summer come and go? How come his arrival in Freiburg appeared to have happened only a few weeks ago? Had not birds, flowers, the sun itself, been those of early summer? And now, leaves were already falling to the ground. And he hadn't noticed it, simply hadn't noticed time escaping him ...

He moved onto the stage, alone under a darkening sky, while the last embers of the dying day flickered on the horizon. The only sounds were those of the wind, and the heavy bell of the cathedral tolling a tell-tale death. A swarm of crows, flying in and out of the spires and vaults of the facade, chased the pigeons off their gargoyle perches. The tower hovered immense over the square, where people moved like pieces on a giant chessboard. Objects of various kinds changed hands out there. It was the hour of commerce, at the very border of night and day, when white becomes black, black becomes white, to eventually merge in a single grey. At the far end of the square, under a street light, a soldier stood smoking a cigarette, his carbine leaning against the lamp post. Above him, several storeys up, Schröder thought he discerned a boudoir beyond a lit window, where a woman, reflected in a mirror, slowly combed her long black hair that reached all the way to her waist. But it might also just be a shadow. In the increasing darkness it would soon be quite impossible to tell whether anything out there was substance or a mere silhouette. Lost in the impenetrable vagueness of the moment, Schröder returned from his imaginary wandering around the square. Göbel came back with a cup of coffee, not strong, but at least warm. Quietly he whispered to Schröder to stay absolutely calm during his approaching interrogation.

– You may not like me, but you have to trust me now.

Göbel sat in his chair, took off his spectacles and tried to clean them with the flap of his shirt. He drank a glass of water, opened a folder and arranged his papers. Schröder observed him in silence. Beatrice came back and went to the same chair at the back of the room where, with the exception of the time during which she had given her testimony, she had been seated all day. Her eyes, dark and inscrutable, seemed to oscillate between an expression of deepest compassion and cold indifference. He knew it wasn't meant that way. Still ...

*

Once the members of the court were assembled again, prosecutor Daniel Nemese smoothed his curly grizzled hair, made sure his suit did not have any undesired creases and made his way to the stand. Beaufort, with the professional countenance of a military officer calmly waiting to put his facts forward, placed his cap on the table at his side.

– Major Beaufort, what is your task as chairman of the Allied Martial Investigation Committee?

– To lead the work of finding and bringing war criminals to trial.

Göbel was about to voice his objection to the prosecutor's innuendo, but had no time to interrupt before Nemese addressed the issue from a new angle.

– How long have you known the defendant?

– Since June this year.

– How did you meet him?

– We had his name in our records, and two soldiers, asking for his identity papers in a random control, saw that he was a medical doctor – in other words, someone we may have been looking for. So they reported his name and his current address, a hotel in town, to us.

– The hearings that you then conducted with the defendant were of an informal nature, and the result of your interrogations proved insufficient to bring charges against him. Is that correct?

– Yes. Dr. Schröder was cleared of all suspicion of wrongdoing.

– Major Beaufort, is it also correct that you met the defendant on the morning of August 24th, at nine-thirty in the morning.?

– Yes.

– Did you know he was coming to see you?

– No. He approached some of my fellow officers and myself as we were on our way to a meeting.

– What did he say?

– He urged us to accompany him to a certain apartment building that had formerly been a convent, a nursing home and a police station, in Günterstal.

– Why did he ask you to do this?

– His purpose was to take us there so that we could meet the concierge who had supposedly seen the body of Dr. Claus Uhland as late as April this year.

– And this concierge was Frau Irmgard Kampa?

– Yes.

– Can you tell us what happened?

– First we came to an iron gate. It was locked. Dr. Schröder seemed very eager to reassure us that he hadn't brought us all the way in vain. He kept ringing the bell. As nobody came to open, he suddenly produced a key to the gate out of his own pocket.

– Did he tell you how the key had come into his possession?

– Yes. He said that Frau Kampa had given it to him

the previous evening so that he could gain access to the apartment which had allegedly been that of the late Dr. Uhland.

– So, in other words, the key to the gate was the key to the apartment the defendant claimed was Dr. Uhland's?

– I don't know that. I only saw the one key, the one that opened the gate.

– Did the defendant explain to you why he hadn't returned that key to Frau Kampa before leaving the premises?

– He said he had forgotten to return it to her.

– Did the explanation seem plausible to you?

– At first I took his words at face value. When we got inside, I began to have my doubts.

– Will you please explain to us what it was exactly that made you doubt his story?

– It's no secret. Dr. Schröder led us right into the concierge's apartment. We found the concierge herself in a rocking-chair next to an open window facing the courtyard. She had been killed. A bullet had gone through her head and embedded itself in the wooden frame of the chair.

– What happened next?

– I decided that we must formally body search Dr. Schröder. We found that in addition to the key, a wallet and his identity papers, he was also carrying a gun.

– Did you know at the time that it was from this weapon that the bullet in the rocking-chair had been fired?

– No, Forensics told us later.

– What did you do after searching the defendant?

– At his request, I agreed that my companions and I should conduct him to an inn nearby. Schröder claimed that a certain person there would corroborate that he had

spent the previous night on the premises.
— Who was this person?
— The landlady.
— What did she say?
— That she had never seen him before.
— And how did the defendant react to that?
— He was extremely upset, especially when the woman told us she knew absolutely nothing about the prostitute he kept referring to.
— What happened then?
— We had to force him to leave the landlady alone. Then we took him to the local police station, where he was taken into custody. The crime-scene was cordoned off. By the end of the day Forensics told me that the bullet we had found in the frame of the chair had been fired from the gun in Schröder's possession, and that the wound in the woman's head had apparently been caused by the same bullet.
— Did you or any of your officers participate in the subsequent inquiry?
— No.
— Why not?
— Because we are not assigned to deal with civil cases. We are deputies of the military department of justice.
— But you did read the police report?
— Yes.
— Was there anything in that report that might indicate that death had been brought about by a weapon other than the one found in the possession of the defendant?
— No.
— Thank you, Major. No further questions.
Nemese turned to the jury and gave the members of the

panel a penetrating glance, as though he wanted to make very sure they hadn't missed one syllable of his simple, but logical and juridically irreproachable examination of the witness.

– Members of the jury. Today the defendant has been given an alibi for the night on which the crime in question took place. Although he and his wife both knew that he couldn't have killed the concierge, he nevertheless led the major straight to the *corpus delicti*. Not only this, he insisted on staging a dramatic confrontation with the landlady of Zum Schwarzen Ferkel, because she refused to admit to having seen him. In fact, Dr. Schröder was furious, although he knew his story to be mere fiction. Ladies and gentlemen, why did he behave in this way? Why was he so desperate to convince everyone around him of the truth of a story which placed him closer to the crime scene, not farther from it? Even during the police interview he stubbornly and self-incriminatingly adhered to the same story. To this day he has cried out for someone to find the corroborative witnesses ... until, suddenly, out of the blue, his wife walks in and provides him with an alibi. Doesn't that just seem a little too convenient? Just a bit too neat? Of course it does, and it would be appropriate at this point to remind Frau Schröder that perjury is a very serious criminal offence, for which she can be ...

– Objection, Your Honour! The prosecutor is threatening the witness.

– Sustained.

– The defendant claims that he acted as he did in order to preserve his anonymity and to protect himself against a presumptive and mighty mysterious assassin by deliberately seeking to get arrested. By thus gaining public attention he hoped to be able to drive his enemy away. But who is this enemy? Dr. Rheinau, Frau Schröder's second husband, is dead; so is Dr. Uhland. So far not one single piece of evidence has been adduced to prove that the defendant's life is in any way under threat. On the contrary. The war is over, and the man himself has been acquitted of the allegations previously made against him. So what was his motive in murdering Frau Kampa? We have ourselves witnessed how the defendant sometimes falls prey to his delusions. Dr. Schröder is, as we have seen and heard, a violent and dangerous man who too often acts on impulse. Provoked by Frau Kampa's refusal to provide the information he asked for, as well as the key to the apartment, he murdered her in cold blood. Frau Schröder is protecting him, naturally. After all, he is her husband. But she's lying, and I urge the court to take no cognisance of her story whatsoever. The gun was found in the murderer's pocket. That's really all I need to say, and all you need to know.

Before sitting down, Nemese was assured enough to give Frau Schröder a haughty look. She instantly darted it back at him from the depths of her dark unmoving eyes. As he sat down he could still feel her eyes fastened on the back of his neck – a heavy smarting sensation, as if a voracious insect had alighted on the spot to inject its poison.

Dieter Göbel rose to cross-examine.

– Major Beaufort, did you not find it strange that a person who was alleged to have just committed a cold-blooded murder would lead you, an official of the Allied court-martial, straight to the scene of a crime? Did you not also find it very strange that he would show you the key which he had obtained in confidence from the victim? Finally, did you not find it very strange indeed that he should have on his person the very weapon that killed her?

– Yes, I must admit that I found it strange.

– Did it occur to you that this behaviour could in fact indicate that Dr. Schröder had absolutely no idea what you were all about to see on entering that room?

– It did cross my mind.

– Did you ever give credence to this doubt of yours?

– Yes.

– But you didn't in any way express your reservations to the police authorities?

– I did tell them that if he were found guilty of this crime, I would consider his behaviour highly irrational.

– So irrational, perhaps, that it might lead one to believe that he must have wanted to be arrested and charged with murder?

– I don't know. Dr. Schröder seemed to me absolutely convinced that he was on the trail of whoever had killed his successor, Dr. Claus Uhland, at Sankt-Anna Klinik.

– Did you believe in his sincerity?

– Well, at first I was sceptical.

– What made you change your mind?

– The man himself. I came to visit him when he was in custody, to ask him if there was anything I could do for him. He begged me not to let the local police get away with their summary investigation. We also tried to find evidence that Dr. Uhland had really lived in that apartment.

– And what was the result?

– All our investigations proved fruitless.

– Whom did you ask for information?

– The landlord, a certain Herr Weber. However, since he represented a new owner, and all the former tenants had been evicted, he no longer had any record of them.

– So what made you finally change your mind about the probability of Dr. Schröder's involvement in this murder?

– This.

To the utter astonishment of everybody in the room, Beaufort produced from his pocket something wrapped in a white cloth. He unfolded the cloth and put a gun in front of him on the ledge of the witness box.

– What is this, Major Beaufort?

– It is a gun.

– What kind of gun?

– A 9 mm automatic pistol containing four undischarged bullets.

– Why do you show it to the court?

– Because it is a weapon exactly like the one which killed the victim.

– And what would that prove?

– In itself nothing. However, the fact is that two days ago Lieutenant Smith, Sergeant Dunbar and I found it in the shrubbery, behind the brick wall which separates the courtyard outside the victim's living-room from the dense vegetation on the other side. This, I believe, renders it a piece of evidence that should be brought to this court's attention.

– Did you and your fellow-officers do this on your own initiative?

– Excuse me?

– I mean, what was it that prompted you to undertake this extraordinary investigation?

– Just a hunch. I had remembered that there was a strange atmosphere in the victim's room. Not only because she had been so brutally killed, but also because of the contrast to that violence of the gentle music on the radio, and the gauze curtain in the open window peacefully stirring in the wind. When we entered there was some Dietrich song playing, and her deep velvety alto at the crime scene – well, it was oddly out of place, not to say eerie. As I said, one of the victim's living-room windows was open. In other words, it would not have been necessary for the killer to enter the apartment. He could have leant over the windowsill, aimed the gun at her while she was dozing off to the sentimental tones from the radio, and pulled the trigger. After firing the shot, the murderer would have wanted to disappear as quickly as possible. But the only way he could have been sure of avoiding notice by any tenant or passer-by, would have been to scale the brick wall in the backyard, over which only the victim had a view. Sheltered by the thicket on the other side he – or she, for that matter – could have disposed of the weapon and left the scene by way of the far end of the park. I assumed that the apartment building and the backyard had both been examined for evidence by the police. However, nobody to my knowledge had searched the dense vegetation on the other side of that wall.

– And there it was, a gun just like the one which was used to take the victim's life?

– Yes.

– Major Beaufort, were you the one who discovered this gun, or was it one of your officers?

– None of us, actually. The weapon was found by our German Shepherd dog. He used to search out mines during the war, and now has been given an honourable retirement. We're fortunate to still have him around.

– How did the dog know what he was supposed to look for?

– Well, he's trained to spot explosives and gunpowder.

– When did all this happen?

– As of today, one week ago.

– Thank you, Major. I present this weapon in evidence to the court.

Theatrically Göbel turned around with the trophy in his hand and held it up for everyone to see. Avid curiosity was written on the spectators' faces, except for Beatrice's, whose eyes glowed dark and inscrutable as ever. Beaufort, who was putting his entire military career and reputation at stake, showed the restraint expected of a strictly neutral witness whose sole concern is to see justice done. Schröder stared at the gun as if he were seeing a ghost, his eyeballs almost starting from their sockets. Judge Giessen frowned, visibly dissatisfied with the irregularities of this case, as new witnesses, testimony and technical evidence kept appearing. His testy expression deepened as the stenographer, who had been busy recording the proceedings, dropped her thick pile of short-hand notes on the floor. The jury had reassumed their aspect of pale sea-anemones swaying in an invisible deep-sea current. This was the moment of truth. Göbel knew that he must succeed now – or never.

– Ladies and gentlemen of the jury. The defendant in this trial, Dr. Hans Schröder, already has his alibi. There is one circumstance, however, that might still seem to cast a shadow of doubt over that alibi. This takes the form of a strange coincidence. At the moment when in his presence the murder victim's body was discovered, Dr. Schröder had in his possession the weapon from which the fatal bullet was fired. Now, we have heard the defendant's wife testify that Dr. Schröder had for many years kept just such a gun in a secret compartment in his writing desk. He was carrying it that morning because he had reason to fear an armed attack by someone who wanted him out of the way. Because this – Göbel moved over toward the judge's bench and picked up another gun from the items of evidence – this, ladies and gentlemen, is the weapon that Dr. Schröder had on his person that morning. And this – he now held up the gun handed into evidence by Beaufort – identical in appearance, is the one that took the victim's life. What does that tell us? First, that the person originally suspected of having committed this crime is innocent. Secondly, that neither Dr. Schröder nor we know who committed this crime. But the fact that we don't know, doesn't make the defendant himself guilty. There is no guilt by association here, and there may indeed be a new investigation and a new trial in due course – let us hope that the prosecution picks the right person to prosecute if and when that time comes. To our present investigation, however, these considerations must remain irrelevant, because we are charged this day not with exposing the real murderer, but with preventing the commission of a fatal error in this court of justice. The only way we can do this is to free the innocently accused, and to do it unconditionally, once and for all. Dr. Schröder has an alibi. His alibi was challenged by the prosecution because of the gun found in his possession. Now that the gun that was actually used in the killing has been identified, your task has indeed become straightforward. All that is incumbent on you is to decide to let the evidence speak for itself, and thus to cause justice to prevail. Thank you, ladies and gentlemen.

– Does the prosecution wish to cross-examine the witness? Judge Giessen asked, in a voice that signified that he too was ready to see the jury put an end to the proceedings unless there was some objection.

– No, Your Honour. But since the defence has chosen to take this court by surprise in deliberately introducing their key witness, Frau Beatrice Schröder – as well as important technical evidence – at the very last instance, we ask for a two-day recess in order to double-check the accuracy of the statements she and Major Beaufort have made.

– Very well, Herr Nemese. This court will be reconvened on November 8 at ten o'clock. Have you anything to say, Herr Göbel?

– Because of my client's delicate state of health, I request that he be taken from his cell to a place where he can be under the surveillance of medical staff until the day after tomorrow.

– He shall of course have to remain in confinement, but I see your point. I shall arrange for his transfer to a closed medical ward this evening. This court is adjourned.

Göbel returned to Schröder and heaved a sigh of relief.

– I think we've done it! he said, patting his client on the shoulder.

– But the prosecutor asked for two days to make inquiries!

– What do you expect? It's his last chance. He hasn't got anything that will stand up in court, and he won't find anything either.

– Are you crazy? He'll find both the landlady and the hooker!

– Even so, what do you think he's going to get out of the landlady? She won't contradict her own story. She has every good reason to keep her mouth shut. And as for the hooker, it goes without saying that she'd only make herself an accomplice by testifying that you were with her. Believe me, the prosecution will find absolutely nothing. Besides, Beaufort is a big player around here. To start questioning his testimony would take more balls than that little French bastard has. He'll be happy to lose this one. So don't worry. And as you heard, I've managed to have you moved to a hospital.

– But I'm fine now!

– Oh, it's just in case. It's a mere formality. You'll get better food, and its easier for people to come and visit. You've already told me you don't want to go back to jail.

– I want to go home.

– Two more days. Two more days, Schröder, and you'll be a free man.

– I wish I could share your enthusiasm. I thought this was all going to be decided today.

– It would normally, but it's late, and the judge is tired. He wants to go home, pour himself a brandy, light a cigar and put his slippers on. That's why the court is adjourned, not because he believes Nemese is going to present new evidence on Thursday. Look for yourself, it's already night.

He pointed to the tall arched windows. Above the hills, among jagged clouds, the thin crescent of the new moon appeared next to bright Venus. The town, dimly lit by street lamps, had almost merged into the surrounding darkness.

The soldier was gone, the boudoir had become a gaping black hole and the square was almost abandoned. Only the cathedral remained, solid, like an enormous missile, aimed at an unknown target. Schröder felt lonely, encapsulated in his own destiny in the eternity of time and infinity of space. There was his wife, approaching him like a beam of light from outer space, but she did not just illumine and soothe his weary heart. She pierced it, ripped it apart, and continued her journey through the void, oblivious of everything except her own motion. He saw her look at him with passion in her eyes. There was no sense of past or future in them; they were simply regarding him with the absolute conviction of female emotion – intense, irrational, unpredictable and profound.

– Hans, she whispered in a muffled voice, – Hans, I love you.

"If you can only keep it up until Thursday", he thought, moved by her intensity, "Then at least we can begin to find out where we stand." But he didn't dare to dim the glare of her regard by expressing his doubts, so he said.

– Let us hope for the best.

– Oh, Hans, imagine what joy this will bring to the children. God, give me the strength to endure two more days without you. She leaned forward and gave her husband a kiss as the guards, closing in on the little group, urged him to leave the court-room. Hans replied to her caress with a faint smile.

The realisation that his children still didn't know that their father was alive, the image of their lovely features, their innocence in the face of so much evil, suddenly overtaking his precariously maintained self-control, proved too much for him, and he was shaking like a leaf, crying in torrents, as the guards helped him out of the room to the Red Cross ambulance waiting in the street.

*

Why had they decided to move him to a hospital? He wasn't sick, he just needed to rest. Perhaps he had already been sleeping for hours. Perhaps they had been giving him drugs. He didn't know. He had no idea how he had ended up in this room. In between their iron bars the windows let through the glimmer of streetlights. To the far left of the room, there was a hallway ending with a solid door. Although there was some light in the room, it seemed faint in relation to the vanishing obscurity of the ceiling. He had the sensation of being locked up in an immense burial chamber, like some corpse, embalmed and prepared for the journey through the regions of the underworld. Above him hovered, invisible, the structure of the tomb, perhaps facing the sun, the moon, the stars, while he himself had been confined to a world bereft of natural light. But why had he, among all human beings, been singled out for this extraordinary undertaking? Why had he been chosen? Had seconds and minutes ceased to exist in this hermetic enclosure, where even the appearance of an outside world, the empty street with its scattered lights, had taken on the aspect of a picture frozen in time? His entire existence, fossilised as it were, was about to unite with some immutable, unspeakable, subhuman entity. Yet the idea of being removed from this mundane scene to play a part in a drama staged by an unknown agent of the underworld, was absurd, especially in view of his imminent release from prison altogether. But there he was, unable to shake off the feeling of having a destiny to fulfil, a destiny in which some sort of sacrifice would be demanded of him. "How many living creatures have to die to redeem one single soul for eternal life?" The question was strange and irrelevant. All the same it kept haunting him with the ghastly insistence of a feverish dream.

He raised himself on the pillows and took a better look round the room. The bed had nothing in common with the primitive bunk on which he had spent the previous nights. It was comfortable, had soft pillows, clean sheets and a thick warm cover. A night-light stood on a small square table beside the bed. Close by the lamp there was a bell to ring, in case of emergency, perhaps, or if he was simply in want of something. This change of environment had been as sudden as it was surprising, and his first impulse was to demand an explanation of where he had been brought. But now something at the far end of the room caught his eye. There was another door standing ajar. Schröder leapt out of bed and at once fell to the floor, convinced he must have been sedated and was only just about to regain consciousness and the ability to move. Carefully he investigated his limbs. Nothing was broken. He managed to sit up. Resting on both arms, he slowly pulled himself up to his knees. Harnessing all his strength, he eventually got to his feet. The entire operation might have taken a couple of minutes to perform, but to him it seemed endless, as if the real task at hand had been to revive an already dead body, raise it up and set it in motion. Feeling reasonably steady, he finally let go of the support of the bed and began, one hesitant step after another, to cross the room.

It was the kitchen all right. The same, with the same pantry and set of shelves and cupboards. In the room next to it he found the writing desk, identical to the one he had already seen. There was absolutely no doubt about it: he had been transported to Dr. Uhland's old apartment, now converted, or rather, reconverted to a closed ward in some sort of hospital. But what was this? So far, Uhland's flat being part of a hospital was only in his imagination. He had seen absolutely nobody around, not even a single guard. The street outside was as empty as before, like a picture frozen in time. Schröder quickly went back to bed, pulled the cover over him and rang the bell. At a great distance he heard it resonating through the corridors outside, to die out in a long languorous silence. He was mesmerised by the void in the wake of the bell, and found himself staring at the door at the end of the hallway without knowing what to expect. Then, as if yielding to an invisible force, it slowly opened, and a nurse in a white uniform appeared. Although a considerable distance still separated them, Schröder couldn't help noticing her thick, shiny black hair and the curves coiling under the tight creases of her dress.

– How are you doing? she asked, and leaned over him so close that he could feel her breast touching his head and shoulder while she rearranged the pillows.

– Not too bad, considering the circumstances, he replied, curious to find out what they really were.

– It's good to see you feeling better. For a while we were all pretty worried that you had lost it.

– Lost it? Lost what?

– We were afraid you had forgotten the purpose of your visit down here. You see, for quite a while there were some doubts as to whether or not you would even come to see us.

– Come to see you? What kind of assumption is that? Who are you by the way, if you don't mind my asking?

– Not at all, doctor. I'm your sister of mercy.

– Of mercy?

– That's right, just relax and watch, and you'll see what I mean.

To Schröder's surprise and steadily increasing excitement she took off her white jacket to reveal a red and black corset, inside which two full breasts were about to break out of their padded prison. It was a déjà-vu, an almost familiar situation; still, he could not recall where he had seen breasts like these before. He was still searching his memory as she leaned over him and gave his bare neck a long, slow kiss. Instinctively, he searched for her mouth, and in the next instant he felt her nibbling his tongue, pressing the embrace further, increasing the intimacy with each and every breath. Slowly, she worked herself down his neck and chest, letting go of the corset. She had reached his crotch as her breasts finally spurted out from their dark caverns to inflame his erect member. She rubbed it against her skin, went up and down over him, pressing and squeezing her breasts tighter and tighter around his throbbing member. Schröder heard himself moan as her quick tongue began to whirl around the fleshy head while she gripped the pouch with her finger-nails – like an eagle tearing a human heart out of its body. Just as he felt that he could no longer hold himself back, she let go, leaving it pulsating helplessly in the air. Then she raised her skirt and descended on him. He felt her hot cavity surround him. Although he was near climax, her movements were so slow and regular that he managed to stay inside her without letting go. The pressure from within became overwhelming, as simultaneously she intensified her thrusts. He threw out his arms, grabbed her pounding hips and pulled her down. A triumphant scream broke from her lips as she felt the convulsive contractions inside her. Schröder had the sensation of being electrocuted. He even smelled electricity in the air. A jolt in the solar plexus spread, lightning-like, into the centres of his brain. A blinding light struck his eyes – the precursor of another nervous attack? Groaning he fell back on the pillow. The sudden unexpected fury of his desire abated. An Amazon, victoriously bending over a dying hero, she lowered her glowing face so close to his that it came within the range of the dim night-light. Only now did he recognise her.

At first he was unable to voice his surprise. He raised his hand toward her, as if reassuring himself that she did physically exist.

– You ... he whispered and turned away. – I knew you would be back to finish me off ... After long hesitation, he continued,

– Can you tell me what I am doing in this place? Who has brought me back to Uhland's apartment? And what are you doing in this hospital?

– How do you know you are in a hospital? Have you seen any medical staff around?

– The judge said they were going to transfer me to one. Do you realise what you have done to me? You almost had me hanged because of that visit to the old woman.

– I had to disappear for a while. Couldn't jeopardise our future together.

– Future? ... Oh, heavens ... What am I doing? Two more days, and the whole thing would have been over. Instead, I am here, here again with you! What happened to my wife? And where have you been? You could have proved my innocence.

– Your wife is doing a damn good job of it right now, isn't she?

– Yes, and why? Because it was the only way to get me out of this, after you let me down!

– I didn't let you down. I had to use you as a cover-up for a while, but I never intended to abandon you. See for yourself, I'm here now, ain't I?

– You used me as a cover-up, what is that supposed to mean, you callous woman? ... ... Oh no, you can't be serious ... Tell me you don't mean that ... Oh no, my God, oh no, not that ... You did it, didn't you? You went back there in the middle of the night. You took the key and the gun from my pocket and went back to the old lady's apartment. Killed her ... in cold blood ... just like that ... straight through the head ... and then ... then you came back, and put the gun and the key back in my jacket. Then you left ...

Schröder emitted a long sigh and looked at her, not quite fully capable of comprehending that he had, at last, figured out the truth. It was like in a costume ball as the participants reveal their true faces behind the masks, like a carnival in Venice, when the alluring figure of an attractive woman, whom one has pursued through an endless multitude of grotesque faces and appearances, finally reveals herself as Death in person ... And in truth, this was the first time that Schröder really recognised her for whom she was. She wasn't just any woman of the street, who had killed a defenceless old lady for whatever coins she had in her purse. She had changed her hair. Before it had been brown and much shorter. Now it was black as ebony and streamed like a horse's mane down her back. In those early days she never used much make-up. But here she was, powdered, painted, with artificially enhanced lips and a body shaped by, and long since addicted to, lascivious pleasure. She had changed, not only as one sometime changes with time, sorrow or fate, but changed as one who no longer wants to be the same person, who has decided to obliterate the memory of the former person, who has decided to burn all her bridges. Yet, she was the Laura Emming he had once known, the girl introduced as his wife's closest friend, around whom he had clustered a host of erotic fantasies, fantasies he had certainly tried to suppress, fantasies which had insinuated themselves into his dreams, in his moments of day-dreaming, into his most secret and unguarded hours. He had always wanted to feel her, touch her, kiss her, to make love to her ... but his marriage vows, his sense of responsibility and loyalty, his love for his wife and children, had always held him back, so that their moments of tender truth had remained late whispers among the rose bushes in the backyard, when everybody else was asleep, an exchange of confidences, sometimes even a long glance itself guilty of adultery, but inarticulate in words and therefore, in the last instance, unspoken.

Thus it had been, and thus it had remained, Laura still being the favourite of Beatrice's friends – what could have been more natural than precisely that she came to visit *à propos* ... By all means a charming, witty girl, with her future before her. He would have to admit, however, that it was her dark, impassioned sexuality that had seduced him from the very beginning, and that her metamorphosis, whatever had brought it about, was not altogether illogical. There had been a leap forward somewhere, but sometimes one has to leap an abyss when the bridge is missing. That she had become a prostitute came as a shock to him, and made his own moral tribulations seem a mere trifle. She hadn't been born in the street; there was a decent family background somewhere; and Beatrice had remained in Freiburg throughout the entire war ... Perhaps there had been a falling out between them because of him? Or had she been disgraced and sunk into poverty for other reasons? Still, she had been Beatrice's friend. How could she have let it happen? The descent from university student to harlot was, if not exactly easy to comprehend, at least understandable in terms of necessity and survival. But only an incurably sick brain would think of murdering innocent people for the mere pleasure of doing so.

Incessantly, the images kept chasing one another through his brain. The Laura Emming, the student with whom he had secretly been in love, or at the very least attracted to, had metamorphosed, first, into an outright courtesan, then into an angel of death. She had also visited him in a dream so convincing that he had been able to foresee many of attorney Göbel's stratagems simply by remembering what, offering to represent him in court, she had already told his subconscious. Student, lawyer, prostitute and murderess in the same person – it simply did not make sense. And how absurd the present situation itself, where one revelation was concealed within another, like a set of Russian dolls ...

Confirmed in his suspicions, Schröder finally shifted his gaze from her intriguing face to get a glimpse of the street outside. From this distance it seemed to have undergone no change whatsoever; there was the same street lamp under the same black sky. Not a single human being in sight. It was like a silent movie whose reel has suddenly come to a halt, stubbornly projecting one and the same image onto the screen. He stared at it for a long, long time. When his gaze returned to the room, it expressed the sadness of disillusion.

– Tell me, Laura, this is not a hospital, is it? This is not even Uhland's apartment. It's all a trick ...

– It's not the way you think. You're jumping to conclusions, just as you did with your wife. Only in her case, you didn't jump far enough.

– Leave her out of this, will you.

– I can't. She is the spider in this web. I had to kill that old woman, because she knew all about us and had threatened to tell the police everything she knew. Besides, everybody knows she poisoned her husband for the life insurance money. She was filthy rich, the old sow. Anyway, she knew that Uhland wasn't dead; she also knew that he wasn't living here for real. But we threatened her so that she would keep her mouth shut and give you the impression that he was dead. Then, when the time was right, your wife was going to inform you that she had remarried, not Rheinau – there was never a Rheinau, he and only he has been an invention – but ...

– Whom?

– Claus Uhland.
– Beatrice? Married to Uhland?
– Yes, but please hurry. We haven't got much time.
– Much time for what?
– To get out of here.
– I can't get out of here. This is a prison.
– Then how do you think I got in?
– They let you in of course. This is a closed ward.
– Is it?
– Of course, don't be silly. How much time have they allowed you? Half an hour?
– They wouldn't say. But since you're asking, let's find out.

Laura rose from the bed, put on her white jacket and wiggled across the room on her high heels. Again Schröder assumed that there must be someone he couldn't see who opened the door for her, but from this distance it looked as if she was herself pushing it open. He saw her body cast an immensely long shadow along the spacious corridor.

– Hello, is there anybody there? Hello! Hello!

The echo of her voice was endless. It travelled along a distance measureless to man. And in the course of its journey it changed character many times. The last vowel ejected into space resounded like the cry of a child, a cat, a deer, an elephant, like thousands of voices merging in one vast murmur, like the sea, or the intense confusion of radio waves emitted from the centre of the galaxy. It became a perplexing multitude, from roaring lion to squeaking mouse to the song of a whale. But whatever its outer appearance, the common denominator was that there was no answer, or, to be quite precise, that even if the message, the question, the call, would one day reach its destination, there would be no one to receive it.

The corridor outside Uhland's alleged apartment was as empty as it had been on that night, many a night ago, when Schröder walked it back and forth. There was no lock, there were no guards, there were no human beings out there. Given the entirely inhospitable nature of that freedom, it was none too surprising that Schröder at first refused to believe that the door had been from the very beginning both unguarded and unlocked. The shock of this revelation hurled him back into the compulsion of rattling the chains. The need to prove to himself that he was in reality held prisoner against his will, was more urgent than ever. In a last attempt to secure the invisible law governing time and space, he clung to his trial like a drowning man clings to the jetsom of his wrecked ship.

– I'm staying here, do you hear me! You're not going to tempt me into breaking out of here before that judge's gavel sounds my acquittal once and for all. It would be incredibly stupid of me, after I've sailed these treacherous waters for so long, to allow myself to strike a reef, and be banned from society altogether, and then, maybe, in the end, still get caught. Can't you see, that trial is all I have got! My entire life is wrapped up in it. If I walk now, I let everybody down: my wife, my children, our future. And you have nothing to fear. Just leave me alone here until they come for me. I promise not to give your secret away. I don't care about what made you become what you are. I don't need your help to be free. My wife has intervened, and she is about to lift the spell you have put on me. So now, go away, and I hope I never meet you again in my life. My wife …

– Hans, your "wife" is married to Claus Uhland. Young Heinz is not your son, but his. She is not interested in helping to get you out of jail. The whole thing has been a smokescreen to protect the two of them. She will rejoice in her heart when you're sentenced, in spite of everything she appears to have done for you. You are not welcome at home. You are a threat to everyone, and they would all prefer that you remain dead. Admit it now to yourself, before it is too late. You married her because she was rich and beautiful. It was to be the perfect complement to your brilliant career. But you never truly loved her, because you always knew, deep down, that her spirit was shallow and her heart of stone.

– Shut up! I forbid you to besmirch Beatrice!

– You can try as much as you want to shut me up, but it won't change the truth. I am the only woman you ever truly loved, and if you don't come with me now, then I am going to turn myself over to Nemese. I'll tell him that you were with me the night the old hag was whacked, except for the two hours when you were gone, believing I was asleep.

– Ha! And who's going to believe you? I saw you that same night in the company of some American soldiers. If you don't watch your tongue, I'll frame you for this and believe me, I'll do everything in my power to see you burn in hell!

– You are pathetic, Hans. I have witnesses. You don't. But I like your spirit all the same. You see, we are two of a kind, you and I. Maybe we won't exactly be happy together, but we would never be able to live without each other. I'm inside your guts Schröder. I am your heart, liver and kidneys. If I didn't know you hated that word so much, I would even say that I am your soul. Or perhaps I should say it just because you hate it so much: I am your soul. But come now, let's go. Only I know the way out of here. We can escape together. No one will ever find us. We can go to Switzerland, or to Sweden. We can even go to South America. Paraguay and Brazil are still havens for people like you and me.

– You slanderous bitch! There was never an honest bone in your body. May the day be cursed that I first met you. May the coincidence be cursed as well that I ran into you after so many years. I was at war while you were earning an easy living spreading your legs for anyone willing to pay the price. And now you – rancorous and vindictive as ever in spite of your innate laziness – can't wait to destroy the only person who ever had faith in you, the only one who has given and opened himself to you without ever asking for anything in return. I despise you, and I despise myself for ever having trusted you.

– Poor Dr. Schröder. Everything looked so fine for you. You had it all perfectly organised: a prestigious job, a beautiful wife, beautiful children, yes, even a hot, temperamental, capricious, full-blooded mistress … or so you hoped. But then you began to question yourself. There was a crack in the armour, and you began to doubt yourself, to doubt that you were able to do what you set out to accomplish. But instead of facing up to your fears, you ran away from them. And while doing so, you made sure that Claus Uhland should be burdened with all the dirty work for which you and your noble conscience were too fine and delicate.

– That's a bloody lie!

– Is it really? What was that contract, then, that you drew up in the form of a last will and testament? A contract in which you entrusted Uhland with the task of taking care of Beatrice and the children in case you were never to return. You were well aware he would not only in all probability take over your family, but your job, too. In other words, you couldn't stand the thought of your own hands being dirtied when you returned home each evening, but you had no qualms about someone else doing the butchery for you and then going home to make love to your wife.

– Stop it! I order you to stop it!

– Why would you accept that? Because you don't love her. Any man truly in love with a woman would do whatever it takes to keep her happy. She would never have held it against you that you were doing what the Reich expected of you, and you know that. But you didn't really want her. Besides, she was a Jewess, and that had become inconvenient as well. And then there were the children, half-Jewish in your eyes, completely Jewish in the eyes of the Nazis ...

– You rattlesnake ... There was never any such agreement between Uhland and myself. I believed he was probably going to remain at his post, that was all. The rest is history. Uhland died three years ago. If he and my wife had an affair before that, and in the belief that I was dead – well then, I shall have to forgive her. After all, he was a handsome man. Like this Beaufort, whom Beatrice suddenly has won over to our side.

– Beaufort's an innocent boy, a tasty morsel for her! She duped him all right, but he doesn't know anything, and he doesn't want to know anything. Right now he's devoured by his bad conscience. He's hoping to return to Canada as soon as possible, planning to leave the army and devote himself to placid suburban life, looking forward to the birth of his first grandchild and making sure the barbecue has enough firewood. Beaufort? Who is he? A pawn, a pawn sacrificed in your wife's queen's gambit. And you had to accept the offer, because all other defences were excluded – right? Well, before you make your next move, don't be so naïve as to believe that your wife hasn't set up the game without placing a king at her side. So listen. What I say now I shall say only once. I offered to escape with you. You refused, assuming that I'm lying to you. Since I understand how confused you are, I shall not hold that against you. I'll even make you one last offer, and this one I don't think you can refuse. I'll volunteer to accompany you to see Claus Uhland. After that you can decide for yourself whether or not he's dead. So what do you say? Please, make up your mind. He's waiting now, but I don't think he'll wait much longer.

Hans doubted that Laura meant anything at all by her rambling talk of escaping together, or meeting Claus Uhland, who by now had become almost a figment of his imagination. On the other hand, the man was apparently involved in this murder case, and whatever might clarify the murky circumstances of the matter was intrinsically of interest to Schröder. And again, what had at first seemed to him a revelation of Laura's guilt, now, on second thoughts, became more open to question, particularly in view of how willingly she had confessed to the abominable act. Laura had in fact all the theatrical compulsions typical of the hysteric. Whatever her true role had been in this affair, whatever the true facts were, one thing was for sure: Laura was herself a candidate for the mental asylum, a typical borderline case. She was absolutely not to be trusted, especially in regard to actions and statements dictated by her jealousy of Beatrice. It was understandable, if not pardonable, that she had lashed out at her in this manner. The only sensible conclusion to be drawn from this show of aggression was that something terrible must have happened between them. "When it comes to love, women fight like cats", he thought.

Nonetheless, a prison without guards, bars and locks was a contradiction in terms, and the fact that the door between his room and the corridor was not only open, but also unguarded, was a temptation that he would ultimately be unable to resist. "Perhaps I am allowed to move freely within the entire building" he told himself, "and if that's the case, why shouldn't I go on a little mystery tour? As soon as we meet some member of the staff I'll tell him to take care of Laura, and make sure she leaves the premises. Meanwhile, I shall have to call Göbel to tell him what has happened." Satisfied with his own shrewd planning, he decided to follow Laura. Apprehensively he looked out into the corridor.

The corridor was even longer and more dimly lit than he remembered it. The distance from one door to the next appeared to be in the order of miles rather than yards, and the lights, although seeming to glare like suns as he neared them, soon lost themselves in space, distant, faint and devoid of outline. The floor itself was uneven, here sloping to one side, there to the other, giving the overall impression of a heaving sea. Once again Schröder was reminded of his physical frailty. He wondered how it was possible that a hospital could exist in which there were no nurses or doctors. As far as the eye could see, there was nothing but this darkened corridor, the parallel sides of which seemed to merge in infinity. Laura kept up the pace, and Schröder, looking back, saw that the door by which they had left the ward had already shrunk to a minuscule red dot lit by the faintest of stars. He had the strong impression that if he were to change his mind now and turn back, he would be incapable, even if he were to walk for hours, of returning to the room they had just left. The sea became stormy too. At times, seized by dizziness, he was obliged to go down on his knees and crawl along the wall for a while in order to regain his balance. Laura waited for him, but she was obviously irritated, and would not help him to his feet once he had fallen. In this manner they continued, slowly moving toward the spiral staircase at the end of the corridor. The scale of their enterprise, however, was such that he could not tell how far they had already walked, or for how long. It seemed as if days and weeks, even months and years, had passed since they had been together in that fateful room where Laura's true identity as well as her deceitful nature had been revealed. With the stormy waves increasing, the lamps not only moved in irregular manner horizontally but also rushed down vertically towards him, only to vanish again in the farthermost reaches of the ceiling. It was like standing on the afterdeck of a ship that was being tossed in all directions by a reckless hurricane, while stars kept peeping through the naked eye of the storm. Schröder was nauseated and felt that he must vomit, but this relief was denied him. There were moments when he had to lean against the walls or fall to the floor to be able to advance at all.

Laura's appearance changed. At times she assumed the aspect of a larger-than-life statue, solemnly striding between rows of temple columns. Forced to the floor, his regard compulsively turned myopic, minutely studying the ochre-red tiles with their curious black design. Every single one – and there were countless numbers of them – had the same geometrical pattern: a spiral in right angles, not unlike one arm of the Swastika, descending into the infinitesimal. He called out to her to stop, his voice a whisper in the roar of the hurricane, and he would lose sight of her until she turned to see where he was, and waited for him to catch up.

– Stop! Schröder cried out, trying to reach for her hand. I can't go on like this. Isn't there supposed to be a staircase at the end of this corridor? Aren't we ever going to reach it?

– If Uhland has been dead in your mind for so many years, it might just take a little effort to restore him to life. But don't worry, we'll be there soon – sooner than you think, in fact.

He wasn't expecting that she meant her words to be taken quite literally, but the mere conjuring up of the memory of the staircase now coincided with its reappearance in space. At the end of the endless row of lights and doors it stood separate from the walls like a desert mirage. The parallel lines of the corridor came to an end, the wave-like motion of the floor stilled and the lights grew steady. When he turned, the corridor revealed itself as being about sixty yards in length. Approximately half-way down, the door to Uhland's apartment stood ajar – Laura must have left it that way. A soft light emanated from the apartment, illuminating the inside of the door and casting a large rectangular shadow behind it.

– Do you want to go back? Laura asked, an ironic smile playing at the corners of her mouth.

– No, no, no ... let's carry on.
– Very well, Dr. Schröder. Here's the staircase.

If the corridor had seemed long to him, the spiral staircase appeared to be endless. The longest spiral staircase he had hitherto walked had been the one leading up to the dome crowning the cathedral in Florence. Half-way up, he and Beatrice, during the course of their honeymoon in Tuscany, had had the most magnificent view of its vivid and candidly cruel representation of the Last Judgement, the centre-piece of which was the devil himself, enormous, part-human, part-beast, entirely terrifying. There had been a guide at the door that led from the narrow balustrade running round the base of the dome. This man had, with Latin eloquence and in gory detail, explained to them that this fresco, for which Vasarí had been inspired by the hellish visions of a Dominican friar, was unique. It was the first pictorial representation in the Western world of the Ottomans' practice of impaling their victims.

– The executioners would stop the process before a vital organ was damaged, though, the guide explained – to ensure that the sensory functions of the nervous system were still intact. Death was consequently slow in coming and, in accordance with the torturers' plan, as painful as possible. The refinement of the Turkish method greatly impressed, even horrified the Europeans of the time, who for the most part relied on the comparatively gentle way of prolonging suffering that comprised breaking every bone in the victim's body and railing it to a wheel. Although those Europeans in their turn had had many occasions on which they could have reciprocated the courtesy shown by the

Ottoman rulers toward their Balkan and Hungarian subjects, the practice nonetheless failed to become a standard feature of Christian torture. As a subject for art, however, it retained a somewhat scandalous, and perhaps for that very reason, popular status. After all, there was an undeniable obscenity in inserting a pole into that particular orifice of the human body, and the European clergy, influencing the killing preferences of the temporal lords, felt obliged to observe decorum in matters of life and death. So hanging, decapitation, and burning at the stake long remained the preferred European way of exterminating the unwanted. Alas, the sobriety of these classical methods is not held in the same esteem nowadays, and the time may be coming when official murder will no longer be considered a reason for a public celebration. The whole thing turns into a mechanical industry, an efficient method of killing, certainly, but devoid both of joy and aesthetic pleasure.

Hans and Beatrice, young, impressionable and newly married, were stunned at such erudition frivolously thrown around in connection with atrocities of this kind. They hardly had time to draw breath, however, before their self-appointed guide waved his index finger in their faces.

– Look there! That's the devil himself, amorphous, chaotic, a Uranus, eating his own children, with a belly – he tapped his own stomach by way of emphasis – that is never satisfied!

Later that evening, sitting in the Caffè dell' Arte, they heard discussions of futurist and surrealist art around them turn into political controversy. They saw hordes of young fascists parading in the streets with banners bearing slogans calling for violence and social revolution. There had been skirmishes with communist supporters, and the morning newspapers were full of obituaries of young people who had lost their lives in this lawless gang warfare. It hadn't surprised them overmuch – the situation in Germany had been much the same at that time – but it helped to convince them that Europe was being drawn into another war. Every day the liberal newspapers advocated mutual respect, understanding, peace and negotiation, but reality itself spoke with an altogether different tongue. There was no doubt that the continent was as a barrel of gunpowder soon to be ignited …

Meanwhile, the Tuscan summer was hot and dry, accompanied by the frenzied percussion orchestra of pine-tree crickets. Hans and Beatrice visited churches and monasteries, offering some cool air in their incense-drowned crypts carved out of rock. They saw ancient aqueducts, theatres and arenas, where the sun mercilessly hammered down on monumental stones, once stained with the blood of slaughtered animals and men. Many centuries had passed since the last gladiators had entered the arena, many centuries had passed since Electra vociferously mourned her father's ignoble death, but the ensuing silence, gently stirred by the feeble midday wind, passing through the grass in the cracks of the slabs, still whispered of the eternal, immutable destiny of man, the endless recurrence of memories, dreams and ideas, and the human sacrifice at the heart of it all.

The cypresses of the modern cemeteries stood tall and dark against the blue sky. In the evening high clouds hovered over the horizon, promising the relief of a thunderstorm which finally loomed away, mission incomplete. They enjoyed cold drinks and cigarettes on terraces shaded by thick vines; they swam in the rivers, laughed at their own jokes for hours, had wine, sausage, ham and spaghetti, and united in nights perspiring with their fluids, their scents and their love. He particularly remembered her dress with irises on a pale yellow background, casually thrown over a chair; the scent of her warm, tanned skin; the little freckles round her nose; the taste of her kiss; her peaceful expression in sleep as she lay on his arm, trustful that no evil could ever touch her as long as he was there. The moon shone through the open French windows and the curtains wafted in the night breeze as she turned round, away from the dark side of the bed, into the moonlight, murmuring, as her eyes rolled, irregularly but gently, back and forth under her marble eyelids. That summer their first child had begun to stir under her heart.

The image of his wife in her prime faded, and the voice of the Italian guide intervened, now magnified, like an echo reinforcing another echo ... "A belly that is never satisfied ... Never satisfied ... Never satisfied ..." He could see the images appear vividly on the dark walls, the whole lot of human sinners, historical figures, demonic gargoyles, each more guilty than the last; victims never acquitted from their trials, condemned to eternal suffering; human souls and bodies shoved into vast ovens, the earth itself breaking up in a sea of sulphurous fumes and fire, swallowing each and every one, like the eruption of Vesuvius, a burning Gehenna, an Armageddon of no return.

How similar the feeling of intense cold was to that of extreme heat! There was a burning sensation in the cold – such as in the winters of the Russian campaign. That was where he learned that hell, as opposed to what people generally assume, is not a hot but a cold place. And the devil, if ever such a figure existed, must consequently be cold. Cold as ice. Colder than ice. Colder than the universe itself ... And yet, in touching him, one would have the feeling of being embraced and consumed by fire ... It was obvious that the devil had to be beautiful too, otherwise how would he be able to seduce? This greatest war had been his doing, and in the end it amounted to nothing more than hecatombs of corpses, piled one on top of another in collective graves. And the pits had not been dug out of piety, but simply to prevent the spread of disease.

But where was the beauty of the Führer? To Hans he had always seemed like a comedian trying to be earnest. How anyone could take his speeches seriously, believe in his ideas, vouchsafe eternal loyalty to him, and promise to take his orders to the moon and back again if necessary, that was the real enigma. To allow Hitler to assume power was like letting a child throw a tantrum in a gun shop. His entire regime was the embodiment of something thoroughly infantile. As a psychiatrist, Hans knew all too well the spiritually crippling effects of megalomania, and he had had more than one Napoleon, Jesus and Caesar on his hands. The irony of it all, was that one of those Caesars had suddenly got the power to initiate the extermination of all the others. And what did all this tell one about the German people? Inevitably, that they were on par with their leader. The German people, nothing homogeneous, a patchwork of races and a chaos of different instincts, probably the most thoroughly mixed people – Americans apart – in the world, suddenly launched themselves on a mission to establish the rule of a pure Aryan race. For millennia to come ... Nothing but madness. The Germans were not like the Romans, slowly and patiently building and consolidating their power over centuries. Germany had only just emerged from the feudalism inherent in its division into principalities and miniature kingdoms. The country was not mature to assume great power; in fact, it had shown itself devoid of common political sense. The megalomania of the recently created German Reich was that it believed itself capable of achieving world dominion by its own means. To be so politically naïve, one must either be ignorant of simple facts, or seduced by the devil, or both ...

In the end, there was no excuse for not knowing, for not being able to foresee the consequences. The basis of civilisation was the ability to foresee to the utmost degree what might happen, according to the well-known principle that everything that can go wrong, will go wrong at some time or another. Civilisation, in the last instance, was synonymous with man's intent to conquer nature, and to render her subservient to his will, thus to reduce the unpredictable to a negligible quantity. In short, civilisation declares war on the reign of chance, until very recently the only discernible force permeating the universe. God has no purpose. Man alone has intention. Facing that contradiction, man finally saw no other solution than to charge God with a mission and to employ the devil to do the job for him. In this way man thought he could claim that he was innocent, that he didn't know what he was doing, that everything had suddenly got out of hand through its own volition.

However, man's only duty in the service of civilisation was to weigh risks and possible gains, to try to foresee the consequences of every endeavour. Hans felt this to be his creed as both scientist and champion of civilisation. If there was to be any truth and justice on earth, it was man's task to define and enforce it. And the weakness behind this line of argument was that Hans, as was the case with so many of his colleagues specialising in different disciplines of the natural sciences, was forced to equate reason with mathematical and logical principles, assumed to somehow 'govern' the physical universe. In the end, even ethics could be reduced to a logical problem. If there is no god, then clearly there is no devil either. The questions of good and evil, crime and punishment, must consequently be judged in relative terms, good meaning that which furthers the interest of any man or group of people who happen to be in power; evil meaning that which opposes them. It was as simple as that.

Meanwhile Uranus, son of Chaos and father of the Titans, continues to devour his own children. The deeper Hans descended the kaleidoscopic spiral staircase, the more this fundamental fact imposed itself on him. Every grand civilisation so far had ended by sacrificing its own human members to the capricious purpose of an insatiable tyrant. Hitler's Germany was only the latest to appear in this series of inspired madness.

– Oh, eternal silence of all who have given their lives on the field of battle. If only for a minute you could speak and tell us if there is anything, anything at all, behind the curtain of glory that you were precipitated against as the wounded bull is driven towards the cape! You believed your enemy to be there, and what you received in return for your attack upon him was the sting of his sword. When death came, he was disguised, invisible. Skeleton, swinging the scythe, mounted on your apocalyptic mare, how much chaff have you separated from the wheat today?'

Schröder heard his voice carried on the wings of eerie laughter. They had arrived at the very bottom of the staircase, and he was laughing hysterically at his own joke about death. Then he discovered the lift and was seized by an indescribable horror as Laura, who had patiently shown him the way, opened the door for him, and he realised that she wanted him to descend even farther.

– No, no, I'm not doing it. Do you hear me! I'm not going down there. Never. Ever.

– Well, she said, and gave him a bored look while examining her fingernails, – Then I can't help you. I thought you wanted to meet Claus Uhland, but now, after all your efforts to find him, it turns out that you don't really want to after all. It was all just talk, then.

– Oh yes, but not that way, please ... Not ... that ... way.

– I'm afraid it's the only way, Dr. Schröder. He's waiting for you. The question is, are you ready to see him?

– But how can he be down there? There are only old cells and catacombs, rats and sewers down there. No human being could stand living surrounded by all that filth.

– Oh, well. He doesn't perceive it that way.

– What do you mean, he doesn't perceive ... Has he become blind and deaf, and insensitive to odours as well?

– No, he just doesn't feel it the same way as others would. Besides, this is just the secret passage he would use every day when returning from his work.

– But I remember you telling me that he took a path through the woods to get to the clinic.

– That's right, but he always left work unseen, by way of the subterranean corridors of this building. That's how we all got to know him. He was very popular with the girls around here – but I already told you that.

– But you don't have the key! Schröder exclaimed, in a last attempt to forestall the procedure.

– You'd be surprised, she answered.

The lift jolted and started to move. Once again, he saw the rough walls, the vaults and the dark corridors vanishing into the void. The deeper they descended, the more oppressive it became, almost as if they were diving down into an ocean, where the increasing pressure forces the explorer of the hidden depths to remain fortified within his submersible, entirely relying on the umbilical cord that connects him to the world above and the artificial light of his vessel. The weight above him was tremendous; in no way could he resist its mass. The few lights visible at this depth were like the fluorescent jellyfish one encounters in the deep seas, strange, electrified, multi-fingered creatures, swimming weightlessly in an ocean of darkness, and soon transported beyond one's field of vision. Schröder, losing all remaining strength in his limbs, leaned on Laura, who tried to hold him up. Eventually he became too heavy for her, and she had to let go of him.

He had sunk into a state of lethargy, but in his mind memories from the past stirred in the form of illuminations. Although the sequence of images was whirling fast, it retained a logical and coherent character, in this way differing from the contorted impressions of a dream. Very clearly, he saw himself pursuing his medical studies at university.

One of his favourite subjects had been pathology, not only for its own sake, and in relation to the latest advances in medical science, but also in its historical context. He could sit for hours and admire the precision of da Vinci's sketches of corpses, made at a time when men had begun to look beyond that which was visible to the naked eye in order to find answers to existential questions. In a significant way, the dissection and resultant mapping of the human interior coincided with the beginnings of the exploration of the universe. The two movements were analogous, not least in the sense that the empirical search for the seat of the soul inside the human body corresponded to the quest for God's abode in the universe. If one were to find the former, one might well hope to find the latter. But regardless of the astounding progress in both medicine and astronomy over the centuries since, neither had been discovered. The question of how to define and prove the existence of the human soul, as well as its corollary, the idea and existence of a universal creator, had remained as hypothetical as when Hippocrates formulated his therapeutic oath.

Nevertheless, it was the search for the material substrate of the soul which had prompted Schröder to take up neurological research. He was fascinated by the potential capacity of the human brain, believing it used only a fraction of its real power. In Schröder's view, although basically proceeding from a materialistic standpoint, there was nothing in the functioning of the brain that excluded the possibility of mental travelling in time and space from being worthy of serious investigation. The fact that the key to conscious mind-travel – it could be a drug – had not yet been found did not make its existence less likely, simply harder to discover. He was convinced such a key existed, and as a young man had dreamt of being the first to confirm this by the diligent application of scientific principles and empirical methods of investigation. In the course of later years of experimental research, he had been obliged to modify his immediate objective and turn to experiments and results more in tune with the ambitions and research projects of his superiors. Hans decided he would not jeopardise his career by announcing as a truth that which still remained to be proven. His thesis, "The Aetiology of Paranoia", was a classic study, thoroughly researched and documented, as well as properly cautious in its conclusions. After defending his dissertation in public in Göttingen in May 1927, he had been awarded his doctorate.

The moment was singularly well chosen, as the event coincided with the 290th anniversary of the university's foundation. Because of this, and as a sort of dress rehearsal for the 300th anniversary, there had been an unusual amount of pomp, one venerable beard and whiskers succeeding another, the dean and professors in their tall doctoral hats, the masters in a state of tense anticipation. The orchestral concert in the Lutheran Sankt-Jacobi church by the Jüdinstraße, had opened, he remembered, with Brahms' Academic Festival Overture, which so captivated and inspired the listeners that they all joined in singing the Gaudeamus Igitur theme of the old student song. Then Schicksalslied by the same composer, a setting of the poem by the genial and schizophrenic Hölderlin, sung by the university men's choir, this followed by Mendelssohn's Reformation Symphony. He remembered the brilliant background to the music, the golden altarpiece with carved statues of prophets, disciples, saints and churchmen. Solemn speeches on the subjects of past and future, tradition and progress, were delivered from the rostrum garnished with laurel and mistletoe; there were endless banquets, a horn of plenty pouring beer from one end and Rhine wine from the other. And then there was Beatrice, the young, beautiful nurse he had just met, so straightforward in her manner and feelings that she did not even try to hide the tears decorating her blushing cheeks at the moment of his triumph.

But outside this exclusive confrèrie of scientists and scholars, the ambience was not exactly gay. Jazz, Charleston, champagne, music hall turns and sweet nostalgic barber-shop interpretations of German folk songs in the Metropolis, could not hide from the astute observer the fact that the liberal Republic was at the end of its tether. Hans, intelligent and alert in spite of his blinkered passion for neurology, had a presentiment of an earthquake still to arrive, for the time being expressing itself as a mounting tension within him, a feeling of impending panic. Strung like a vibrant cord, he was appointed assistant physician at the renowned psychiatric clinic of Eglfing-Haar, where he was to remain and dutifully perform his professional obligations for three years. It was during this time that he proposed to and married Beatrice, who until 1928 worked as a nurse at Göttingen Universitätsklinik.

The train of images, hitherto almost in chronological order, then took a sudden backward leap, and Hans saw himself as a young boy. His grandparents used to live in an old house in the village of Calw in Schwaben. Together with his younger siblings, Grete and Ernst, Hans used to spend his summer vacations there. From an early age accustomed to trekking in the hills, he often went on long solitary excursions, during which he looked for new specimens to add to his collections of insects, especially butterflies, as well as geological samples. He often stopped for no reason at all and just listened to the peaceful sound of the brook, to the wind rustling in the leaves, and the birds chasing through the air. Sometimes he saw falcons hovering among the clouds far above a distant hilltop. At such moments he was seized by the grandeur of creation, feeling the presence of an immense being of which he was a minuscule, yet intrinsic and inalienable part. Perhaps it was this childhood experience, that everything on earth exists for a reason, that formed the basis of much of his later views on man and nature. To him the psychological deviation from a norm defined by the social structure of human beings was not alien to nature. On the contrary, even perversions were encompassed by the great being, in whose mind there were no such chimerae as good or evil, useless or useful, nor a distinction between sick and healthy. One could learn from everything, and Hans, curious, at times even dreaming and poetical, wanted above all to learn and get to know the world. In the course of time his butterflies and minerals were exchanged for the incredible variety of mental aberrations classified under the heading psychopathology. Luckily for him, however, there still remained moments when he looked upon this strange fauna as the great being himself upon his many monsters, and he came to the, albeit philosophically vague, conclusion that everything had its place, otherwise it simply wouldn't exist.

It seemed that Hans had to some degree inherited this gracious attitude toward life from his grandfather Wilhelm, who in his day had served as a minister of the Protestant church, and who had also been a Protestant in more than just a formal religious way. An advocate of sobriety in matters of faith, Wilhelm Schröder had had difficulty in accepting the dogma of the virgin birth and also that of the holy trinity, holding that the transubstantiation of Father and Son into a whimsical third entity represented an attempt to replace God with something even greater, and that the very meaning of a unique God, responsible for the entire creation, thereby was lost in speculation and theological subtlety. For this Wilhelm had not only been hated by Catholics, but on several occasions reprimanded by the bishop's office in Tübingen Diocese. Thus, it was in the last instance quite a miracle that he managed to retain his position until, hinting at his mature age and happy to grant him a pension before it was due, they could urge him to retire. In the autumn of his life, Wilhelm eventually reconciled himself with the official view of the church, but seemed at the same time to somehow have lost his faith. Apart from pronouncing grace at mealtimes, he no longer appeared to have much interest in practising any religion whatsoever. Nonetheless, it happened that Hans, who slept in the bedroom next to his, heard him move around restlessly in his chamber, loudly complaining that demons were assailing him, pouring out proverbs to fight them, singing psalms and praying to the saviour to heal the wounds that the soldiers of Satan had left in his heart.

In the morning following such a night, his grandfather was exhausted, and his grandmother – a loveable grey-haired woman, who in spite of the gentleness of her nature had always stood by her man's side and stoutly defended him against slanderous accusations – came to cleanse his profusely perspiring body with the aid of soap, a bowl of water and towels. Hans stood in the doorway and watched his grandmother at work, while Grete and Ernst had respectfully taken up positions in the adjacent room. Grandfather himself was semi-conscious, yet majestic as an afflicted prophet with his long white beard and disorderly hair. Later the same day, the good spirits would usually return. No mention as to the causes of his distress was ever made; even the slightest insinuation on the part of the grandchildren was met with grandmother's categorical disapproval.

Hans recalled all this in the most minute detail, down to the very words and gestures of their daily doings and conversations, but then, as suddenly as the images of these happy times had appeared, the air turned frosty and the sky grey. He saw the graveyard in Calw, where on a cold February morning they had said farewell to Wilhelm, and then, in the middle of November barely three years later, to his wife Elisabeth. Hans' father, Gerhard, had only one brother, in need of money for his Hamburg trading business, so it was decided that the house should be sold, and the money from it divided between the brothers. Gerhard lent his share of the proceeds to his brother. But as the brother some years later tragically perished in an accident at sea, and his company was run down with debt, Gerhard never saw that money again.

Gerhard worked as an engineer, first with the German State Railways, then at AG Siemens in Berlin. Later he became independent, and set up his own electrical business. The company survived the ordeal of the First World War, but during the depression of the 1920s it too faced bankruptcy. Gerhard had to try to find suitable work, but it wasn't easy as employment was scarce and the national economy shaky. Although fundamentally of jovial disposition, these blows of fate emphasised his melancholic streak, and he grew somewhat taciturn, accusing himself of having been a neglectful father, and society as a whole of being corrupt. He had his drinking bouts as well. Luckily, he was not a violent man, and he never caused his wife, Lotte, or the children physical harm during his morose moments. Besides, he was often overcome by guilt at squandering household money. By the middle of the 1920s he managed to pull himself together. He found himself a respectable and quite well-paid job as an engineer at Krupps Industries in Düsseldorf, and moved there with Lotte. The children by then were all in their twenties and doing well. Hans, who had won a scholarship and received a very favourable mention from his school, left to pursue his studies at university. Ernst wanted to become an engineer like his father, and Grete, a sweet-looking blonde girl, had hopes of getting married. While waiting, she helped an uncle on her mother's side to grow and sell vegetables.

On the surface everything looked fine again, Gerhard having come full circle. His remaining problem was that he resented being an employee. For him it was a failure, and since he couldn't see how he himself could be blamed for the downfall of his business – Gerhard had always been a conscientious and hard-working man – he started to look about for a scapegoat. Like many other people, he began identifying the problem with the Jewish dominance of the press and finance. Although he did not share the racial bias of the Nazi party – to him Jews were simply a too-influential clique of people – he began to spoil family and other conversations by strewing pejorative remarks round, his leitmotif being the infamous slogan, "Jews are our misfortune". A consequence was that he became estranged within his own family circle, as all the children had Jewish friends both at school and elsewhere. When nobody would listen to him at home any more, he went to the beer halls and attended political meetings. However, Gerhard's quest for independence made him a less than suitable subject for party membership, and he was not willing to work for an organisation whose goals did not, in the last instance, coincide with his own. After all, Gerhard simply wanted his private business back. These people on the other hand wanted every enterprise to become subservient to the state. That was wrong as well! Dissatisfied with the propaganda, he stopped attending meetings and he never held membership in either the NSDAP or any other radical political organisation.

By now his wife Lotte had to endure most of his complaints about the lamentable situation of the nation. To her the notions of right or wrong in society were of far less concern than the question of cohesion and solidarity within the family. She would therefore do her best to get Gerhard to understand that if he continued in this way, he would end up as a grumpy old man abandoned and despised by everyone. For a while it seemed as though Gerhard would heed her warnings, but then the moment came when Hans proudly introduced his beautiful fiancée Beatrice to his family. Father, at first thoroughly charmed, changed his attitude completely when he found out she was Jewish. There was a terrible scene in which father accused son of being a traitor, a mere puppet dangling from the strings of unscrupulous businessmen. Hans, his soul in flames, left the house swearing never to return. Lotte was destroyed and fell ill. From now on the issue of marrying Beatrice became just as much a matter of protest against his father as an act of love. Hans refused to admit that the one thing had anything to do with the other, but if he had listened to his heart alone, and not to the sound and fury enveloping it, he might have asked himself why on earth it was that this hesitation continued to exist within him, even when everything spoke so clearly in Beatrice's favour. However, on Betarice's incentive, Hans made a last effort to mend fences, and he never forgave his father for refusing to come to the wedding. It was the final breach, and although Hans was in fact relieved that his father didn't turn up to poison the atmosphere with his acrimonious remarks, he was soon to realise that from then onwards, the parting of their ways was as inevitable as it was irrevocable.

In October 1939, only months before the outbreak of the war, Gerhard suffered a haemorrhage of the brain from which he failed to recover. For one week he lay paralysed. Then he died. Hans did not visit him, and father and son were never reconciled. Nonetheless, it turned out that Hans had not been disinherited. In response to his mother's repeated pleas, Hans attended the funeral, where he met his siblings and the rest of the family, united in the feeling of burying the hatchet with the old man. It was never openly stated, but it was clear that everybody now regarded Hans, the eldest, as head of the Schröder clan. Since no pronounced anti-Semitic opinions were held by other members of the family, there were reasons to hope that things had finally taken a turn for the better.

On the other hand, the political situation had deteriorated to the point at which any gesture of peace and understanding was regarded as being antagonistic to "the will of the people's soul". Hans returned to Freiburg, feeling more alone than ever, profoundly worried about the future. His father's death had deepened his acute sense of responsibility, particularly in regard to his own children. And the one thing he wanted to make sure, was that they should never have to be ashamed of their father's actions. At all times he should be able to look them in the eye and explain what he was doing. He wanted to give them that elementary notion of honour and respect in the absence of which human dignity and freedom of choice cannot truly exist. In no other way did he want to influence their choices in life. All this implied that he did not wish ever, or in any respect, to resemble his father. Yet there had once been brighter days; days when father and son had wandered about as if in a garden of Eden; happy childhood days when Hans' father was the greatest man who ever lived, and the two of them were invincible, together; days when they were doing woodwork in the cellar, building model railways, listening to music on the radio and visiting the zoo; days when Hans' dearest wish had been to become exactly *like* his father ...

The descent from those heights of bliss and limitless confidence had been like a violent crash into the reality of life on earth; and here he was, his father dead, once and for all. Now it was all up to him to create the family life he had always wanted and missed for so long. It was up to him to remake himself in the image of the father he had once known, and to send to oblivion the one that had turned his wrath, frustration and jealousy against him. It was a work of therapy, of self-healing. In the process he needed to convince himself of Beatrice's loyalty, and of his sincere love for her, since once the old man had been laid to rest, it had become senseless to pursue love and marriage as a revolt against something. The pretext had fallen. Now was the moment of truth.

Arriving at the bottom of the shaft, the lift stopped. Schröder, trying to hide within himself, had shrivelled up in a corner. He turned away his eyes from the wrought-iron gate as a prisoner in a dark solitary cell, who when the door is finally swung open, averts his gaze from the sudden glare of daylight. Contrary to his expectations, the corridor at the bottom of the complex did not present the same unforgiving aspect as all the others they had passed. It didn't meander at odd angles, nor did it abruptly ascend or descend. Instead it extended in a straight gallery, its architectural style being more reminiscent of the Uffizi Palace in Florence than of the dungeons of an old prison. There was concealed lighting along the walls, which themselves supported a vault made up of squares of what appeared to be exquisite polished marble. The air, again contrary to expectations, did not smell of mildew or dust, nor was it heavy to breathe, but seemed light, almost rarefied. Twin lines of Greek columns were painted white and inlaid with gold.

The sudden change of atmosphere had a reviving effect on Schröder, who now slowly got to his feet and walked out of the lift cage. Each of his steps resounded clearly, as if echoed back to him from the vaults of a cathedral, but as soon as he stopped the sound died. A little farther along the aisle new phenomena captivated his eye. On both sides, between the row of columns, showcases the size of coffins had been placed, containing all kinds of natural wonders and monstrosities. One of these exhibited an enormous hound with no fewer than three heads protruding from its neck. In his day Hans had seen some specimens of Siamese twins, both human and animal, some of which could probably still be found in the collection of natural oddities at the Museum of Natural History in Salzburg. But this was not just some random zoological anomaly. This was a veritable freak of nature. It was an adult animal, big as a calf, that must have led a long, healthy, and, above all, ferocious life before being killed, preserved and put on display. The three heads were all equally well developed, showing magnificent rows of teeth that could rend any animal to shreds. Three pairs of voracious eyes must have given the animal panoramic 360° vision, the six pointed ears exceptional hearing, and the long muscular legs the strength of a lion and speed of a panther. Provided that the beast had been able to coordinate its various nervous impulses and obtain a degree of co-operation between its heads, it must in fact have been a lethal machine such as the world has not seen since the last Tyrannosaurus Rex walked the earth in search of prey. Or rather, since palaeontological evidence suggested that the giant saurian had in all probability been a slow-running scavenger, this was a real killing machine combining the savage gluttony of the giant lizard with the fierce agility of the sabre-toothed tiger. But how had it been possible for three different brains, and consequently the beginnings of three cerebral cortices – that is, three nervous systems – to function in concord? One head might see something here, another something over there, while the third wanted to sleep. Unless, of course, they had been forged as a team, knowing by instinct that they would survive together or not at all. An anarchy of will was the one great danger they faced, so, as long as each head subordinated itself to the common belly and its needs, the organism would remain practically invincible. Since the animal had obviously attained maturity, there could have been one iron will dominant over the others', one head perhaps that was in command and obeyed by the others. The middle one? Although identical in appearance to the other two, it might have been the general, constantly processing the information provided by the subordinate heads; ordering attacks and retreats, ambushes and strategic withdrawals to lure a victim into his trap ... But once the jaws had sunk into the prey, anarchy and destruction could be unleashed again without danger, since it wouldn't matter which head fed the belly as long as it was fed. "What a ghastly sight it must have been to see this beast tear its prey apart," Schröder thought. And where had it been born? It seemed unlikely that present-day Europe would be able to produce anything like this. Asia then? Or Africa? It was some kind of dog, for sure, but bigger than any he had ever seen, and certainly totally wild. The only master this creature would have obeyed was death itself, he concluded, and moved on to the next showcase.

Inside was an open sarcophagus, its lid left leaning against the far side of the case. It contained the remains of a mummy, judging from its size probably that of a male person. The body was surrounded by precious stones and jewellery, tools, baskets that had once contained various foods, and weapons, such as a spear, a bow, arrows with different heads, some of metal, others of stone, others still of animal bone. On the chest, above the heart, rested a skin purse and some gold coins. His hands had been arranged to clasp it, so as to give the impression, perhaps, of one asking to be favourably received in the next world by virtue of his earthly riches and pious veneration of the gods. Beneath the purse, on the belly of the mummy, a little parcel could be seen, containing nothing but a few rough, circular items of a yellowish, almost golden colour, perhaps pieces of bread, or some kind of glazed biscuits. The wrapping on these mysterious bread rolls bore a number of hieroglyphs. At the very end of an obviously long and elaborate sequence making mention of the papyrus, the crocodile, the ibis and the god Anubis, there were three letters written in Greek: CBR. What most intrigued Schröder, however, were three small human skulls, obviously those of children, laid at the feet of the embalmed corpse. Each one had been propped up so that its mouth remained open, and where the tongue had once been, a gold coin had been inserted.

Next came, not one single case, but a long series of cylindrical glass vessels arranged on shelves and containing various extreme, abnormal and deformed human embryos preserved in formaldehyde or alcohol, some of them in very advanced stages of development, some even consecrated to science after birth. An array of megalocephalic and microcephalic heads alternated with embryos having no limbs at all, or too many, or just four but in all the wrong places. One foetus displayed the almost unheard-of anomaly of having legs instead of arms, and arms where there should be legs. There was an abundance of embryos in which normal development had been held back because of a monstrous growth in some other part. There was for instance one case where the face had become one big nose, and another where the head of the child was no more than an amorphous carbuncle attached to an enormous cauliflower ear three or four times its size. Some cylinders contained embryos that had no reproductive organs, others hermaphrodites of all kinds. There were human heads with ears that had retrograded into gills, and where the fingers had grown far apart, though they were still connected with tissue so as to give the creature frog palms and perhaps the capacity to both live and swim under water. There were seemingly human foetuses covered in saurian scales, others with fins and yet others having kaleidoscopic insect eyes. A child, or rather an indefinable creature having left its embryonic stage behind, looked like something that had been put together by the dismemberment of a small human body. It looked as if the body parts had been reassembled at random and finally blindly glued together. The gem of the collection, however, was neither a foetus nor a baby of any species, but an adult dwarf, normal for his kind in most respects, except in this, that it possessed an enormous male reproductive organ emerging from right under a vagina. The creature was thus endowed with the capacity of mating with itself, if not actually of making itself pregnant ...

Amazed, Schröder stared at this apparition, quite unable to determine if it wasn't, after all, some kind of projected image. Walking around the transparent case he was unable to convince himself of the insubstantiality of the macabre figure inside it. On the contrary, closer scrutiny made it seem more and more real to him. The paradox of a higher organism's being capable of reproducing itself was as revolting as it was alien to biological science. It implied a contradiction in terms, an organic machine that sustains its own motion by its own means throughout all eternity. In other words, it represented a closed system of reproduction, an organic test tube, as it were, in which egg and sperm carry identical hereditary traits. It should consequently produce any number of doubles, or natural copies, of itself, in this way prolonging its own ephemeral physical existence indefinitely. Provided there was a womb inside that creature, the exact replication of a life form was at least theoretically possible. Thus, in a sense, the secret of eternal life had been discovered. Only one would have to abandon entirely the romantic notion of an old man and woman sipping *aqua permanens* from an Arcadian spring, to be transformed into two beautiful naked children innocently uniting under a shower of fragrant spring flowers on the eve of divine creation. Eternal natural life was indeed possible, but it wasn't beautiful, poetic and romantic. It was grotesque. At the expense of being a monster, one could survive forever. Eternal life as experienced by a degenerate dwarf ...

At some distance along the arcade Schröder now perceived light coming from an opening on one side. As he moved nearer he noticed that the lights themselves were dimming. A putrid odour reached his nostrils, a stench of sewers so intense that he at first reeled backwards and almost fell to the ground. Then came the real shock. Seeking a way to avoid the smell Schröder looked around for an escape. Since the closest appeared to be by way of the chamber from which the light emanated, he made a quick decision to defy the horrid odour of putrefaction and to boldly launch himself forward. At the same moment he saw that he had stepped into some liquid or other. In trying to step back out of the puddle, he trod into mud. By now the realisation was inescapable – he was standing in a lake, about one inch deep, primarily composed of urine. The bottom sediment of the lake was apparently of various ages and states of decomposition, but homogenous insofar as it was composed of human excrement. Panic mounted inside him and, although he had for a long time been oblivious of Laura's existence, he now desperately called her name, begging, imploring her to take him out of there. But the only thing he heard was his own voice, sounding like the cry of a wounded animal. The echo of his terrified bellowing finally faded. Schröder tried his best to avoid stepping in the faeces all around him. Zig-zagging, he reached the opening at the side of the corridor gallery and turned into the adjacent room in an attempt to get away from the filth. At the far end of this fairly spacious room he discerned a familiar writing desk on a platform at some height above the shallow lake. Behind the desk a male figure was sitting, apparently busy signing some documents. His right hand, after having written down some words on each paper, was lifted as the left hand removed the sheet and added it to a pile. Having covered half the distance toward the man and his desk, Schröder moaned. The other put down his black fountain pen, looked up, sheltered his eyes with his hand, as if trying to locate a creature through dazzling light, and then rose from his chair with a welcoming smile.

– Ah, Dr. Schröder, if you only knew how happy I am to see you again!

– Uhland? … Is it you?

– Oh yes, it's me all right. But come – let's get you out

of that awful mess first. You see, we have had some terrible problems with the pipes lately, but they're working on them, and soon this inconvenience should be taken care of for ever.

– Inconvenience?

– Yes, I mean the stuff from the sewers. It's not, hmm, very pleasant ...

– Not very pleasant?

– Ah, well, there you go. We'll get you some fresh water, soap and towels in a minute. I know this is all most unfortunate, but apart from that you have to admit that the location is quite extraordinary. By the way, did you enjoy my little exhibition? I call it Sankt-Anna Collection. It took us quite some time to get it all together, but it's nice, isn't it? And the best thing is that nobody knows about it. We are at the cutting edge of science down here, Schröder. And this is just the beginning. Ah, how happy I am that you could finally make it! It has been such a long time since we had a good talk together. Now, you go and wipe off your shoes, and then you must tell me all about your adventures.

Uhland stretched out his hand in a friendly gesture. Schröder not only noticed that the hand was meticulously manicured, but also that, in the stench of the gutter around them, it smelt of Eau de Cologne. Mixing as it was with the smell of filth, the scent was utterly nauseating. Schröder felt the urge to vomit right in front of him, but by a supreme effort of will, he held himself in check once again, and forced Uhland to yield as he approached the desk on which the documents were stacked. A quick glance was quite enough to convince him of their real nature. He turned and looked the other man straight in the eye.

– What the hell is going on here, Uhland?

– Research – the most promising research you could possibly dream of, I have results that …

– Are you out of your mind? Don't you realise the war is over? You can't do this. They'll hang you if they find out.

– They will never find out. That's the reason we had this place constructed in the abandoned mine shafts under Sankt-Anna. The only unfortunate thing is that we had to pass between the communal sewers in some places. From time to time there are still leaks, as you can see.

– This is not Sankt-Anna. The hospital was many miles from here. Besides, as we both know, it's not operational any longer. I have been there myself, and it is all shut down. So what kind of private show are you running down here?

– Let me tell you. But first, allow me to clean your shoes, dear colleague.

Uhland made Schröder sit on a chair while he himself leaned down and began to wipe his shoes with a sponge which he first dipped in some detergent, then in chlorine. He polished the shoes and buffed them with a waxed cloth.

– They're saying you're dead, Schröder finally said, after incredulously watching Uhland move around on his knees, as if applying ointment to his feet.

– Well, that makes two of us, doesn't it? Anyway, so much the better, since we are both obviously of better service to science officially dead than officially alive.

– What do you mean?

Instead of answering, Uhland ushered Schröder to a narrow door at the end of the platform. Behind the door a staircase led upward. As they both mounted, the odour from the sewers gradually receded and was replaced by that of anaesthetic and disinfectant. He could still clearly discern the sweet smell of Uhland's cologne blending with the smell of chlorine from his own shoes. They entered a square room lit by a single light bulb, and containing little more than a film projector, a few plain chairs and a screen.

– Please sit down, Dr. Schröder. Let me show you how we continued the project after your alleged demise. It was all conducted along the general lines that you had already laid down before moving on to still higher tasks within the organisation ...

– I was sent to the front!

– Oh yes, so they kept telling us. But we knew better, of course. Especially since the attestations and reports came back from headquarters bearing your signature.

– I had nothing to do with it!

– Oh, really? Well, we knew you were with us in spirit all the same. Look, and judge for yourself.

Uhland switched off the light and started the projector.

– We have recorded every stage of experimentation. It was all classified material of course, and only I of the local staff knew that there were hidden cameras. So what you are about to see has by a twist of fate become my private collection, as the programme was terminated toward the end of the war, and orders were issued to destroy all remaining evidence pertaining to the T4.

– What about your staff?

– They had to be taken care of as well.

– You mean they were killed?

– Removed, yes.

– And you yourself. Why didn't they kill you?

– Because I was already presumed dead, and then I had

your personal protection, of course …

– I don't know what you're talking about, but I guess there will be plenty of time for you to explain yourself once you have been brought to justice.

– Oh, don't get all worked up now, Dr. Schröder. You know it's not good for your health.

– To hell with my health, and yours! I know about the destruction of the wards, too. The first thing I did upon arriving in Freiburg was to go and check the wards. There was absolutely nothing left of them.

– That's right. But even when they were in use, they were not directly connected with T4-related activities. The actual research centre was situated down here. Now look. Initially we conducted many experiments in which viruses of communicable diseases were injected into the patients. In the interest of our medical industry, demanding some means of producing efficient vaccines cheaply in great quantities, we administered typhus, yellow fever, smallpox, polio, malaria and dysentery to a great many people. This for instance is an example of remarkable resistance. This incredibly robust human specimen, a nigger sentenced to life for having raped and killed seven women in Tunisia, was brought here with a group of other coloured felons. He was given yellow fever and became very ill. However after seven days he began to recover, and would undoubtedly have survived if he had received nourishment and proper care. Even after twelve days, deprived of food and water for the last three, the man was still alive, as you can see. He was even capable of demanding his right to be released from the experiment, since he had survived it. In the end we had no alternative but to inject him with thanatoxin.

Eventually the epidemiological project had to be abandoned because of the great risks the medical staff were running of contracting diseases involuntarily. In addition, cyanide gas, in the form of granulates called Zyklon B, and other chemicals introduced into these hermetically sealed chambers were dangerous to handle, and the premises had to be closed for days before we could use it again.

We then concentrated on studying the effects of sterilisation by X-ray. To this end we used some convicts, but mostly Jews and Gypsies selected for deportation. The results were encouraging. Here you have our contraption. In one of the wards we had people lining up to register for what we told them was a medical examination. At the counter, behind which a nurse was sitting, they were told to fill out a form. This procedure took about two minutes, during which time each individual was exposed to powerful radiation. This smiling woman, for instance, who believes that her mentally retarded daughter is about to receive medical care, has just been rendered sterile by a high dose of radiation. The procedure itself is painless for the patient, and the nurse is protected against the harmful rays by a thick lead shield placed between the inner and outer walls of the counter. The outcome of this series of experimentation was very positive in both male and female cases, the sole inconvenience being that the patients would not for ever remain unaware of their inflicted infertility. There were also some secondary effects, such as skin rashes, disturbances in the endocrine system and a heightened risk of contracting lymphatic cancer.

The clinical euthanasia programme, properly speaking, was carried out in two ways. Efficient especially in cases where the patient had no or very little awareness of his own state of mind, the first method simply consisted of a progressive diminution of food intake until the patient succumbed due to lack of nourishment. It was a practical and convenient method. It had the advantage as well of allowing certificates stressing alternative causes of death to be issued and sent to the patient's relatives. In this way there were few objections on the part of the relatives to the procedures, which were always carried out gradually and under the greatest possible discretion.

With other patients, such as the hyperactive, schizophrenic and the mentally retarded, we used carbon monoxide gas. The patients, moved from their original place of detention by way of three or four intermediary stations, were finally committed to Sankt-Anna. They were sent to the shower rooms, and here we see a group of backward children, some 50% of them Mongoloid, about to enter the dressing-room, where nurses help them to take off their clothes. As you can easily verify by their smiling faces, they have no notion what is going to happen to them. The staff was instructed always to treat them cheerfully and with indulgence, so as to make the transition from dressing-room to the showers as smooth and undramatic as possible. Even when in the shower-room, the majority of the subjects remained unaware of its actual purpose. There were real soap, brushes, sponges and towels to hand, and the showers contained temperate water to preserve the impression of a weekly bath. The carbon monoxide gas from two diesel-engined buses was then introduced into the showers through the ventilation system. Odourless and unnoticeable, it had a subtle effect. As you can see with these images captured one hour later, everyone present in the shower-room is peacefully asleep. Only on very few occasions were there scenes of panic. It was really one of the easiest and most cost-effective means of bringing about a truly merciful death. And the administration in Berlin declared itself very satisfied with the implementation of the programme, and urged us to continue on a larger scale. But then we ran into logistical problems. It was unavoidable that some members of the German population would observe the transfers from time to time. Patients were always transported in buses with tinted windows, but during transferral the kitchen staff, for instance, might observe something that was not meant for their eyes. Or there might be mischievous schoolboys hiding behind dustbins in one of the exchange zones. Soon enough, there were rumours of people disappearing without trace from the national hospitals. Since transports therefore had to be protected by enhanced security methods, a special security force was trained for the purpose. But this also meant higher costs, and demands for more manpower. So in the end, even the initially promising carbon monoxide method proved hard to apply in accordance with industrial principles. Luckily, I was not to be in charge of these operations after 1942. Instead I was entrusted with far-ranging responsibilities for a very interesting part of the preventive eugenics programme destined to succeed the preliminary elimination programme. I was to bring into being an era of medically controlled as well as judicially approved births. In short, my task was now to study genetic manipulation and the possibility of producing ideal human beings.

– You are a very sick man, Uhland!

– Maybe so, but my goal is to create health. Think of it

realistically, Schröder. Even the race of which we are members will soon be just another relic of the past. In the middle of the war I realised that the Führer, although in principle right about the necessity of selective birth control, had nevertheless – and possibly under the influence of bad advice – taken the wrong path. There is no such thing as a pure Aryan race. It is a myth. Medical and biological science hold the keys to the future inasmuch as they will soon help us to overcome the cumbersome procedures of bringing suitable men and women together for procreation. Even the eugenic birth programme *Lebensborn* had its unavoidable limitations. It catered primarily to the SS and eventually ended up in assuming economic and social responsibilities which stood in no defensible ratio to the possible benefits. Women in the Lebensborn programme didn't even have to work, although there were no men to provide for them. It was a pure expense. The system was both costly and time-consuming, and would ultimately have been ill-suited to satisfy the ever-growing demand for an increase in loyal, perfectly adaptable and productive citizens. Lebensborn was based on the idea of promoting an Aryan aristocracy. Today, genetics tells us that there is no such thing as blue blood. The elite we want is an elect society of highly efficient brains, veritable masterminds. But this is not primarily a racial idea. The notion of the innate inequality of the races is outdated and fundamentally false. On the contrary, the differences are all in the genetics. Though we can't expect a spontaneous increase in the creation of genius, artificial insemination may one day help us at least to make it appear less randomly. We don't quite yet have the tools in our hands, but there is no question that we keep moving closer by the day to the heart of the problem. Meanwhile, as we try to solve the mystery, we must ensure the steady regeneration of workers and civil servants in the general fabric of society. As for women, we shall discreetly influence them in their preferences and choices.

– So your idea is to force women to get pregnant by artificial means, and then you and your like will make sure that the male hereditary traits are the ones best suited to deliver workers to this colossal beehive.

– Oh, no, that's another obsolete idea. Forcing people to procreate in a certain way will always in the end create resistance and resentment. The new solution is radically different. Instead of forcing a preventive eugenics programme upon the population, the propaganda must be fashioned in such a way that women learn to do the right thing themselves. And the first step in this direction is not, as Hitler believed – or pretended to believe in order to keep up the appearance of an alliance with the Vatican – to reinforce the family structure, but to weaken it. Close families are in fact rather unwilling to accept binding loyalties outside the bloodline. In this respect the family is conservative, and an obstacle to the machine of the state. Families must instead be dissolved, and female sexuality given free rein.

– But that will result in chaos! And cause a revolution!

– Exactly. But we can also foresee that wherever woman turns, she will eventually need protection, a roof over her head, and economic as well as social security for herself and her children. Thus, the idea is to expose women to men who are sexually very active and fertile, men who can satisfy a woman's immediate desire and then be disposed of once pregnancy has been confirmed. The disposal of the inseminator will be made all the easier since the women themselves are no longer interested in keeping a traditional family structure together, not to say, constitutionally incapable of it. And, true enough, the progress of eugenics has been slowed down by the restraining idea and reality of the family. We must begin to consider human beings exactly as we regard other animals. As far as breeding is concerned, this means that a woman – given that she is physiologically and mentally sound – does not wish to couple with a genetically inferior male. Like a mare she will prefer to be impregnated by the best and strongest stallion – that's all. Many of our former colleagues, unfortunately, were still too prudish to admit this fundamental truth, believing that there was some inherent prerogative in white skin, Germanic virtues and Norse mythology. The sooner we stop regarding the problem as a question of finding the right Aryan man for the right Aryan woman, the sooner we will move closer to understanding the real issue. The final solution presents itself with the clarity of a revelation. It is the Negro – the word taken both literally and metaphorically – who will help us to build the future state. Hundreds of years of enforced slavery have made Negroes physically strong and enduring. They were a reliable source of manpower throughout the southern states of North America, the Caribbean and South America until the dawn of industrialisation, when machines began to replace them. Supported by the victorious ideas of democracy and liberal capitalism, the physical as well as the psychological liberation of the Negro is bound to coincide with the liberation of woman. The two will eventually find each other by virtue of an inexorable logic, the common denominator being that a woman, at heart, instinctively identifies with and feels herself akin to a slave. The foremost social engineering problem of the future is therefore that of finding a way of controlling and using the power provided by a race of manumitted slaves.

– Oh yes, brilliant! Schröder exclaimed. – And how are you going to get these people here in the first place? By sending brigs to Jamaica and the Gold Coast, shanghaiing as many vigorous natives as you can, shipping them to Hamburg and then spreading them all over Germany like so much manure? Has your brain gone soft, or what? Do you seriously believe the world to be some kind of private laboratory, in which you personally can decide what kind of homunculus to produce next? There is no way that the genetic quality of procreation can be controlled, even on a limited scale. You can't tell people with whom they are supposed to mate and whom they should reject. You …

– Old Schröder, always impetuous, always taking everything just a bit too literally! Uhland sighed. – There will of course be nothing of the sort. Blackness is just the symbol, if you will. What we have in mind now, Schröder, is something infinitely more sophisticated. Of course we won't force anyone to do anything against his or her wishes. Be assured, there will be enough placid Aryan specimens left to survive into the future. What I am proposing is a very subtle method of gradually improving the genetic quality of any given population, the steady regeneration of more and more average, more and more qualitatively even populations.

First of all, since the future will see spontaneous immigration from African and Arab countries as a consequence of the collapse of colonial and imperial power, Europe will see itself invaded by the same peoples she once subjugated.

No need to look for the Negro in the Caribbean; he will be here of his own volition. The innate female instinct for natural selection and improvement of the species will then do the rest. There will certainly not be a massive racial suicide, since a majority of Aryan women will still continue to look for the social and economic security a responsible white man is capable of providing. But look at America, where the dreaded racial war I'm predicting is already in full swing, where the ruling class, once almost exclusively Anglo-Saxon, is in steady decrease in both number and effective societal power. The America of the future will afford the spectacle of a gradual but relentless dethronement of a once predominant caste. The difference between them and us is precisely this, that they will perish by it, whereas by having the foresight to be aware of what so-called liberal democracy holds in store for us, we will prevail. Our society will be a mimicry of those other, degenerate, societies which are in the making in those parts of the world where the strident cry for equality between men and women, as well as between the races, has become the norm.

So let us act in accordance with ancient wisdom. The Jesuits well knew there was no individual salvation in store for the common man. But they knew just as well to keep quiet about it, so as to avoid social distress and upheaval. The same applies to the future race of new slaves in society. They must never know that they are being used in the service of something higher, something beyond personal ambition and greed. The trick is precisely that we must give – not only to men, but to the coming generations of women too – the impression that they are free to pursue their own luck by their own desire.

By way of propaganda, what the Americans call advertising, we can, given time, make superior black male specimens attractive to average and less than average white women – this already implying the improvement, not its opposite, of the genetic material. The only thing we need to do is gradually to remove the taboos regarding primitive man that are at present ingrained in these women, and replace this image of fear with one of comfort. The state must guarantee that no woman who allows a Negro into her bed would have to endure the occasional capricious violence and social irresponsibility of the savage. Consequently, the ideal citizen of the future is of mixed genetic background, a mulatto in all respects, considerably weakened in his spiritual integrity, but endowed with easy talent, and strong in his social ambition. And for this very reason, future man will have as his overwhelming ambition the total adaptation to existing circumstances.

We will ensure there will be no path to success other than that of bowing beneath the yoke of spiritual mediocrity. We will discourage all general education that does not have as its aim the building of a people fit for the kind of society we want. The people should be given the chance of free movement and interaction with one another – even to express their personal feelings and opinions – but the slightest transgression on their part vis à vis the legal system must be severely reprimanded, if necessary punished. And the brilliant thing about all this is that the women themselves will be the first to cry out for the punishment of the men who dared to beat them. And we will condemn them, not in terms of general racial prejudice, but in setting an example to others. Men will realise that it is better to leave women when they begin to expect men's subservience to their social and economic needs, and instead, leave all that to us. We will then make sure that the men work, and that they pay their taxes and their alimony. We thereby also make women economically dependent on us, and we take over the responsibility for bringing up children in the images of our future citizens.

The women, recognising the general unreliability and innate promiscuity of the coloured man, will willingly turn themselves over to us, being happy to accept the new kind of slavery with a human face that we offer them. This won't happen straight away, and it remains, at a theoretical level, at odds with the idea of family life and family values. Nevertheless women, each having children by two, three or more different and in effect anonymous men, will eventually, by virtue of their demands for emancipation and freedom from cultural restraint, find themselves joining informal female groups, or herds. In a sense they'll begin spontaneously to form a kind of matriarchal society in which men have been reduced to the role of inseminators, and in which each child is brought to up be complaisant, and in all its actions, however disparate they may seem, to pay tribute to the Queen.

– To the Queen?

– Yes, Schröder, this is the very essence of the plan, the "Nucleus of the Poodle", if you will! We will place a woman at the head of society, as prime minister, as president, a Führerin for both men and women. Her message to the world will be one of peace and understanding – except in the case of sexual transgression – and she and her acolytes will ensure that men employed in fathering children stay in line. Men will never again create havoc, because they will now be controlled – with our deliberate consent – by women ... But of course, this is only the outward aspect of the power structure of the future. In reality we will be more securely in control than ever we were in the Nazi era. We run business, we make sure that the economy works, we build and construct, and we select the work-force and make sure it meets our standards. With the aid of more and more sophisticated diagnostic techniques and methods, we doctors become the ultimate guarantors of a healthy and vigorous population. In a society where women are free to satisfy their physical and biological needs, there will be no interest in giving birth to infants with mental or physical defects. Such children would reduce available leisure, and in obliging women to nurse their own children also give them a guilty conscience.

As I said, the children must be healthy, and by the aid of continuously refined diagnostic techniques we will always at an early stage of pregnancy tell women carrying deformed or brain-damaged children that they had better do the right thing. Considering that the fathers are not recognised as such, abortion should be easily arranged and readily agreed to. It is of course necessary that women themselves are not made to suffer feelings of guilt on this account. Rather they should be congratulated on doing themselves and society a great favour by not bringing defective children into the world. Women prone to miscarriage should not initially be sterilised, but offered the possibility of artificial insemination. In such cases the entire pregnancies would be under surveillance, and doctors would have the right discreetly to terminate those pregnancies in which the foetuses do not meet certain pre-established standards. This programme can be regulated in detail, and the questionnaires put to prospective mothers must be formulated in such a way as to avoid giving rise to suspicions of the imposition of a general eugenics programme.

The media must be rigorously controlled by us, and the best way of bringing this about is to allow women to set the level of debate. All attempts to go beyond their intellectual and spiritual level will then naturally be perceived as threats, and the debate, with its pros and cons, will be kept within proper limits. In this way we create the illusion of freedom of choice – this is in itself much more in tune with the world now rising like a phoenix from the ashes than any openly tyrannical and dictatorial system ever was. Rule by flattery and indulgence, and prepare in secrecy for the entry of the stage managers, that's what the future holds in store for people like you and me, Schröder. As doctors, we have the unique opportunity to become the engineers of this development. The very best way to ensure the eternal supremacy of the ruling hierarchy must be to find some way of connecting high intelligence with a 'natural' inclination toward homosexuality, that is, to the cult of the beautiful man and mind. Such was the case with the Greek philosophers, who were the jewels in classical Athens' crown. You see, nothing else could stop women eventually succeeding in bringing all men, even the spiritual elite, under their dominion, and thus, ultimately, corrupting them.

Schröder, who had long since ceased to pay any attention to the obscene content of Uhland's monologue, nonetheless felt weirdly fascinated by his appearance. Although Uhland had hardly changed his tone of voice, and had retained the same body posture throughout the interminable exposition of his perverse ideas, he seemed to Schröder not only a man of a thousand faces, but of a thousand forever changing faces. Most of these were disturbing, as ugly and deformed as his collection of monsters, but when he unexpectedly evoked ancient Greece he assumed the guise of a stunningly beautiful young man, yes, as the very incarnation of the ideal he was propagating. For a short, fleeting but undeniable moment, Hans even perceived the alarming reflection of himself as a young man in the other's face. A fraction of a second later it became the face of his father, then that of his oldest son ...

– Stop this ludicrous fantasy! Schröder interjected. – I have heard enough! You don't even have the slightest idea what you are talking about, and you go on as though the Thousand-Year Reich, in spite of its utter defeat and final destruction, was still to come. It's over, Uhland, and you will surrender yourself to the authorities, but not before telling me here and now what you have done with my wife and my children!

– Ah! Considering that there are scientific gaps that you have not yet been able to fill in because you haven't had the time to take a closer look at our recent results, I can understand that you don't want to believe me. However, what I have been talking about will happen, regardless of whether we want it or not. We are far ahead of our time, Hans. That the once-subjugated people will rise from the urban ghettos of the world is certain. The question before us is: are we going to let them have their way, or are we going to predict, prognosticate, control and monitor their ascent, so that in the future we remain the rulers of men and women, and do not become the ruled? If we don't realise in time what's happening in the world, reality will take us unawares, and some centuries from now there will be as little left of western civilisation as there was of Rome after it was sacked by the barbarians. The psychological weakness of the old Romans and the Achilles heel of the Greeks was their fear of female sexuality. We, the doctors and psychologists of the future, must fully understand and obligingly meet this particularly delicate problem half-way. In this sign we shall be victorious, and I am confident that you will come to the same conclusion once you have had time to study the facts.

Schröder stared as if hypnotised at Uhland's face, now immobile like that of a statue. It didn't betray the slightest indignation or impatience. He saw the immaculately white collar, the wax-like hands, and felt the lingering presence of sweet aftershave. This animal in human disguise, this so-called medical doctor, this demon, had not only taken over his job and carried it to abominable extremes, he had also moved into his house, taken sexual and spiritual possession of his wife, and, of course, indoctrinated the children, his children ...

– What have you done with my wife and children? he hissed at Uhland and approached him menacingly.

– Don't worry, Hans ...

– Dr. Schröder to you. Where are they?

– You will see them shortly. But before you get too worked up, let me just show you this. From his inside pocket Uhland pulled out a piece of paper.

– What's this?

– It's our agreement, Schröder.

Hans took the paper and looked at it in bewilderment.

Then he remembered, and his eyes went to the bottom of the page from which each word flew like an arrow, " ... and if I should perish in the war, I hereby entrust to my colleague, Claus Uhland, the task of taking all measures that he deems necessary to protect my wife and children. I also certify that it has been agreed that if my wife, Beatrice, has nothing against this, and Claus Uhland so wishes, he may marry her."

– Do you recognise your own signature?

– It has been falsified before.

– No, Hans, it hasn't. You signed all these documents and attestations before you left, to relieve me of the burden of doing so myself. Well, I kept them, but I never used them, since I conveniently changed my name to Rheinau upon marrying Beatrice. In this way we all survived. When we finally dissolved the fiction, I reassumed my old identity. My death in 1942 was staged as a security measure, so as to relieve me of personal responsibility for whatever had been done at the clinic. It was all carried out in your and Rheinau's names. Then you unexpectedly returned, and we had to create a new scenario, one that would inevitably compromise you to the point that, if we were to go down, you would have to go down with us too.

– Why do you keep saying 'we' when it's all your doing, Uhland?

– Because it wasn't just him ... I was in it too.

Her voice reached him from the door. Hans turned and faced her in the doorway, an apparition, casting an enormous shadow across the room. Uhland walked up to her, laid his arm around her shoulder and protectively escorted her to the centre of the room. Hans and Beatrice stood at a few yards' distance from one another. She watched him intently for a moment, then broke the silence.

– I too had assumed that you must be dead. And then there was your letter, which Claus showed me. We figured that once you were gone, it wouldn't do you any harm to be connected with the programme.

– What about my reputation? What do you think future generations would have thought of me? What do you think our children …?

– At that time we all still believed that Hitler would lead us to victory, and that you would go down in history as a national hero.

– So you did know what was going on at the clinic?

– I had no idea. Claus only gave me the letter to read. He then proposed to me, saying that I was free to regard his hand in marriage as a mere formality.

– Did you?

– At first, yes. But then, as we got to know one another, I actually began to like him.

– You mean, you fell in love with him?

– Well, I …

– Don't lie to me! Were you or were you not in love with this man?

– Yes! I loved him …

– And you still do!

– Hans, for God's sake! By a curious twist of fate, he is my husband. What do you want me to say? You even expected – even wanted it to happen!

– Maybe so, but why the make-believe? Why didn't you tell me the truth from the beginning? Well, I'll answer that question for you. It was because my return was nothing but an inconvenience to you. It was because at the time of my removal, long before my alleged death, you were pregnant with his child, the same that you had me accept as my own. You had given yourself to him long before I died. In this way you already had me killed. You, you broke up our marriage. It was dishonoured and disgraced, it was a shambles. And I, the laughing stock, was reduced to the pitiable cuckold's role! But then again, you could not let me disappear before I had provided the two of you with a perfect alibi. This I did. Not for you and not for him, but for the sake of our children, that is, the ones I might still have the right to consider mine.

Beatrice's features, at first distorted by wild emotion, suddenly became pale. Then her face froze completely.

– What do you mean, I broke up our marriage? she said.

– It had long since ceased to be. It was a lamentable travesty, but I did nothing to spoil it further until I realised that your affair with Laura wasn't just a fling, but had become an extra-marital institution in its own right. Do you think I didn't know what was going on between the two of you? For years I tried to look the other way. For years I tried to deny what I knew deep down to be true. You never loved me. Our marriage, as far as you were concerned, had been no more than a strategic move in your own rebellion against your father. You wanted me to be there, to fulfil my duties as a wife. Meanwhile you refused to consider the consequences of your own actions. I loved you, Hans. To me our marriage was a dream come true. But you didn't want it to last – you wanted her instead! One day she confessed everything, how you had been meeting in secret for years, how you used to send her flowers and gifts. She told me about your promises, your protestations of unwavering love, your fits of jealousy, your need to control and restrain her. And do you know what? I didn't have to force it out of her. She told me everything because she felt sorry for me. I was mourning the loss of a man who had never truly belonged to me, who had long since ceased to love me, who perhaps had never loved me. She couldn't bear knowing that I was living an illusion, which if it were allowed to keep on ruling my heart would prevent me from getting anything from my life before it was over and forever done with. She anticipated my growing old without recompense, and although she knew that I would reject and loathe her for the rest of our lives, she was willing to risk it, even to become a prostitute to save me from the disgrace of your betrayal. It wasn't easy to accept the truth. After all, she was my best friend. But I'm nonetheless grateful for what she did, and we have become reconciled. Let me just add that she wasn't just 'forgiven'. She still owed me a favour. It then so happened that Claus and I had to ask a particular service from her. She performed this to our satisfaction, and she was granted her one wish, which was to get you out of prison. Everything taken together, you are guilty of many things, Hans, only not of the particular crime of which you have been accused. Now, fortunately, all this belongs to the past, and you are free to take her with you.

Schröder listened to her contemptuous speech, tension mounting within him. Now, as he finally began to understand how the entire plot had been put together, he also realised what a disruption to a smooth-running machine his return had caused. Whatever Laura's real part was in all this, she had been perfectly right about one thing – notwithstanding that in view of the 'real' facts her words had been rather an understatement –which was that nobody was happy to see him back alive. Calmly he answered,

– How singular to hear you speak in such a distant, detached manner, Beatrice. It is almost as though we had never even known each other. What happened to your heart? Have you forgotten all the wonderful moments we had together? The joy of seeing our family grow? The hardships and the difficulties we overcame? Have you forgotten? I can see that your heart has turned to stone, that the one person you once needed is needed no more. But tell me now as our ways part: Did you ever care about me, or has all this, from the very beginning been nothing but a grand illusion, something I just dreamed or made up during years of pretended domestic happiness? Tell me, please, Beatrice. How could I have been so mistaken?

– Hans, listen to me, she said in an unsteady voice. – I loved you so much, so much. I always wanted the very best for you. I hoped that I could be the person to make you happy, to take care of you, to support and to love you. If it were possible, I would still have wished today for nothing else than for us to live as we once did, as man and wife. And I would have easily forgiven you your affair with Laura, if it were not for a feeling, a deep-seated, melancholy and truthful feeling, which tells me that it is your destiny to live and die with her, that you two really belong together, and that you should accept it, not as a curse, but as a promise, a possibility, a fresh start in life. If you want it, she will stay with you to the end of your days. I love you Hans. For the sake of that love, I'm willing to let you go.

Beatrice made a conciliatory gesture and moved forward to embrace Hans. He did not respond.

– Clever, very clever, he said. – But of course it's just another of the lies you had to tell to cover up the fact that you were Uhland's lover even before he became a murderer, and turned you into one as well, it seems. I know you need this story to cover yourself. You even congratulate yourself on having secured me a false alibi by seducing Major Beaufort. In this way you managed to convince yourself that you still possessed a shred of decency. But that decency proved to be your greatest weakness. Like a cat with its tail ablaze, you keep spinning around in circles, unable to extinguish the fire. Your mistake was not to have me killed right away. Besides, and as if it ever mattered to you, I might just add that I was never in love with Laura. You invented that story to justify your own adultery. Then, to make yourselves accomplices, the two of you made her into a murderess, too.

– Oh really, is that so? In that case, why don't we ask Laura herself?

Throughout the course of these revelations, Schröder had quite forgotten Laura and the role she had played in bringing him into contact with Claus Uhland. But no sooner had she come into his mind than her haunting presence materialised on the threshold, her black hair glistening in the naked source of light behind her. Her reappearance was perfectly timed, like a theatrical entry. As she grew taller in the doorway, Claus Uhland and Beatrice slowly moved away in opposite directions and took up positions outside the widening cone of light falling through the doorway. Their faces grew dark and anonymous as did their bodies, now hardly more than two contours, barely distinguishable from the surrounding darkness. Schröder stared at Laura in disbelief. From the moment they had met again in the empty hospital, she had seemed more and more a figment of his own imagination, a fleeting impression, a dream, an almost immaterial spectre, leading him through secret galleries and chambers deep beneath the surface of the earth, and finally abandoning him there. For this reason it didn't surprise him that her voice, although in fact he could see her lips move as she spoke, appeared to emanate from inside his own head, and that she herself was a mere projection, conjured up by the great silent sphinxes on either side of the doorway.

– Hans, the game is up. You were my lover while you were married, and not only that, we were together before then. In fact, as long as I can remember, we've always been together, you and I. Don't judge your wife too harshly. How can you expect her to have acted differently in the circumstances?

– But Laura, what are you saying? First of all, we were only talking and talking during all those years. There was hardly as much as a fleeting kiss on a cheek as a sign of farewell. It is only recently, in extraordinary circumstances, that we engaged in the act of love. Secondly, that man is a fully developed monster, a predator with a human face. How could she even consider allowing him around the children once she had found out what his daily work involved?

– It isn't just recently, Hans. I see how you still refuse to admit the ultimate truth about yourself ... During all this time Beatrice never knew, and she never cared to know, what Uhland was up to. Even now she is only pretending to be involved in the murder, whereas it was a business deal strictly between Uhland and myself. Besides, he was always kind to her, affectionate and mindful of her needs. But she was first and foremost in love with you, and she would have accepted without hesitation the sinister character of your assignment at Sankt-Anna. The only thing she expected of you was that you should be more in love with her than with your own moral principles. The moral dilemma you invented for yourself did not simply entail a clear-cut distinction between good and evil, but also your heroic choice between them. You and I know perfectly well that there is no such thing as a confrontation between good or evil. We know that there is no God, and that creation only means what man intends.

No, your hesitation and vacillation had their origin only in your cool and scientific mind. You realised that parts of the eugenics programme could be of tremendous scientific importance, but also that Hitler was not in the long run going to win the war and secure peace for Germany. In deliberate opposition to his orders, you decided, as Pilate did, to wash your hands of the whole business. This was because what mattered more to you than your own wife and family was that you should be remembered as blameless, leaving behind an unusually interesting and intriguing dossier on paranormal phenomena for someone else to read and carry further. In this way you hoped to be able to live on in spirit. But your pioneering work would only stand a chance of being discovered, accepted, properly evaluated and taken further if it remained free from all associations with Nazism. Your sole concern was to save for the future the results of your research. To that end you were willing to sacrifice your family, knowing very well that Uhland, in the last instance, was going to do all the dirty work for you. Look at his results. Immoral? Certainly, but an important step has been taken towards replacing evolutionary chance with careful, deliberate selection. Uhland himself may be mistaken in the details, and it's true that his Negro programme has some questionable features ….

– Questionable? Schröder seized Laura by the shoulders and shook her hard.

– Questionable? It's no more than nihilism, and not even a lucid kind of nihilism, but a myopic obsession with the prospect of another devastating world revolution. An ever-expanding bureaucracy, such as any modern society will support in peacetime, doesn't need the virility of African tribesmen to thrive, but placid, inconspicuous worker bees, technicians, engineers, in short, decent people capable of checking the charts and running the systems. It's all down to that, and the future even of genetics depends on what the system can and cannot digest. It is not the other way round. That man is a lunatic, and an idiot as well!

– Or perhaps he has probed a little bit deeper into the psychological intricacies of the problem, and is willing to look into the future and not to flinch in the face of a reality still only in the bud … Eventually the barbarians became Romans too, didn't they? So this time it did not begin with Christianity and Ostrogoths, but with Josephine Baker and jazz music. Don't we all remember Hitler's dismay at the achievements of black athletes at the Olympic Games before the war? If he had been smarter, he might have used them for his purposes instead … Perhaps Uhland wanted no more than to provoke you, to rub a little salt in your wounds, so to speak. But even your indignation in this respect is still only a camouflage, a facade behind which your moral problem lies. The deeper significance is hidden in your own heart. The truth is that the only person you have ever loved in your life – except me, to whom you are indissolubly attached by obsessive sexual attraction and repressed desire – is your own self. The reason for your not playing ball with the Nazis was purely egotistical. And it's this that makes us two of a kind.

Now, by the grace of these two pillars on either side of me, we can leave together and be on our way to Brazil by tomorrow. Hans, don't even think about staying! If you do, you'll be dragged back to that court-room to find that your wife's testimony has been overturned, and you'll be put away for life. As things stand, Uhland is the one who has to remain incognito for the rest of his life, while you still have years of fruitful public research ahead of you – perhaps there is even a breakthrough awaiting you in the realm of telekinesis? Now, what do you say, Hans? Shall we go?

– You deceitful, slanderous bitch ... You didn't hesitate to paint the devil on the wall! And she was more than willing to be seduced by the sweet charm of your lies, wasn't she? You are a murderess too, Laura – that says it all. Where are my children? Laura! Beatrice! Uhland! Where ... are ... my ... children?

Schröder approached Laura, put his hands around her neck and began to shake her furiously. Neither Uhland nor Beatrice made a move to come to her rescue. They remained absolutely still as statues in the darkness. Laura, now unable to defend herself, was pushed backwards. She stumbled over a chair, lost her footing and suddenly fell back headlong down the narrow staircase. Schröder saw her tumble down the stairs and come to a halt, unmoving, at their foot. He then switched on the wall-light to illuminate the chamber, and ran into it to find his wife and Uhland. But the room was empty, save for the projector in the middle and the screen on the wall at the far end. Confused, Schröder again turned to the one door that led in and out of the chamber. Here he beheld his three children on the threshold. They were holding hands, watching him intently.

– Oh my God! Schröder cried out ecstatically – Thank God you're all alive and safe! Look at you, you have all grown so much! Is that really you, Renate? How old are you now … Oh, you are so beautiful, you look so much like your mother. And Peter, what a beautiful young boy you are, you look so much like your grandfather when he was your age. How old are …?

– Dear father, I'm sixteen years old. Peter is twelve, and little Heinz …

– I'm not little, I'm seven years old, and I started school this year, the youngest one said, and stretched out his hand to pass something to his father. Hans, whose sight was dimmed by tears, moved closer towards the child, and, trembling with agitation, caressed the little boy's head. He looked searchingly into the eyes of the child, who seemed at first a little shy in the presence of this man whom he had seen only in photographs. The boy lowered his gaze and stood indecisive.

– I know you don't remember me, but you need not be afraid, Schröder said with emotion. – For a long time I had my doubts, but when I see you eye to eye like this, I detect a familiar trait in the line of your forehead and eyebrows. There is something in your look that tells me that you really are my son, after all. Now tell me, do you know this to be the truth?

– Yes, father, I am your son. He raised his head and gave him a long melancholy look. Schröder felt his heart filling with an immense joy. At last, after so many lies, false accusations and guilt, he had found, in the pure heart and eye of a child, something that he could still believe in. Here he had found something that was imperishable, and more worthy of trust than his own soul and the fateful decision it had once been wrapped around. What did his lifeless soul matter compared to the fact that his children were healthy, and could now begin to hope for better days? The lovely shapes of their youthful limbs, the light of their eyes, the melancholy of their secret longings struck him like hammer-blows.

– Children, he said, his voice muffled. – I'm home. Everything is going to be all right again. Do you hear me? Just fine ... He embraced Heinz, then reached with his hands to the two other children.

– Father! It was Heinz again who stretched out his little hand to pass over to him what it was that he had kept hidden.

– Father ... Aunt Laura said we should give you this before you leave us.

Hans looked down at the boy's open, slightly sweating palm in which two ancient coins glimmered, and then into his son's eyes, whose melancholy expression now seemed transfigured into a steady silvery shine.

– We made you some cakes too, Renate said, and had Peter hand them over.

– Real honey buns! For your trip. She gave him a faint smile.

– Dear children, that's so nice of you! But of course I'm not going anywhere now. I will be staying with you for ever.

– Father! Renate leaned forward and gave him a long kiss on the forehead. – Father, I know how you feel, and I know how you have been looking forward to this, to coming home and living with us. But it is not possible.

– Not possible? What do you mean? Oh, but of course, I can live somewhere else and come and visit you …

– No. You can't, father.

– Why? Why can't I?

– Because … Because you are not coming home. You are not coming back. Father, you are going away forever. We have only come to say goodbye.

– That's ridiculous. Laura was an evil woman. She was punished, and she is no more. You must forget everything you know about her. Do you hear me? Do you hear me?

– Yes, Peter said hesitantly and with regret in his voice. – Yes, we hear you. But, father, it's like this. When she died, you died too.

– You have to leave us, father, Renate concluded gravely. – Now, turn round and enter Hades, the house of the wide gates, in peace. We will always remember you. We always loved you, we always will. Farewell …

– What is this all about?

– … Farewell …

– What?

– … Farewell …

Schröder was overcome by the sensation that his two oldest children had merged into one terimorphic body crowned by two heraldic heads. Seen through the misty veil of his tears, they actually looked similar to that eagle-like figure behind the judge's bench, the court emblem. Not until now did it dawn on him that the trial proceedings had been going on all the time, only under different forms and guises, and that the final, irrevocable, verdict was being announced to him by his own children ... "By the supreme cruelty of this court ..."

While the sentence was being pronounced, the heraldic figure composed of his two oldest children began to darken. In vain did he try to address them. They had spoken, and in silence they slowly vanished. Stripped of almost everything that had bound him to his earthly existence, and in a last attempt to hold on to whatever remained of his world, Schröder locked Heinz in an even tighter embrace, determined not to let him go. The heraldic emblem was fixed in mid-air before the little door that led to the staircase, visibly the only way out. Gradually the animal filled the doorway, while at the same time turning into stone. Schröder saw the cone grow pitch-black from the centre outwards toward the rim, and while a huge heavy slab depicting the heraldic figure began to fill the doorway, he saw the eyes of the beautiful boy in his arms fade like two silvery coins, silently slanting deeper and deeper into dark water, until they could no longer be seen.

*

– I'm too young to die. Take my life and live it for me, the boy in his arms had whispered. – Now, is the bell swinging in the wind? Now, is the bell swinging in the dying wind – now, now, now ? ... Can't you hear the wind?. . The snow in the wind, the snow in the wind? ... Now ... Snow ... Come snow ... Schröder had taken the pillow and placed it over his head, and pressed and pressed until the chest no longer rose and fell. The fixed stare of his glazed eyes. Schröder, seized by horror, was haunted by the dead man's soul, or so it seemed. There had been a moment of absolute identity and brotherhood between them, such as can only occur between men who know that for the same inescapable reason they are about to meet Death. He felt as if he had been staring into the dead man's eyes for a million years, and had thereby acquired a strange knowledge. Where had he been travelling? He only remembered the boy's eyes, there was something about those eyes ...

He pulled out his gun. Everything that had passed seemed so far away now. "My father used to have one," he thought. "Strange that he managed take his life with one of these, even though he was almost completely paralysed ... Now I shall have to do the same. No matter how hard I tried to avoid it, Father, fate itself wanted me to follow in your footsteps. Maybe everything happened the way it did just because I tried so hard not to become like you. I didn't want to have anybody but myself to blame. I was looking for a way to free the scapegoat by turning myself into one. That way I would absorb the shock. Nobody else would be involved, and life would continue. Perhaps there would still be a chance for some love and respect in this world. I hoped that one day my wife and children would have reason to feel gratitude, that they could be proud of their father. I was hoping that I, Hans Schröder, could make some difference in the world by refusing to submit to the tyrant. But it doesn't make any difference. Dead, we're all the same. And it won't matter that I believed I did the right thing at the time. I thought that even if I were to die in the war, at least I could face my destiny as a man. Now I'm not so sure any longer. I'm not even sure I understand the difference between dying as a man and perishing as a beast. But before that moment comes, there is a difference, because the animal has no choice, whereas every man has eventually to face the consequences of the choices he has made in life. That's the law. And I really don't know, but I think it was all in vain, and that neither gods nor men ever take pity on each other."

He raised the gun and pointed it at his right temple. Just as he was about to pull the trigger, he discovered a piece of paper sticking out from inside the dead man's uniform. Although it seemed completely meaningless to do so – maybe he was just playing for time, begging for a last distraction like the condemned man's last cigarette – he pulled the torn and blood-stained paper from the pocket. It was a letter. Written by the man himself, but of course never sent. It read,

Dear parents, dear sister, dear Laura,

I don't think you will ever receive this message from me. But I write it all the same. I know I shall die today. We are waiting for the Russians to attack us. Our commander has said that we will not surrender, and that the Führer expects each one of us to stay at his post and

defend his beloved Fatherland. I know the Führer is still alive, but when I see the number of tanks and guns that the enemy has, I realise that he too will soon be dead. But I shall still fight for him, as I shall fight for you, and for the future and glory of Germany. Goodbye dear parents, goodbye dear sister. May God always be with you.

Your Heinz

"His letter makes him seem even younger. I wonder who that Laura is. His girl-friend? Dark hair, slim waist, bosom ... She'll wait for him for a while. Then he'll be reported missing, and she'll mourn him. But then she'll make herself forget, and get on with her life. The boy's right. Once here, there is no choice. I'd better get ready myself ... By the way, Uhland, I really did find out how the other side works, only the margin is not wide enough to allow for my proof. You see, they did at one point during the campaign send me a portion of a little-known substance, with an accompanying letter saying a certain Dr. Hoffman in Switzerland had discovered it more or less by accident in 1941. Hoffman had isolated the active chemical agent, lysergic acid, which afforded such relief as to make men face death bravely, so they thought it might be useful in easing the pain of the mortally wounded. I tried it on a few occasions, but it seemed mostly to give the patients vivid hallucinations, sometimes accompanied by unbearable anxiety. The drug came in tiny crystalline squares and could be mistaken for anything, breadcrumbs, even. Knowing that, for me, everything was about to come to an end, and to forestall the Russians, I swallowed a large amount, and then injected into my own veins a dose of morphine big enough to kill a horse three times over. To no avail. I can feel it wearing off now, although, technically, I must already be dead. But there is something about that acid. It's not wearing off. Uhland, you are not going to believe me, but I visited the future and came back. In fact, I didn't simply visit it, but lived the future, too, a future I will never in this reality live to see, yet it somehow appeared to me ... Can't really remember how, though. And when I think of it, it may be just as well.

The future isn't a place you'd wish to visit before your time, especially not as a consequence of a dream. That's what it was, you see. For a moment I was hoping that the Russians would come round and spare my life because I was a doctor, even though I knew very well that they shoot anything that moves. I can hear them coming closer and closer now. As I said, the margin is not wide enough for my proof, and as there is no post or telephone, I send this brief summary on another wavelength. And if you don't receive the message, or choose to ignore it, maybe someone else will get it. Anyhow, this is the way I see it.

"The parallel world exists, and it is certainly in many respects ahead of ours in time and space. However, if you enter it as a consequence of an illusory dream, you introduce distortion into that dimension because your wishes necessarily turn into their opposites. Fear, hatred, frustration, jealousy, anger and desire begin to contaminate that other realm. You perceive this reality as an eerie dream world, in which all living beings pass each other by with simply no real communication between them. Everything becomes part of a world that is almost a world, but without soul or spirit. In such a state, even the most flagrant immorality seems completely natural and inconsequential. And the reason for this is that the other realm, seen through the eyes of vicarious wish fulfilment, is dead. It seems to live, but it doesn't. All feelings, all thoughts, all movements, are simulated, and you yourself move about only by virtue of the artificial energy of your own illusion. A further consequence is that all identities become interchangeable – one person appears in the guise of another, and so on and so on. Not even your own self remains the same ... The illusion spins a web, a cocoon, if you will, around you, so that at the end you're wishing for nothing more than to continue to believe in this imaginary world of your own making. And the horrible thing is that as long as your desire is stronger than your sense of reality, it works. Slowly and inexorably, though, it turns into a ghastly nightmare, which can only end with the revelation of death itself.

I can feel myself returning from a long, scarcely believable journey through the realms of the unknown and perhaps, ultimately, unknowable. I have no more than very dim recollections of what I saw and experienced, but something tells me it was just as much a hell as my present existence in the antechamber of death. So, in the end, the two worlds converge. Whatever we do, wherever we turn, we end up facing the same unalterable fact – it's all inside us. That's why we, each and every single one of us, is responsible for – everything ... I could go on endlessly, but time's up, I'm afraid. I can hear the Russian tanks rolling over our last defences. I must hurry up and join the vanishing point where the two lines converge ...

... Farewell, Beatrice, love of my life. Did I ever wrong you? I hope not. Farewell, Renate, Peter and my youngest child, with the same name as that young soldier. Farewell, little boy that I never came to know. Farewell, Sister. Farewell, Brother. Farewell, Mother, and farewell – I guess I'll have to forgive you now – Father. Farewell, dear colleagues. Adieu, Dr. Uhland, and good luck. The other, the real future, if you live to see it, is in your hands ... What? What is the secret? But I told you. It is all inside ourselves, I already told you ... Hitler, Stalin, Devil, God, all of them are ... inside ... us ... If only it wasn't so damned cold, so burning cold ... Oh, there they are, the honey biscuits for Cerberus. Thank you, children. It wasn't just a wish that you would be alive when all this is over, was it? And I mustn't forget the coins for the ferryman ... Divine singer, why didn't you trust me? I would have followed you to the end of the world, and beyond. Now that your sweet music is heard no more, my life has turned into endless misery and sorrow ... It's getting darker now. Your face has disappeared, merged with the sun ... out of reach ... All that I can see now is you, you, forever silent house of the wide gates ... Oh, Santa Anna! Holy Santa Anna! Pray for us in our moments of despair. Pray for us in the moment of our death ... Santa Anna ... Santa Anna ... Beatrice ... Laura ... Uhland ... Why have you locked me up in my own hospital? ... Why are you experimenting with my brain? ... Oh, no more sedatives, no more morphine, no more drugs ... Let me out of here! ... Let me out ... Let me come ... Snow ..."

Three hours later the Russians crushed the remnants of the Wehrmacht at Stalingrad, and summarily executed any

German soldier found still alive. When they stormed the cellar which had functioned as the German's last medical ward they met with a curious sight. Most of the dead were lying alone on the floor or in cots, but there was one dead man lying on top of another corpse. When they turned him over they saw that he had shot himself with the gun still dangling from his hand. In itself there was nothing strange about that, but what awed everyone was the expression on the man's face. The bullet had entered his skull between the eyes and slightly above the root of the nose. His eyes, however, wide open in death, emanated such peace and serenity that it seemed as if he had simply forcibly opened his third eye, and by way of this spiritual organ received the light.

*

Epilogue

– Mother, have you seen my dress?
  – No, Renate, and how many times do I have to tell you that you can't always expect me to keep track of all the things that you whirl up like a tornado.
  – Oh, mother, don't be so dramatic. I was just pulling your leg. It's here in my hands.
Renate, blonde and blue-eyed, peeked around the corner and glanced mischievously at her mother. It was a fine day. Early spring, the first flowers in the flower-beds, the whole town swept clean of snow, gravel and mud. Not a green leaf on the chestnut trees yet, but buds in the making everywhere. Beatrice looked back at her daughter, and had to smile.
  – This coquetry obviously runs in the family, she sighed.
  – Well, don't just stand there. Get ready. We haven't got all day.
  – But the birthday party isn't till three o' clock!
  – Yes, but we're going to the cemetery first. And we'll need to buy flowers before that. Now, stop arguing with me!
  – Oh, Mama …
  – Yes? What is it?

– Can I borrow one of your dresses?
– No.
– Not even this one?

Again Renate appeared in the doorway. This time she held another dress in her hands. Beatrice was about to give her a well-calculated scolding, when her gaze became enmeshed in the texture, shape and colours of the dress. The rebuke died in mid-air.

Renate made the most of this opportunity.

– I mean, since you obviously don't wear it any more. It's old, isn't it? Look how short it is, it must date from the '20s! What did you do – did you dance in it?

Beatrice put aside the glass bowl she was polishing and moved over to her daughter's side.

– This dress ... she said, and caressed its folds dreamily. – This was the dress I wore on the first night that I had a date with your father. He was very fond of irises, and he particularly loved the combination of yellow and lilac.

– Where was this?

– Göttingen, in the month of May, 1927.

– May I?

She held it up in front of the mirror. She turned to her mother and said,

– I look like just like you, don't I?

– All right. But look, it's quite thin, the best satin. Wear a coat over it, and don't ruin it at the party!

Peter and Heinz could be heard fighting over something in Peter's room. Beatrice ran upstairs to get them on their way as well.

– He hit me! Heinz cried out, still nevertheless keeping a firm grip on the much-coveted model car.

– Let him have it now Peter, she said. – You two get dressed as well.

– Where are we going?

– Out.

– Yes, but where?

– You'll see.

When the children were finally ready, shoe-laces tied, Beatrice collected them outside. They set off toward the centre of town. There was a soft breeze in the air, just strong enough to chase the last dark clouds beyond the Black Forest. Although it was still cool in the shade, the sun spread warmth wherever it could.

At twelve o'clock they all met Claus in the square. He was in a good humour.

– How did it go? Beatrice whispered to him. She was a little concerned that her husband had been summoned to a meeting with the Allied Forces Investigation Committee.

– Oh, fine.

– What did they ask you?

– Oh, they just wanted to see that our records from Sankt-Anna were in good order, and that we had never been involved in the euthanasia programme during the war.

– And you were able to explain everything to them?

– Oh yes. There was solid documentation. After your former husband's departure, Ward-D was closed for good, and demolished. To make a long story short, the case is closed, Beatrice, and it will never be opened again.

– Oh, I'm so relieved. And I'm proud of you, standing up to them, being so strong and manly. I'm happy for us. Happy that the war is over, that there will be a new summer, new flowers and vegetables in the garden. She leaned forward and gave him a tender kiss. The children whirled round them, playing catch.

On this first day of spring, the cemetery was full of people honouring their dead. Claus stopped at some distance from the monument and fished a cigarette out of his case, while Beatrice brought the children right up to the fence that surrounded the obelisk. The inscription was not in large letters, but in the sunlight all the names on it could be read clearly even from a distance. Toward the bottom of the second column on the stone commemorating the Unknown Soldier of the most recent war, the name Hans Michael Schröder was inscribed. Beatrice knelt down, kissed the roses in her hand, and slowly dropped them inside the fence. Two teardrops, big as pearls, detached themselves from her eyes and ran down her cheeks. She felt her heart give an extra beat, and a cold shiver run down her spine. Next to her, Renate prostrated herself as well. The boys were told to take off their caps and remain silent. Beatrice stayed motionless for a minute, then rose and turned round. It worked as a signal to the boys, who couldn't help chasing each other round the column.

Claus had finished his cigarette, and advanced to join them. He lifted his hat, bowed his head an inch, and remained for a brief but courteous moment in that position. He then put his hat back on, and raised his head. When the family were ready to leave, they called to Heinz, who came running for all his seven-year-old legs were worth. He stopped in front of them, and said,

– My father was a great man, wasn't he?
– Your father *is* a great man, Beatrice said.
– No, no, no! I know, he was! He was, he was! And he

stamped his little foot as hard as he could, and ran ahead of the family towards the high wrought-iron gate at the far end of two almost interminably long, sun-caressed walls.

That evening, after the children had gone to bed, Claus and Beatrice shared a bottle of white wine together. Their conversation had faltered for a moment, but suddenly Beatrice reanimated it.

– Tell me, Claus, what did you really think of Hans' research into paranormal phenomena? You knew, of course, that he had a theory that the events of the physical world run almost parallel with another, more or less identical but spiritual, or ethereal, world. He said he was trying to discover a method of measuring the time-delay from the moment something happens in the super-sensible world to its entry into the physical. According to him, this delay was always in that direction, from the super-sensible to the physical, never the other way round. What do you think?

– I think Hans had a lot of very interesting ideas, only in this case it is hard to find ways of verifying them. The study of paranormal phenomena is a relatively new discipline, and only a few people are qualified to pursue it in a scientific way that doesn't lay them open to charges of charlatanry.

– Well, you see, I was thinking… Before Hans left, he entrusted me with all his notes from various experiments. Let me show you.

Beatrice left the room, went upstairs and returned with several files containing both hand-written and typed material.

– Here they are, she said. – I'm quite unable to determine the worth of these records myself, but I know that it was his dream to see an institute for paranormal and neurological research established, with him in charge. Maybe you have colleagues who might like to look his notes over, and who might profit in their own research from some of his results. After all – who knows?

– Dear Beatrice, I'll be more than happy to look after Hans' legacy. No later than tomorrow, I'll make sure that it will fall into the right hands. You're such a beautiful woman, Beatrice, and you know how much I care for you and the children.

– I love you Claus. I really do.

Next morning, Claus began his new job as head of a special department within the newly formed Bundesrepublik for the "Establishment of social welfare, insurance policies and the implementation of a judicial system guaranteeing non-violation of the human rights of deranged subjects within the public health care system." The department was beautifully situated in the centre of town, opposite the cathedral and with pleasant views of the surrounding hills. There was a tiny hint of green among the branches of the trees this morning, but the night had brought frost and his room still had to warm up. Claus Uhland had cold hands. He placed them on the tiles of the stove, and let the warmth help his blood circulate. When his body had reached a comfortable temperature, he was ready to start the day's work. His secretary had piled it neatly for him, but – oh, he had almost forgotten. On the top of the stack of files needing his attention lay Hans' files. Claus opened one of them and began to look over some pages at random. He turned twenty pages forward, turned back, opened a new file, then, after a short investigation, closed that one as well. He then walked to the door, made sure it was locked, and returned to the desk. He took the files and pushed them under his left arm. With his right hand he opened the brass doors of the stove and introduced some sheets into it, seeing blue ink, red pencil and printed letters catch fire and vanish like salamanders. For a good half hour he kept feeding the fire, positively surprised by the amount of warmth this odd kind of fuel was able to generate. After making sure that every last page was on its way to obliteration, he just stood there and watched them burning. He lowered his neck an inch and murmured into the furnace,

– I'm convinced you would have done exactly the same thing as I once you had become acquainted with all the facts. But remember, Schröder, this is unfortunately the last service I can do you. I can't risk sticking out my neck for you any longer. You have to take care of yourself now, all right? Well, that's all, I'm afraid. Goodbye, dear colleague. And good luck.

Nobody in the square noticed the phenomenon; everyone was too busy selling and buying merchandise at the Monday market to even have time to look up. But if anybody, against all odds, had at this early hour lifted their eyes to the level of the rooftops, they would have witnessed a stream of incandescent material spurt forth from one single chimney, transform into soot, and gracefully, as if in slow motion, fall upon the roof, and there to come to rest as a thin layer of black snow.

*

Lars Holger Holm's new novel *Come Snow* is a compelling detective story caged in a nerve-racking drama. Comprehensively researched and documented, it emulates the style and manners of the epoch, and while not necessarily based on a wartime case, remains in a superlative sense a true story.

Its moral quandary assumes gigantic proportions. A trial leads to the centre of a labyrinth in which human insidiousness reveals itself as both protean and eternal. Blurring the edges of perception and reality, the crime at the heart of this darkness is so unspeakable that even the idea of punishment becomes irrelevant.

PHOTO: KENNETH GENESER

Holm: *"This book draws inspiration from literary sources and three major motion pictures;* The Serpent's Egg *by Ingmar Bergman,* Angel Heart *by Alan Parker, and* Brazil *by Terry Gilliam. I express my gratitude to these writing directors."*

Other books by Lars Holger Holm
at Leo Publishing:

Fawlty Towers – A Worshipper's Companion

Dionysos – A Sinuous Essay to Divine the Universe